The Embedded

Book One

Jamie Shemesh

Copyright 2009 – 2023

ISBN: 978-1-960399-43-4

Cover illustration and design by Mattine Jensen

Request for information at Jamie@JamieShemesh.com

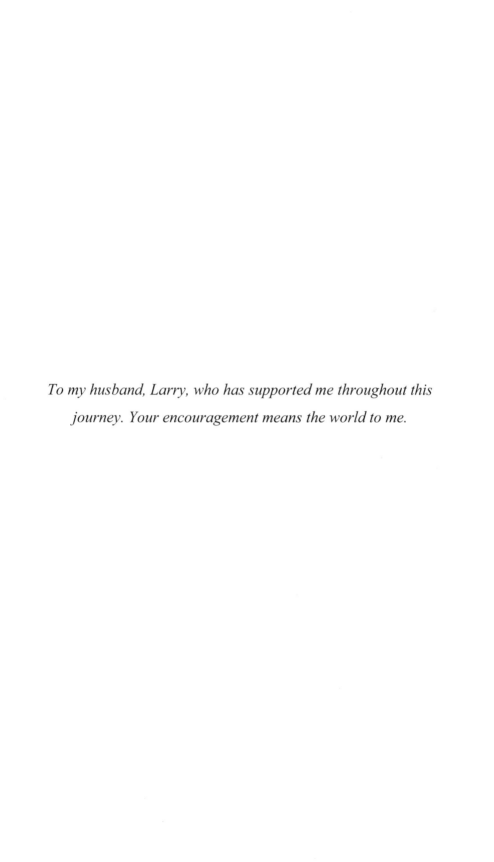

To my husband, Larry, who has supported me throughout this journey. Your encouragement means the world to me.

Vengeance is a monster of appetite, forever bloodthirsty and never filled.

Richelle E. Goodrich

Table of Contents

Chapter 1

This time it was worse. The words, written in black, heavy strokes across Avery's locker, stood out in bold defiance- "Go Home Goth." She faced the locker, clenching her teeth to force back the stinging tears, but also to prevent the electricity from running through her body. She knew that it would be a horrible scene if she unleashed her emotions, a scene that would be unforgivable to her parents. A scene that would make her more of the outcast she already felt she was.

Avery slowly turned around. She could see Charlotte, surrounded by her posse; her mouth turned upwards in a smirk. Clad in his varsity basketball jacket stood Brandon, slapping the shoulders of his jock buddy. Her eyes focused on Lucy- cast downward as if she placed the wrongdoings of all the students of Stanton High upon her shoulders. Most were laughing, whispering, or pointing.

Through the haze, Avery could see one face, a face that she caught fleetingly through the crowded hallway. Ryan. Her heart was beating so loudly, she was certain he could hear it. Her pulse raced, and she could feel her left palm getting hot. He stood in the background, looking devoid of emotion. His jet-black hair barely clipped his neck, and his bangs carelessly fell over one dark, brooding eye. His eyes locked on to hers, and he stared as though transfixed. The intensity of his gaze rattled her, but she could not look away. His eyes were dark green with tiny flecks of gold. They reminded her of her own eyes. Slowly, he turned and walked down the crowded hallway, his hands stuffed into his pockets.

Avery turned around, opened her locker, grabbed her second-period books and slammed it shut. *When was this going to stop?* she asked herself.

It was already two weeks of pure hell since Avery and her parents moved to Willowdale. It wasn't like things were any better in the last towns from which they had moved, but the hatred was getting worse.

Avery's parents made her promise that she would not do anything that would initiate another move. They made her swear that she would not use her powers. The guilt from knowing she was the cause of the accidents was just too much, and Avery pledged that she would control her powers and remain trouble-free. But today, the hatred welled up inside of her.

She quickly walked to her class, where she found the chair nearest the door and hunkered into the seat. Her left hand was throbbing, and the tiny crystal embedded into it was glowing. She pulled her black sweatshirt sleeve over her hand.

Math class was brutal. The minute hand seemed stuck. Every nerve in Avery's body was electrified. She tried to calm herself. *Just think about exponents*, she thought to herself. *Think about algebraic equations*. When she arrived in Willowdale, Avery was placed in all the honors classes. She heard the whispers that some students were now calling her the Gothic Geek. Avery pleaded with her parents to move to an urban setting. She craved anonymity. No one would look down upon her. There would be no one looking, period. But her parents insisted that small towns were ideal for their jobs. Talia was the proprietor of a small antique shop out of their home, and Steve had his own carpentry business. They believed that the small suburban towns were best for Avery. They would allow her to be a *normal* girl.

Ha! How far from the truth was that! She thought over and over.

The bell finally rang, and Avery sprang out of her seat. She couldn't wait for the day to end. She swore she would restrain from using her powers. "We can't move again," she heard her parents tell each other night after night.

The move to Willowdale had been sudden. Avery's parents knew that if they stayed in Lincoln any longer, people would begin to act upon their suspicions. The whispers at the supermarket, where Avery's mom, Talia, shopped, were already audible. The pointed looks at Avery's dad, Steve, at the lumberyard were now obvious, and the all-too-familiar taunting at Avery's school had progressed rapidly. Avery's parents pleaded with her to dress like the popular girls. They tried to reason with her that if she did, she would fit into the suburban landscape. Her mom brought her bags of clothing from H&M and American Eagle. She would send Avery links to "cute" outfits on Forever 21's website, but she shook her head every time and explained that it was not her. The harassment continued.

However, it was not just Avery's wardrobe that made their moves inevitable. It was what happened when she became upset. It was the electricity that coursed through her body and out of the barely noticeable crystal embedded in the palm of her left hand. It was the sprained ankle of one of the cheerleaders that occurred right after she had made fun of Avery's black studded necklace. It was the bloody nose of the basketball star immediately following the bogus invitation asking her to the Homecoming dance. Avery desperately tried to control her emotions, but again and again, the powers overcame her. Soon the family was looked upon as lepers and ostracized from each of the small, quaint towns they longed to call home.

"Wait up, Avery," Lucy called, running to catch up. "I am sorry about your locker. You don't deserve that kind of treatment."

"Whatever." Avery slowed a bit to let her only friend catch up with her. "I am used to this. The weird thing is that I don't know why I attract so much attention." She looked down at her outfit;

black combat boots, studded choker necklace, and chains swaying out of every zippered pocket. "Well, maybe I do."

Avery started to laugh, something she hadn't done in some time. Tears welled up in her eyes. The tears were a pure emotional release, the result of her alienation.

The two of them walked to Spanish class. Lucy always made her feel a little better. Avery met Lucy on her third day in school while precariously balancing a tray of meatloaf and mashed potatoes. Lucy waved her over and moved aside to make room on the long lunch table bench. Shots of poisoned looks pierced Avery from the others. But Lucy acted like it was no big deal.

At first, Avery was hesitant. She geared herself up for some practical joke. But after five minutes, she realized that Lucy was genuine. She was the opposite of Avery. Just five feet tall, she had red hair that tumbled past her shoulders. Freckles dotted her pale cheeks, and her eyes were the lightest blue Avery had ever seen. Lucy was so sensitive and worried about everyone and everything. But she was well-liked by her teachers and peers. No one appeared to understand how the two of them clicked and became fast friends. Lucy accepted Avery for who she was and did not care what others thought.

As much as she wanted to, Avery could not confide in Lucy about her powers. She vowed never to mention them to anyone. Her parents were the only ones who would understand her gift. *It's not fair,* she thought. *My parents have each other. I have no one.*

Chapter 2

Eighteen years ago, Talia met Steve at a local antique fair. Her hair, as black as ebony, was what initially attracted Steve to her. But when she turned, she took his breath away. Her complexion was smooth as glass, and her eyes were the color of malachite. He watched her move from aisle to aisle, picking up curious objects along the way. He noticed how she caressed each one, holding it up to the light, tilting it sideways, and gingerly placing it back down on one of the long, slatted tables that flanked the aisles. Her fingers were long and graceful, bare except for the one tiny crystal ring on her left pinky. He watched as she negotiated a price with the vendor, her focus intent on getting the best deal.

He followed her, aisle after aisle. He could not get enough of her. She was a magnet pulling him forward. Finally, as if sensing she was being followed, she swiftly turned around and met his gaze. Her penetrating eyes locked on to his. Talia was twenty and a senior majoring in Art History at the state university. Steve was a mere twenty-two and majoring in partying. He had flunked out during his freshman year at State and then tried community college. But school was not "his thing," so he began his carpentry business.

The two became inseparable, and one month later, they were married in a small civil ceremony. Talia had explained to Steve that she had no family and had been living on her own for as long as she could remember. It was always that subject that Steve could not pry out of her. Her eyes frequently would hint at some pain, but in a flash, it was gone.

Steve came from a huge family of Irish and Italian descent. They had very little money to spare, and thus, the small ceremony on a quiet hilltop. It was perfect.

Life was bliss. They rented a tiny one-bedroom apartment, but it was filled with love and a homeyness that Talia could never have imagined. She had just graduated and was looking for a job. To make ends meet, she hand-designed business cards advertising her expertise in antiques and quickly built a small clientele. Steve joked that it was the beautifully embellished cards that built her business, but he knew that it was her innate talent for locating objects of great beauty and uniqueness that made her business flourish. Her taste was impeccable, and people flocked to her. Just two months later, she leased a small space nearby their apartment and opened her own antique shop.

Steve was also building his business. He was so deft with his hands; he could create anything. Quickly, he began to establish himself as a master carpenter in their small community. He worked out of a rented garage space, busy designing and constructing everything from a sturdy oak dining room table and chair set to the delicate intricacy of a honey-maple cradle. And so, it was in this tiny apartment, just six months later, that Talia received the news.

For two weeks, Talia kept the news about her pregnancy from Steve. Her emotions were running wild, scared one second, excited the next. She didn't know how her husband would react. They had been married after knowing each other only a month, and now she was pregnant six months later. The main reason why she lay awake at night was what she had kept hidden from anyone for the past five years.

Saturday began like any other Saturday. The only different thing about it was the secret. She knew that she had to tell him but could not force it out of her mouth. They had woken up to the delicious smell of coffee wafting through the apartment. Steve joked that their coffee pot with its built-in timer was the best wedding gift they received. The night before, Talia was sure to measure out six scoops of decaf. She was already thinking about the pea-shaped baby growing inside.

They spent the morning leisurely reading the newspaper. It was their weekend ritual.

Having a baby would certainly put a kink in that, she thought.

When the last section of the paper lay crumpled on the floor, Steve drew Talia in close. "I think we should throw a housewarming party. We are finally settled, and I want our families to meet. It's time to include them in our lives."

Talia began to protest. She tried convincing her husband that they were just newlyweds and that family somehow always managed to put a dent into new marriages. She began to tell the story about how a friend of a friend's distant cousin ended up housing her in-laws for five months just after their marriage. She went on to say how this poor girl, so crazed by her in-laws, ended up moving out with just the food processor and the clothes on her back.

Steve knew she was joking, but still, he looked at her incredulously. He didn't get why she was so adamant about not including her family. He understood that they were not close, but certainly, she had to have feelings for them. They were her family, after all. Steve reached into the pocket of his robe and pulled out a piece of paper. "I already made a list of my family members and their address. All I need to do is add yours."

Talia whirled around. "You want to do what?" She questioned. Her eyes were ablaze, her back rigid, and her fingers flexed. Her pinky on her left hand twitched. "I thought I was doing a good thing. It's your family, Talia. I would like to meet them and get to know them." Steve moved over to envelop her in his arms. At that moment, a jolt struck. He reeled back in agony and held his throbbing right hand. "What…?" Talia's eyes flashed a greenish-yellow hue, the gold flecks glistening, and she darted over to the corner where she crouched in terror.

"Get out of here now!" she bellowed. "Take your list and leave!"

Steve's eyes widened as he watched Talia writhe in pain. His gaze traveled to the crystal ring on her pinky. He stood immobilized as tiny sparks emanated from the crystal. Slowly the sparks abated, leaving Talia's tiny body shuddering as small flickers of light encircled her body.

And then, as if the ordeal were just a mirage, it was over. Talia stood up and slowly walked over to Steve, who was planted firmly in the same spot from where he watched. She placed her arms around his waist, and began to sob quietly at first, then sobs so strong that they uncontrollably racked her body.

"Shh, it's going to be okay," Steve whispered in her ear. He had no idea what he had just witnessed, but he did know that he loved his wife. Whatever had happened, he was going to stand by her side. He led her to their favorite overstuffed chair. Slowly, he stroked her hair and eased the stiffness in her back. Her sobs soon became a whimper which finally subsided. Her eyes were closed, and her head rested upon his shoulder. All was quiet except for a strange crackling noise that seemed to come from the crystal in the ring. Both their eyes stared intently at the dainty pinky ring. Talia lifted Steve's chin up to meet her gaze and began speaking.

"I was going to tell you, but I just couldn't seem to get the words to come out of my mouth," she murmured. "Every day since the time we first met, I was going to tell you. But something inside of me resisted. I am so sorry, so sorry."

Chapter 3

The Leirion comprised only thirty families. They found a place to call home on the mountaintop Oros in the northern part of Greece. They were a peaceful group with powers that were determined according to the member's position in the clan. The people of Greece believed that the Leirion were named after the Greek white lily. It was rumored that at night when the wind blew, one could often catch its sweet-smelling scent.

The clan did not always live harmoniously. Not too far from Oros Mountain was a small village called Matas. It was in this village that the Leirion lived alongside another group of witches and warlocks who called themselves the Sethos. The Leirion lived simply, and they used their powers only if necessary. No one knew how these clan members first received their powers, but the legend was that when the sun and moon were created, they sent their light cascading through the night sky. That light became embedded into the crystal of the small ring that was on each of the original clan members' left pinky finger that was present at birth. Even the men wore the ring. The chief had the most powerful crystal. Yet he, too, kept his powers at bay. The Sethos clan lived at the other end of the village. They also received the sun, and the moon's energy, except their powers, lay in the crystal in a small pinky ring on their right hand. For centuries upon centuries, the clans coexisted. Life was simple, and all were content.

During the last century, the younger Sethos realized that they could do so much more with their powers. They thought little of waving their hand to conjure a pile of gold coins or causing the farm equipment to cultivate the field under its own power.

Over time, the heightened greed, arrogance, and impulsivity of the younger Sethos ultimately divided the two clans. The Leirion could no longer bear their flagrant disregard of the laws bestowed upon them by the clans' God and fled the village, finding their way to Oros Mountain. There they scaled the crag and began their new life. The Sethos remained in Matas, and the two clans never again came in contact.

The Leirion were self-sufficient. Despite the rocky soil and dry climate, they were able to live off the land. Rumors circulated that the clan could crack open the parched soil with one penetrating stare, and a shoot of asparagus would spring forth. Also, regardless of the poor weather conditions, their cattle were always fat, their sheep plentiful of wool, and their cows abundant of milk. The children were home-schooled and were educated in the fields of art, music, and literature. It was also believed that when the air was still, the sweet notes of children's voices and the melodic plucking of a harp could be heard from the top of the mountain. But these were all rumors, for no one did attempt the dangerous climb up the steep mountainside. From time to time, a clan member would venture down the mountainside, believing that life was better "down below." However, the Desertion Decree, written by the first clan members, stated that once a member left, he or she could never return. Perhaps then, those rumors began with those insisting on abandoning Oros Mountain without thinking of the repercussions it would cause.. The Leirion lived peacefully for fifty years on Oros Mountain. Babies joyfully entered the world, and the elderly passed on, arms opened to welcome their next journey. Although the clan had powers that could immortalize their kind, they did not believe in such practices. They let nature take its course, no matter how difficult it could get at times. And for half a century, that was how they lived.

Peace prevailed until one year, the Leirion welcomed identical twin boys from one family and a beautiful baby girl from another. The mothers were best friends and raised the babies together. All three of the children had powers, but it was the dark-haired beauty who held the most. She was enchanting. Her green eyes, tinged with gold flecks, captivated all the members of the clan. They were fascinated by her intelligence, beauty, and the intensity of her powers.

Like clan members before her, the small crystal ring that was present at her birth was the source of her great powers. The ring grew with her as she grew. As with the rest of the clan, the girl knew that her powers should be used only as a necessity, and all stressed that normalcy was how their god required them to live. From time to time, however, displaying an innocent defiance to her parents, proving that she was still, after all, a teenager, she would wave her pinky in the air and send a bolt of fiery light from the crystal. She would make the flowers dance, and the cows produce chocolate milk. She would laugh, her eyes sparkling in the night sky as lightning struck and rain fell upon her in silvery droplets. She would dance and sing, her voice enrapturing the twins who competed for her attention. They were fifteen, and a day before their sixteenth birthday, both would ask for this young girl's hand in marriage. And she would have to accept one of them to be her husband.

As the boys grew, so did the competition. They acted like spoiled teenagers and would use their powers to try to outdo each other. One would send out sparks to ignite the buckets of milk into flames, while the other would tip the cows over.

The girl knew that she did not want to spend the rest of her life with either one of them. They were insufferable. She pleaded with her parents to let her make her own choice for marriage, but they explained that it was not up to them. On the tallest of the courtyard walls that surrounded the outer ridge of the mountain was carved The Promise of Betrothal. It was this written decree that the clan members must adhere to or suffer the consequences. Still, she beseeched her parents, to no avail, that it was a new world, a new time, and that she should be able to choose with whom she wanted to spend the rest of her life.

One very black night, when the stars had finally shut their eyes, the girl ventured outside to breathe the succulent air. She knew she needed to come to terms with her life. She looked out over the ridge of the mountain and closed her eyes. Just then, the twins grabbed her and pulled her to the ground. Their breath, laden with alcohol, sent fear coursing through her body. Their faces were contorted with anger, and they pressed their weight upon her and vehemently tried to force her to decide. The girl knew at that point that she had only one choice. She lifted her left pinky, and jolts of electricity coursed through the crystal and into the boys' hearts. They flung back into the tallest courtyard wall. She could smell burning flesh but refused to turn around. The girl waved her crystal ring in the air, sending sparks of love to her parents, and ran down the mountain.

Chapter 4

"So, you see, I have not seen my parents for five years," Talia said softly. "They must think that I am dead, or perhaps because it looks like I have disgraced my family and the other members, they have considered me dead all the same. I have often thought about going back up the mountain, but it is the law that once someone leaves, they cannot go back. I have spent endless hours looking deep into my crystal, trying to coax out some sign that my parents are doing well. But nothing. I am ashamed of my powers at times. I will never forgive what those boys tried to do to me, but the thought of having killed is too much to bear."

Talia stopped speaking. Her eyes glistened, and her cheeks were flushed. She twirled the crystal ring around and around her finger and waited for Steve to say something, anything.

He brushed his lips against hers and murmured, "My poor baby," again and again until Talia fell asleep.

While Steve continued to stroke Talia's hair, thoughts were flying wildly through his head. My wife's a witch? My wife grew up on a mountain? There was so much more to talk about, but he did not want to wake her. Although the story was unsettling, he still felt intense love for Talia and knew they would be able to weather any storm.

The sky was black when Talia opened her eyes. Steve's arms were numb, but he did not want to move. When she saw him rubbing them vigorously, she joked, "Would you like me to use my powers to speed up your circulation?" Her eyes had their usual sparkle, and her body was relaxed.

"Hmm, could you do that?" he joked back. He looked at her and knew everything would be okay. Talia explained how at just fifteen, she was on her own.

For the next two years, Talia relied on her powers in ways that no one in the clan would have approved. She herself was ashamed but had had no choice. She extracted money from people's bank accounts with the swift wave of her crystal ring and was able to set herself up in a small apartment. She picked a remote spot so she would not be too conspicuous. She became a voracious reader and consumed hundreds of books.

"Having powers does have some advantages," she said with a twinkle in her eye. "I was able to read at super-fast speed and absorb vast amounts of information. During this time, I became interested in art history. I knew I wanted to pursue a degree. When I was seventeen, with the powers from the crystal in my ring, I created a credible bio and became the high-school student that every university was dying to accept into their prestigious institution. And you know the rest. I am so sorry that I never mentioned this to you.

But our relationship happened so quickly, and how do you tell your husband that you are a witch?"

Talia stood up and began to pace. She walked over to her husband, placed his hand on her belly, and whispered, "I have something else I need to tell you."

"A baby?" Steve repeated the phrase over and over, uncertain that he hadn't heard her correctly. He lifted her and began to twirl. "Uh, you might want to put me down. Morning sickness just doesn't happen in the AM," Talia joked. "So now you can see why I am scared. It's hard enough knowing you are going to be a dad after six months of marriage and when we are just starting out, but it's even scarier to know that the possibility of giving birth to a baby with powers is very real."

Steve gingerly placed her down on the floor and hugged her once more. "I love you, and I love our baby, whether she is mortal or a witchlet."

"A witchlet?" Talia tossed her head back and laughed. All her worries melted away. She knew that her life would be complete.

Chapter 5

Avery slammed the front door and stomped up the stairs. She hated her life. She just wanted to climb back into bed and sleep the days away. She could hear her mom climbing the steps. *God, why did she have to make a bad day even worse? Couldn't she just leave me alone like every other teenager's mom did?* She thought.

Avery's mom softly knocked on the bedroom door. She didn't want to answer, but then guilt washed over her. She forced herself up from the bed and swung the door open.

"What's up, Mom?" she asked with an exasperated sigh.

"Lucy's mom called. She told me that Lucy came home very upset today. She said something about your locker being vandalized." Avery retreated into her room.

"Avery, please tell me what happened."

Avery looked at her mom's pleading eyes. She gazed down at her mom's crystal pinky ring and then at her own crystal embedded into her palm. Why couldn't they just be "normal"? Why did Lucy have to say anything? She was her only friend at school. Avery knew she meant well, but at this moment, she just wanted to be left alone. Avery held her mom's hand and touched the ring.

The crystal sizzled and sent tiny sparks into the air. She then touched her own crystal. It hissed, and effervescent light shot into the air. Avery knew that her own powers were much stronger than her mom's, and Talia told Avery repeatedly how the slightest shift in her emotions could set off her powers. And being a teenager just made things worse.

"I didn't do anything, Mom. I promise. I just went on with my day." Tears spilled out of her eyes, smearing her heavy eyeliner. Her pouty lips, painted with a dark maroon stain, trembled. Avery pushed her long black hair out of her emerald green eyes and looked up at her mom.

"Everything about me is abnormal. Look at me." Avery stood. Her body was lean like her mom's, but even in stocking feet, she had a good five inches on her. That, she knew, she got from her dad's side. "I am like a giraffe!"

Avery plopped back on the bed, tears still streaming down her face.

"I know, honey. I know that you did not do anything. I am so sorry that you thought I would not believe you. I am so sorry that you have to put up with all of this." She stroked her daughter's silky hair and pulled her close. "It will be okay. Don't worry. You are my baby, and I will always protect and love you."

Now, Avery pulled back. "I love you, Mom. You know I do, but I must work this out for myself." She touched the small crystal in her palm. "When did you know? When did you and Dad realize that I was like you?"

"We didn't know at first. We were looking for the crystal pinky ring, and when we did not see it, we thought you were mortal like your dad."

"Were you relieved?" Avery asked.

Talia smiled. "Either way, we knew you were perfect. Your skin was the softest pink, your lips were like rosebuds, and all your fingers and toes were accounted for. That's all that mattered to us."

"So, when did you finally realize I was a Leirion?"

"When your dad and I brought you home from the hospital. Your dad's mom crocheted you the most beautiful sweater, booties, and hat. While we were struggling to get your tiny fists through the sweater, your fingers kept poking through the holes, and that is when we saw it. There was a fleck on the palm of your left hand. It was so minuscule that even the doctors did not see it. I had never seen this, and I could only assume that the crystal embedded in your hand meant that the new generation of Leirion would have much stronger powers. Your Dad and I knew we would have to raise you not to rely on them or abuse them. But from the time I told your dad I was pregnant and who I was, we both knew it would not matter whether you were a Leirion or a mortal. Our love for you, even before you were born, was immeasurable. We want you to be happy. That's all we've ever wanted."

Avery ran her fingers over her palm. "It's so hard. Sometimes I feel like I don't have the control I once had. Every day is becoming more of a struggle to keep my powers intact."

Talia looked into her daughter's flashing eyes. "You must, Avery. You must."

The alarm clock blared. Avery hit the snooze button and rolled over. She dreaded another day filled with snotty girls, idiotic boys, and boring teachers. *Why can't I just be home-schooled like my mom was when she lived on the mountaintop?* She only had this year left and couldn't wait to be finished. Finally, she trudged over to her mirror. She looked closely, and for the first time in a very long time, Avery liked what she saw.

Her skin was smooth and free of makeup, her hair, still straight even after her tossing and turning throughout the night, and her eyes were shiny. She touched the mirror as if afraid that it was someone else staring back at her.

A thought of Ryan raced through her head. *Would he like what he saw?* Ryan was the one guy who rattled her to the bones. They never spoke in the two weeks that Avery had been attending

Stanton, but she always felt that he was watching her. Some days, the wispy hairs on her neck would stand up, sending goose bumps down her arms. On other days, her left hand felt like it was on fire, and her eyes burned. They were strange reactions, and she just chalked it off as a crush that she had on him.

Avery dusted her high cheekbones with rose-colored blush. Instead of the heavy black eyeliner rimming her eyes, she used a soft brown and filled her lips in with a soft pink lip gloss. *God knows I have enough makeup*; she laughed to herself. *My mom must own stock in Sephora.*

Avery left her hair straight and combed it till it was a shiny black mane. She dressed simply, a pair of Levi jeans and an American Apparel t-shirt. Instead of the heavy chain necklace, she fastened a simple gold locket. Avery stared at the mirror once more. She liked what she saw staring back, but at the same time, a feeling of sadness washed over her. *Is this the real Avery, or is the Gothic version the real Avery? Who was the real Avery?*

Avery crept down the stairs. Her mission was to get out the door without her parents seeing her, but no such luck. Her mom was in the kitchen, reading the front page of the newspaper while gripping her cup of coffee. She looked up and nearly dropped the mug.

"Don't say a word. I figured, if you can't fight 'em, then join 'em," she replied.

"You look beautiful." Her mom set her mug down on the table and walked over to her. She stared into Avery's eyes. "Do not let your appearance color who you really are. You are an amazing girl with or without your powers, and I only want you to find happiness."

"Thanks, Mom." Avery gave her parents a quick hug and ran for the bus.

The fifteen-minute bus ride felt like fifteen seconds, and Avery dreaded going into the school. She felt like everyone was staring and whispering about her. She couldn't wait to get her driver's license. Although she was already seventeen, her parents wanted her to wait a couple of months so she could practice more. *Deep breaths, Avery, take deep breaths*, she told herself. She faced her locker. The custodians must have painted over the harsh words during the night, but their impact was still etched into her heart.

"It's a good look for you, but I thought you looked cooler the other way."

Even though she had never heard that voice before, she knew who it was. Avery whirled around and found herself face-to-face with Ryan. He stood close to her, a little too close. One hand was resting on her locker just above her head, the other pushing his stubborn bangs out of his eyes. *Those eyes,* she thought. She could not resist staring into them. He was taller than she, and his jaw, chiseled stone. He did not budge, his hand still firmly planted just above her head. She could feel the crystal pulsating. She could see a faint shadow of stubble on that perfect jaw, and yet she could not look away.

Avery could smell the leather of his jacket, and she fought the urge to wrap her arms around him. *What is wrong with me? I am acting like all the other girls at Stanton.* She swore to herself that she would not turn into one of them.

Finally, she broke his gaze and slid under his arm to free herself from captivity. "Uh, I guess I'll take that as a compliment," was all she managed to muster. *Oh my God,* she internalized. *I sound like a blubbering idiot.* Avery turned, her long legs taking graceful but purposeful strides to get away. But Ryan managed to jump ahead.

"I guess what I meant to say was that you look good no matter how you dress. I'll see you around, Avery." He held her gaze for a moment too long to be considered polite, turned, and sauntered off down the hall.

He knew my name! Avery thought. She opened the door to her math class, took a second-row seat, and sat up straight. *Maybe today will be a great day after all*, she thought.

As he rounded the corner, Ryan took one last look at Avery. Everything about her was perfect. He used every ounce of control not to run his hands down her glossy black hair. And her eyes; he tried to resist looking into them but found them mesmerizing. She was beautiful, just like he was told she would be.

Ryan pushed open the door to his science class. The cool metal door was a relief against the hot pulsating crystal embedded in his right hand.

Avery was waiting for the inevitable. She knew that the morning was going by far too well for something disastrous not to happen. She could feel the stares, but often they would turn into smiles.

"Hey, Avery, how's it going?"

Avery looked up from her locker and came face to face with Peter Saunders. He was a senior at Stanton, the captain of the varsity football team, editor of the school newspaper, and president of the senior class. He was well-liked and gorgeous.

"Uh, hey," she faltered.

"I was wondering if you were going to the football game Friday night. There's going to be a party afterward at my house. Maybe you can stop by."

The crystal in Avery's hand sent off little sparks of energy. She wrapped her hand around her bookbag strap tightly. He was so cute; his hair spiked in every which way, clearly something over which he had no control. His eyes were the softest blue, and his body was lean and muscular.

"I am going with Lucy, and the party sounds like fun. We'll be sure to stop by," replied Avery, her legs secretly doing the happy dance.

"Sounds like a plan." Peter touched her arm.

His touch sent off a spark that even Avery could not control. It traveled up her bookbag strap and down Peter's arm. But instead of reeling back in pain, terror, or disbelief, he looked straight into her eyes and smiled. Avery felt her cheeks reddening.

"Uh, gotta go, or I'll be late for my class," she stammered. She took off down the hall. Avery spotted Lucy and ran to catch up. She grabbed her arm. "You will never guess what just happened."

"I have a clue. I saw the two of you talking."

"He seems sweet," Avery said. "But I sounded like a blubbering idiot."

Lucy laughed, "Don't take yourself so seriously." She hugged Avery, and the two of them laughed all the way to class.

Ryan watched from the end of the hall. *God, she was so beautiful. What did she see in that Peter? Just another jock that uses his status to get what he wants.* Ryan knew that really wasn't true. Peter had the reputation of being a good guy. He watched the exchange between the two of them. He sensed the electricity that Peter felt when he put his hand on Avery's arm.

Jealousy bubbled inside of him. She should be his. He had a connection with her. He knew she felt it, too. He wanted to touch her but knew it was too dangerous. He wanted to place *his* hand on her arm but knew that she would detect something too familiar. He craved to touch her face, her hair, her graceful neck.

"Hey. You coming, or what?" asked his buddy Mike.

Ryan shook his head, relieved to be pulled out of his trance.

With one last look at Avery, he curled his hand into a fist and spoke so quietly that only he could hear himself. "Don't worry, Dad. I will keep my promise."

Chapter 6

The sun rose, casting its rays across the village of Oros. Like every day, the adult Leirion started their morning with the same ritual they had performed for centuries. With their chief leading the ceremony, they gathered inside the long meeting house that connected all their simple but sturdy stone homes, clasped hands, and thanked their God and ancestors for bestowing upon them such good fortune. They looked up to the open window on the roof and watched for the morning dove to greet them, acknowledging their thanks. But today, something was amiss. There was no dove. In its place was a hawk. The Leirion knew what that meant. The bird's ominous wings flapped rapidly. "Something is dreadfully wrong," the chief announced in a hesitant voice. They ran out to the courtyard. There, lay the two boys.

Wails of unadulterated grief erupted from their parents. Darius lay in a pool of silvery liquid. Alec lay on top of him. Rivulets of silvery liquid oozed out of Alec's back. Sobs racked his body as he tried to use the crystal in his ring to bring Darius back to life. Tiny sparks shot out but petered before they could touch his brother.

Another cry filled the air. "Where is Talia?" Talia's mother frantically searched the courtyard and all the common areas. She ran back to the house only to find the bed still neatly made.

At that moment, Alec looked up at the girl's mother with eyes so cold that it seemed like her tears could freeze on the spot. "She killed my brother and tried to kill me as well," he said venomously.

The mother dropped to her knees. *It could not be,* she thought to herself. *My sweet Talia could never do something so evil.*

Suddenly he was upon her, clawing at her face like a ravaged wolf. He grabbed her pinky ring and pressed his finger into the crystal. "Make him come back to life!" He screamed into her agonized face. "You have amazing powers, just like your evil daughter. I order you to bring him back!"

"You know I cannot do that. It is against the Orders of Life. Accept his death. His soul has already left him." The mother looked at him. Her gaze was unfaltering. "Where is my daughter?" she asked. "What have you done to her?"

He slowly stood up. "Your daughter is in hell, and there she will rot!" Alec stared into the mother's eyes. "I swear upon my brother's grave that I will avenge his death!"

The burial for Darius was quick. If one waited too long to bury the body, its powers would poison the ground. And so, at the edge of the mountain, the Leirion held a brief ceremony, and Darius's body was lowered into the ground. A hedge stone carved out of granite marked his grave, and a tiny lily was planted firmly into the dry soil next to him.

From that moment on, the village was never the same again. Mornings of gratitude ended. The crystals in the clan members' rings had lost their powers. The cattle became weak, the sheep lost their wool, and the cows' milk dried up. The ground hardened, and crops withered up and died. Despair permeated their lives. One brother was dead, one brother's grief consumed him with such hatred and revenge, and one daughter was never to be seen again. The Leirion were now divided, and the contrasting loyalties caused more strife. The young villagers knew they must leave their home of Oros mountain, for they still had much to do on this earth. The elders accepted their destiny and stayed behind. They believed in the afterlife and were not afraid to begin their next journey.

With the barest of essentials, the clan members and their children descended the mountain. They did not know what to expect. They knew they no longer had any powers, and so it was up to their knowledge and wisdom to find their way in this new life.

It took the Leirion five days and nights to travel down the mountain. The journey was arduous. The sides were steep and rocky. Many of the clan members suffered immensely. Their legs were blooded from the jagged rocks, and their palms were calloused to the point that they were uncertain that they could hold on for much longer. They begged to be left behind on the side of the mountain, but the other clan members would not hear of such a thing. The air was bitter, causing many to heave in spasms and be unable to catch their breath. The wails of pain mixed in with sorrow seemed to permeate each member's soul. The only food they had was what was left before their powers had run dry, and that was saved for the children.

The clan was so divided with grief that the two groups could not bear to be near each other, and so they descended the mountain on different sides. Talia's mother and father led the way down the north side, while Alec's parents led the way on the south. The pain in each mother's heart from losing a child was so immense that neither one of them knew how to forgive the other. Where they were to end up, no one knew. Finally, after what felt like an eternity to these villagers, the two groups arrived at what would be their new homes. They were about forty miles from each other, and that was far enough for wounds to begin to heal.

Life began to resume some normalcy. However, many of the clan members found it difficult to obtain jobs. But they were a resilient group and knew how to make the best out of the worst. Talia's mother and father slowly weaved together a new life, the hole in their hearts never mending completely.

Alec's parents also began to find a spot in their hearts where the memory of their son Darius could finally lay dormant. Although they did not see Talia's parents, they found a way to forgive. This was the way of the Leirion, and many times Alec's mom would look out into the vast sky and yearn to speak to her dear friend.

One clan member, however, could not forgive. With each year, his resentment smoldered. His heart was stone, and no person could chisel out even a fragment to be let in.

A year later, with only a duffle bag of his few belongings, Alec left the village. He traveled aimlessly, taking on odd jobs to survive. He had a mission to complete. He knew that he had broken his parents' hearts, but he only wanted one thing, revenge. It had to be the sweetest revenge. He knew that his ring was now useless, and so he yanked it off, and with all the strength he could muster, threw it without even a thought to where it might land.

Every night he thought about Talia, how she rejected him, how she killed his brother, how she ruined his life, and how she destroyed his powers. He knew he had to be patient. He would wait for as long as it took.

Chapter 7

Talia and Steve woke up to snow blanketing the frigid earth. On days like these, they were grateful that they worked so close to their home. The sun's rays were beaming through the antique shop's window so brightly it was blinding. Talia walked over to draw the curtains when she heard the chime that hung from the door of her antique shop play their sweet melody. "May I help you?" she asked the stranger who entered the store. He looked to be about her age. He wore a black wool coat, black turtleneck, and jeans. His hair was jet black, and his eyes were shielded by dark sunglasses.

"I am looking for a gift for my parents' twentieth wedding anniversary. I believe that crystal is the theme for that year. Cost is not an issue."

Talia's back went rigid. The man's voice sounded oddly familiar, but she could not place it. "I believe that crystal is for the fifteenth anniversary and china is for the twentieth. We have some beautiful china tea sets I am sure your parents would adore." She led him to a small aisle in the back. His presence was disturbing. Maybe it was because she was alone in this tiny shop with a stranger, and Steve was not home. Usually, men did not shop in Talia's antique store. She showed him an array of delicate tea sets, commenting on their origins and patterns.

The man shook his head. "No, thank you. I am set on crystal. I'll just tell my parents I am five years behind." He let out a little chuckle and strode over to a crystal chandelier hanging from the ceiling. "She sure is a beauty," he whispered as if he were speaking to himself.

The sun's rays filtering in through the window caught the hundreds of crystals strung from the chandelier and sent a multitude of rainbows dancing across the shop. "You know what they say about crystals," the man said softly, staring at Talia. Talia felt herself taking a few steps back from this man. "Rumor has it that crystals have powers, healing powers. If you touch a crystal, you can feel its vibration." He paused, continuing to stare. "I'll take it. My parents will love looking at it and remembering their twenty years together."

"It certainly is exquisite. I am sure your parents will love it. I will have to dismantle it and wrap all the crystals separately. It will take some time for me to pack it up. Would you like me to ship it to your parents' address? You can fill out a card right now, and I will box and wrap it beautifully." She pointed to the rolls of wrapping paper.

"No, I will take it with me."

"Very well, then. Give me about an hour. Would you give me your phone number, and I can call you when its ready?"

The man shook his head. "I would rather wait."

Talia looked at him quizzically. She wished he would take off his sunglasses. Not being able to see his eyes unsettled her. "Well, feel free to browse around." She walked over to the corner and pulled the step stool over to where the chandelier hung. But before she could climb her first step, the man rushed over to her.

"Here, let me. I can see you are in no condition to be climbing ladders." His gaze lowered and settled onto the tiny bump of her belly.

Talia felt herself blush. "Thank you," she said quietly. "I didn't think I would be showing this much at eight weeks."

Alec looked into her eyes. Her dark green eyes were still flecked with that amazing gold he had remembered. *God, she was still so beautifully mystifying,* he thought. The heat that she gave off made him break out into beads of sweat. As he watched Talia wrap up each crystal, he was acutely aware of how the crystal in her own pinky ring sparkled brightly. Because Talia had disappeared before the clan members had discovered his brother and him, she maintained her powers. Talia's powers were always the strongest of the three children born that day, and he knew he must be careful.

"Here you are," Talia said to him after she counted the thick pile of crisp one-hundred-dollar bills. "I know your parents will enjoy this for twenty more years."

The man did not move to take the box. He stared into her eyes. Talia resisted the urge to yank his glasses off, but she would look like a madwoman; especially after the amazing cash sale she just had. "It was a pleasure meeting you," she said.

In one swift movement, he took her left hand and placed his over hers.

"What a beautiful ring," he murmured.

"It is my wedding ring," Talia replied, pulling her hand from his.

"Wedding ring?" the man questioned.

Talia let out a nervous laugh. "It was my husband's grandmother's ring. She must have been quite a bit smaller than I since it only fits on my pinky."

"Your husband is certainly a lucky man."

Talia blushed. "That's very kind of you to say that, Mr.--"

"My name is A--"

Talia stiffened.

"Adam. You can call me Adam."

Talia made herself relax. *She was losing it today,* she thought. *It must be my hormones doing crazy things to my head.* She looked down at the man's hands as they grasped the bulky package. They were ungloved. The fingers were slender and bare. "Goodbye, Adam. Thank you again."

She closed the door, slumped into an antique rocking chair, and stared at the large pile of money. Somehow, it did not make her smile.

Alec shoved the package into his car. Staring at the small door of the antique shop, he exhaled a long breath. Three years of searching. Three years of all his energy spent looking for her. Three years of working in crappy jobs and living in a tiny roach-infested one-room apartment finally paid off. *It could not have gone any better*, he thought to himself. "A baby," he said aloud. Turning the key in his ignition, he pulled slowly out of the graveled driveway. At that moment, he knew that his plan had changed. "See you soon, Talia. See you soon," he laughed to nobody.

Talia heard Steve calling her name and then the chimes.

"What are you still doing here? I saw the lights on while driving home. It's dinnertime, and you are working too hard in your condition. When was the last time you ate?" Steve rubbed her hands. They were ice cold. "What's the matter, honey?"

"I had the most unsettling customer today. I felt like I knew him. He bought that crystal chandelier that you just hung up in the shop. You know the one that we bought at the estate sale?"

Steve chuckled. "How can I forget? You made me dig deep into that mouse-infested box to locate every crystal. And then you made me Windex *every* one of those crystals. Boy, the things a man does for love."

Talia managed to smile, but Steve could see the tiny lines that furrowed between his wife's beautiful eyes. "Well, I guess the fruits of your labor paid off because, without a moment's hesitation about the exorbitant price, he just purchased it."

"But that's great, Talia. Isn't it?"

Talia shook her head. "Yes, it is, but the man just gave me the chills. I guess it's just pre-baby jitters that have gotten me so on edge." She patted her belly and smiled. "I just can't wait until our baby is born."

Steve smiled back. "Me either. Come on; let's grab dinner at Alfonso's to celebrate your huge sale."

"I should warn you, though. I am eating for two now, so our profits might not be as huge." Talia hugged her husband. "Let's go. I am starving.

Chapter 8

Can Friday go any slower? Avery thought as she counted the minutes in her last-period class. Finally, she was going out. The football game sounded like fun. This would be her first. But the thing that she looked forward to more than that, was Peter's party.

I wonder if Ryan's friends with him, she thought. As cute as Peter was, she could not get her mind off Ryan. Her heart raced when she thought of him against her locker. And to make matters worse, Ryan was sitting in the back of the classroom. Chemistry was the only class they had together. Not that it would have mattered. Except for that one time, he never uttered a word to her.

The thought of him made her shift uncomfortably in the small wooden seat attached to the desk, causing her arm to fall to her side and hit the edge of the desk. Just then, she felt a small current of electricity leave her palm. *Oh my god,* she thought frantically. She was afraid to turn around.

"Not now, not now," she whispered. She willed herself to turn her head. A tiny spark traveled quickly across the floor. The teacher spoke monotonously, and the students seemed to be in a trance from boredom. She watched the spark pick up speed until it came to a dead stop in front of Ryan.

Avery watched as Ryan bent down and placed his right hand over the spark. His hand was illuminated, and a fiery red current shot out of his fingers. He closed his fingers into a fist, and the sparks ceased. Avery stared as Ryan raised his head and met her gaze. His green eyes were much like hers, except now, his looked like cold, hard marbles. Avery blinked and quickly turned back towards the front. Her eyes were fixated on the clock, silently pleading for the hands to move more quickly. The bell finally rang. Avery shot out of his seat and rushed out the door.

"Bye, Mom. Lucy's parents are going to pick us up from the party." Avery and Lucy jumped out of the car and headed toward the bleachers. She was excited but also nervous. This was sort of her debut, and she hoped that Lucy's friends were going to accept her.

"Avery," her mom called out. "Have fun but remember, keep yourself under control."

"What was that all about?" Lucy asked.

"Nothing. She's just paranoid after seeing all those videos on TikTok of teens going wild. I mean, really, first Facebook and Instagram, then Snapchat, and now this. Why can't parents just stay off our social media and stick to Facebook?"

Lucy laughed, "I know what you mean. My mom is constantly trying to follow my friends and leave a comment. I call her the 'Stalker'."

Avery and Lucy walked over to the group of kids. She recognized most of them. Charlotte and Brandon were there. Her heart skipped a beat, and she held her breath.

"Hey, Avery," Brandon said while linking arms with Charlotte. "Good to see you." Charlotte just nodded and pursed her lips to force a smile.

Well, one out of two isn't bad, Avery thought to herself.

"Come on, Brandon. Everyone's waiting for us up in the bleachers." Charlotte practically pulled his arm out of the socket while she led him away. Avery did not like that girl, and it took all her energy not to let her emotions stir up her powers.

"I guess we should also find seats." Lucy led Avery to a section of the bleachers. She heard someone calling her name. She did not have to turn around to know that it was Ryan.

Ryan was walking nonchalantly up the asphalt track. Lucy raised her eyebrows and quizzically looked at Avery as if to say, "How do you know him?"

Ryan had an air about him that had all the students at Stanton turned off but, at the same time, intrigued. He did not go out of his way to make conversation with anyone. Even to the teachers, he was indifferent. But he had charisma. He had the reputation of a Bad Boy.

"I'll catch up to you, Lucy. I will only be a few minutes."

Lucy shrugged and walked to find the group saving seats for them.

Avery waited for Ryan. She was not going to act like she was some stupid schoolgirl crush. He walked slowly-- *too slowly,* she thought. *He really does think he's all that.* He kept his right hand shoved into his low-slung jeans. Despite the chilly night air, he wore only a black T-shirt.

"So now you're in with the popular group." His voice was husky, and goosebumps blanketed Avery's arms. "You are finally getting what you wanted all along."

Avery shot an angry look at him. "How do you know what I want? You don't even know me." She turned and started to walk away.

"I know more than you think I do."

Avery swung around. Her green eyes focused upon Ryan's. The gold flecks mirrored the gold in her eyes. He moved closer. He took his hand out of his pocket and touched her face. Intense heat scorched her icy cheek. He grabbed her left hand and clasped his right hand around it. Their crystals touched, sending electrifying currents coursing through her body. He pulled her even closer, and his blazing lips touched hers. The rough kiss almost sent her reeling backward. Avery could not believe how strong the powers from her crystal were at that moment.

"What do you want from me?" Avery demanded.

Ryan gazed at her once more and whispered, "Everything."

Chapter 9

It did not take long for Alec to set his plan into motion. He traveled to Greece to the village of Matas, where he knew the Sethos had settled. He remembered the endless stories his grandparents and parents told him and his brother about this clan and how they used their powers for selfish reasons.

Alec knew he would have to find someone quickly to father his child. Talia was already eight weeks along. He had no power or money to offer, but he did have the power of seduction and knew how to execute it. It took him five days to meet the perfect woman. Her name was Korinna. She had golden hair and light blue eyes. She looked nothing like Talia, and that was what he wanted. Alec also learned from one of the villagers that just a year before, Korinna had married a mortal.

Korinna's husband, Ben, was a photojournalist. He had been sent from the United States to follow a lead about a group of people living in Matas who claimed to have special powers. This was Ben's first job as a reporter and the first time since he was hired six months ago that he was given the opportunity to travel abroad. He was both excited and apprehensive about the assignment. He had spent four years majoring in journalism at Fulton University, a major in which his professors had drilled into him that his job was to only report the cold hard facts and remain objective. And traveling this far to find a "clan of witches" did not jive with his pragmatic side.

A day after Ben arrived in Greece, he met Korinna. The two had fallen in love instantly. Korinna confided in Ben and told him she was a Sethos. She showed him what her powers could do, only to prove that witches did exist.

For two weeks, the two were inseparable as Korinna showed Ben the sights of Matas and explained Sethos' history. Korinna knew that it would prove to be detrimental if Ben wrote an article about them, and she expressed her concerns to him. Love overpowered Ben's need for the "story," and the two were married at the end of the second week. They had a quiet ceremony with just them and the chief initiating the service, and nine months to the day that they had consummated their love for each other, Korinna gave birth to a beautiful baby boy. Korinna loved her son and husband intensely, and she and Ben vowed to keep her powers a secret. She remembered all too well, the harm and destruction that the powers could garner, and so she wanted nothing more than for them to act like a "normal" family. It was those memories that also made her use her powers to perform one last act of secrecy, an act that only she was ever to know about.

Married life was easy at first. Korinna learned to cook instead of just waving her hand and creating a three-course meal.

She savored the time at night when she would rock her baby to sleep and sing the most mesmerizing songs. She could not get enough of staring into his crystal-blue eyes and smiled to herself while she watched him struggle to keep them open while she sang. She loved her baby son and husband so much; she would sacrifice anything for them.

But one snowy night, when the baby was just three months old, Korinna and Ben got into a huge fight. It was over something silly, but it had escalated into the two of them calling each other hateful names.

Korinna, in a fit of anger, waved her right hand and sent off shocks of electricity. The bolts were headed straight for her husband and son. Korinna ran to them and shielded their bodies with her own. She absorbed the shocks into her own body, leaving Ben and her son unscathed.

Ben knew that Korinna risked her own life for them, but he was too worried that when the next time her anger boiled inside her, they would not be as lucky. On that snowy night, while she slept exhausted from the ordeal, Ben took his son and left. Korinna was afraid of her own powers and feared that if she tried to find Ben and their son, she would end up hurting them.

From that day on, she spent her days as a recluse. After a few weeks, no one tried to break the hardened shell she had created for herself. Until Alec came along.

Alec wooed Korinna, promising his undying love for her. Korinna did not know Alec's plan. She did not know where he had come from or that he, too, had once been a warlock. What she did know, was that he showered her with the attention and the love that she so craved. Korinna told him about her powers and what had happened to her. And all the time, as she was pouring out her heart and soul to him, Alec remained a mystery.

A week later, they were married. "I want a son to carry on my name," Alec told her as they lay in bed. He touched the small crystal set in Korinna's right-hand pinky ring. Alec knew that she would give him whatever he wanted. But to his surprise, Korinna bolted up and looked at him with such grief that it seemed, at any moment, her body would crumble into ashes.

"No, I can't go through that again," she sobbed. "I just can't. I miss my son so much, Alec. I can't bear to lose you or another child if my powers take control of me."

Alec stroked her hair. "Shh, that won't happen." His voice was like syrup, and it seemed to calm her down. "We will have the most perfect son, and neither he, nor I will ever leave you."

Korinna looked at him. Her blue eyes were flecked with silver. Alec felt the smallest pang of guilt, but he knew what he had to do. And so, with their bodies locked and small currents igniting, they created a baby boy.

Chapter 10

Avery and Lucy stood elbow to elbow in the crowded room of Peter's basement. The music was blaring, and Avery could not believe how many kids were crammed into the space. She recognized many of the faces, but she was trying to find Peter.

She felt a tap on her shoulder, and as she turned, found Peter grinning at her and pointing at the stairs. Avery followed. "How did you like the game?" he asked her when they reached the top.

Too flustered by his touch, Avery stammered, "it was good." *Oh my god, I am such a dork*, she thought.

Peter smiled. "I see you're a real big football fan." He laughed.

Avery blushed. She scanned the room for Lucy. She didn't want to leave her standing by herself.

As if sensing her thoughts, Peter said, "She's fine." Avery found her friend and saw Peter was right.

Lucy was surrounded by all the cheerleaders. They were all laughing, throwing their heads back as if someone had told the funniest joke.

"Lucy's a nice girl," he continued. "I am glad that the two of you are friends." He looked at Avery with a meaningful stare; his eyes glinted with silver specks. "Choose your friends wisely, Avery." He then smiled and laced his fingers into hers.

Avery needed to calm down. The feel of Peter's hand made her heart race.

"So, it's great that your parents let you have parties at your house. I could just see my mom saying, 'yes, darling, no problem.' to a houseful of teenagers." She rolled her eyes and laughed.

Peter looked at her. At once, Avery knew she had said something wrong.

"It's just my dad and me, and he's really cool--for a dad, that is. He's upstairs in case he needs to throw someone out. I never knew my mom. My dad told me she left when I was only three months old. I don't remember anything about her, and I guess it's better that way. Sort of like she never existed in the first place."

"I am so sorry," Avery said softly.

Peter gently squeezed her hand. "I have a really fantastic dad. He even came to my second-grade "Mom and Me" tea. You should have seen the stares, but he did not care. He sipped out of that teacup with his pinky pointed straight out and nibbled on the sugar cookies that we had made in class."

Avery laughed. "I hope I can meet him one day."

"That can be arranged," Peter said, giving her hand a tiny squeeze.

The night flew by. Avery had to be home by twelve. "I might turn into Cinderella," she joked to Peter. She didn't want to leave, but Lucy's parents would be picking them up any minute.

Peter placed his hand in the small of Avery's back and led her to the outside patio. The air felt good on her hot cheeks. She didn't know if it was just the stifling heat inside, or how Peter made her feel. She let out a tiny shiver. Peter pulled her close.

"I really like you, Avery." He held her face with his hands. They felt so cool. His lips were soft as they barely touched hers-- not like Ryan's. *God, why am I thinking of him?* She shut her eyes tighter, trying to block out any more thoughts of Ryan.

Avery returned his kisses and began to feel the tiny sparks shooting out of her hand. Panicked that Peter might feel them, Avery opened her eyes, and she watched as he continued to hold her face. He didn't seem to notice. His eyes opened, and he stared at her. "You are so beautiful," he murmured.

"Ahem, are you ready, Avery?" Lucy stood at the slider leading onto the patio. "I'm sorry, but my parents texted me and said for us to be outside in two minutes. God, I can't wait until I get my license. Two more months, and I am free!" she laughed.

Embarrassed, Avery broke Peter's hold and looked at Lucy. "Yes, I will be out front in a minute." She felt every nerve ending in her body tingle. She was flustered and excited at the same time. "Well, I guess I will see you Monday."

Peter took her left hand. "Can I talk to you this weekend?"

"Definitely."

He held her hand a moment longer and then said, "You better go." Avery shook her head and headed toward the front yard.

"Well, I see you had a great time," Lucy teased as they sat in the backseat of her dad's car.

"The best," Avery whispered back, not being able to hold back her smile.

Chapter 11

Alec's plan was working perfectly. He and Korinna along with their baby boy, Ryan, moved to a town close to where Talia and Avery lived. He followed their lives closely and waited patiently for the right time to seek revenge. When they were forced to relocate due to Avery's "mishaps," so did Alec and his family. This did not make Korinna happy, but she loved her husband with so much passion and devotion that she abided by his wishes.

Unlike Korinna's former husband, Alec demanded that she use her powers. Although he did not mention this to his wife, he felt that he was entitled to benefit from them after all the suffering he was put through in the past years. He persuaded Korinna to flourish her right hand in large, sweeping motions to create piles of money, enabling them to buy the biggest house in the neighborhood and live extravagantly.

These extreme actions did not come without a hefty price. Korinna's health began to deteriorate at an alarming speed. Ryan acted just like his father, self-absorbed and insolent. Unlike his father, whom Korinna believed to be born a mortal, Ryan was born a warlock like herself and used his powers from the crystal embedded in his right palm in dishonest ways. He felt studying was a waste of time and would use the crystal to extract the answers from his teachers' brains. He made friends by using his powers and did not need to keep them around unless they served his purpose at that given moment. Despite all that, Korinna loved her son, and Ryan doted upon his mother.

It was a Friday night, and the two had just finished watching *Charlie and the Chocolate Factory,* starring Johnny Depp. Korinna read Ryan the book when he was a child, and it became his favorite. It was one of those rare occasions when he wasn't out with his friends. Korinna made her famous chili popcorn, and the two sat together until the credits were rolling. As Korinna watched the screen turn to black, all she could think about was how the characters' greed and spoiled ways led to their demise.

Ryan rose to take the dishes into the kitchen, but Korinna gently took his hand and sat him back down next to her. Her voice was strained. "I want you to be a good person, Ryan. I have seen what my clan members have done in the past. These behaviors will only lead to tragedy. Please, for me, give up your egotistical ways."

Ryan patted his mother's knee. "Come on, Mom. It is all in good fun." He tried his hardest to sound sincere. "You have given me powers, so why shouldn't I use them?" Ryan hugged his mother. "Now, let me get those dishes for you. You look so tired tonight. Don't worry. Everything will be fine." Korinna slumped back into the couch. Every nerve in her body told her otherwise.

When Ryan turned 16, tragedy struck. The family had moved again, following Talia and Avery to Lincoln. Alec and Ryan were outside when they heard a painful cry. Korinna was lying in a pool of silvery liquid, her body writhing in agony. Although Alec's machinations had led him to marry Korinna, he had learned to love her. She was filled with a goodness that carved out a small place in his heart. But his revenge was stronger, and often he would lie in bed, torn between the two feelings that kept him in constant turmoil.

Ryan hovered over his mother. He waved his right hand furiously over her body. "Get up!" he cried.

"No," she whispered. "It is my time to go. I cannot endure anymore. Alec, whatever it is that torments you, please make peace with it. Ryan, my love, please put an end to your malicious ways before it is too late for you. I love you both, but I must now let go."

With one last breath, she was gone. The silvery liquid pooled, and all was silent.

Grief consumed them. Alec, just as he had done many years before with his brother, laid his body over his wife's. Ryan crouched by her side, his fists pounding into the ground. His tears cascaded down his face, and as he wiped them away with the palm of his right hand, they sizzled in anguish.

"I killed her! It is my fault. She begged me to stop," he cried uncontrollably.

"You must not blame yourself. I pushed her too hard. I should have listened to her pleas. Just know that she loved you with all her heart, and her memory will remain with us forever."

Alec placed Korinna's body on a crimson velvet chaise. He knew where he had to bury her. She needed to be next to his brother on Oros Mountain.

At eleven fifty-nine, Alec and Ryan stood over Korinna. She finally looked at peace. Ryan took his dad's hand in his right one and placed his left hand on his mother's shoulder. With all the energy he could muster, he propelled the three of them out into the night air with such force that it sent excruciating pain through him and his father. Ryan welcomed the pain. He knew it was a small price to pay for what he and his dad had done. At midnight, they arrived on Oros Mountain.

The village was deserted. Small hedge stones dotted the landscape. Alec bent down to read each name. In a corner, lay the bones of the last Leirion.

"He never got the chance for a proper burial, Dad," murmured Ryan. "We need to do that for him."

Ryan directed his palm down toward the hard, cracked ground. He closed his eyes, and within seconds, two large rectangular holes were etched into the soil. He picked up the bones of the villager and gingerly placed them into the first hole. "Rest peacefully now," he whispered. The gentleness in Ryan's voice formed a lump in Alec's throat. *This is the boy I should be raising,* he thought. But that thought was fleeting, and only vengeance remained.

Ryan then lifted his mom. He held her close and rocked back and forth. Finally, he placed her in the second hole. He covered her with the soil moistened by his tears and turned away. He did not want his father to see him like that.

Alec knelt beside Korinna's grave and whispered goodbye. "There is one more thing I must do, Ryan," he said, trying to regain his composure for his son's sake. "I must see my brother's grave."

He walked around the perimeters of the mountain. He looked for the small stone marker. In the far-left corner of the mountain lay the grave. "Take care of Korinna. I promise you that I will make Talia pay for what she has done to us." Alec walked over to Ryan and grabbed his son's hand. "I am ready to go now." Ryan closed his eyes. His right hand shook, and in a matter of moments, they were back at the house.

Alec knew that his plan would keep him focused during his time of grief. A week after Korinna's death, he finally sat Ryan down and told him about his past. He spat out Talia's name as if it were poison when he talked about his brother's death. What he did not mention, however, was how he and his brother tried to force themselves upon Talia to get her to choose. He finally told Ryan about Avery and how it was not fair that Avery had a mother and a father. He played upon Ryan's grief. He did not mention how he used Korinna, his wife, Ryan's own mother, as a pawn in his game of deceit. He did not mention how Ryan was conceived just to get back at Talia. No, he would carry those omissions to the grave.

Ryan sat transfixed. His skin was ablaze. The sparks from the crystal in his right palm sent shocks through his body. His whole body felt ravaged. He was drained of energy. He felt cheated. It wasn't fair that this Avery still had her mother. Ryan listened intently to every word his father uttered. "I will keep my promise to you," he replied softly to his dad. "I will make Talia and her daughter Avery... pay."

Chapter 12

Avery could barely keep her eyes open while she fiddled with her locker combination. Since her "newfound" popularity, she spent the night accepting Instagram and Snapchat friend requests. When Brandon and Charlotte popped up, she was reluctant. Fearing that she might be considered a snob, she hit 'Accept.' Before Friday night, Lucy was Avery's only follower, even though Avery had yet to post on either. But by morning, she had 52 friends added to her list and 45 Instagram followers. *Well, I would say it was a successful night. I guess I need to start posting something;* she laughed to herself. Avery sighed. *Is this what I really want, though?* Dressing as a Goth backfired on her. She thought that she would be left alone, only to find out that she was harassed and tormented by her peers. She realized she needed to change in order to control her powers. But she knew that being popular would come with its own challenges. Just sensing the jealousy from Charlotte made her crystal once again, emit tiny sparks. Avery swore to her parents that she would control them. She wouldn't be able to forgive herself if they had to pick up and leave Willowdale. Avery also realized that this was the first time she had friends and was beginning to enjoy her senior year.

Avery caught up with Lucy after school on the way to the busses. Lucy was with Morgan and another girl she had never met.

Morgan was petite like Lucy, but she had ultra-blond hair with two thin strands of purple running down the sides, framing her waif-like face. The other girl was tall and muscular. She stood at eye level with Avery. Avery had seen her play basketball during gym, and she knew that she was an athlete.

"This is Samantha, but we call her Sam," said Lucy.

"Hi," said Avery. "You're in my gym class. You're a great basketball player."

"Thanks. But volleyball is my sport. You should try out for the team, Avery," Sam said. "You have the long limbs for it." She laughed. "Tryouts are this Thursday. I played JV last year, and I'm trying out for Varsity."

"I don't know," Avery replied. "I have been told that sometimes these long limbs have a life of their own, and not in a good way. I can be sort of a klutz."

"Well, think about it. Maybe I'll see you Thursday."

Lucy gave Avery the once over. "You know, you should try out. You would probably be decent enough to make JV."

Avery laughed. "Not Varsity, huh? Well, maybe I will. I'll run it by my parents and see if it's okay with them."

"So, did you see Peter today?" asked Lucy. "It looked pretty hot and heavy between the two of you Friday night."

Avery blushed just thinking about that night. "We passed by each other a few times, but we didn't have time to talk. Although we did text all weekend."

"That's good. You make a cute couple," Lucy said. "But what's with you and Ryan? He looks at you with such intensity that even I feel uncomfortable. Don't get me wrong, he is totally hot, but I get this weird feeling around him. I did not want to leave you two alone. I was just about to come after you when I saw you walking up the bleachers."

Avery looked at her and laughed. "Take a breath, Lucy. One, Peter is a great guy, and I do like him--a lot--and two, Ryan is not my friend. I wish he would leave me alone. I don't know what he wants from me, considering we have said about ten words to each other. And anyway, he wasn't in school today."

Lucy raised her eyebrows. "Looking for him, I see."

Avery reddened. She knew she was lying. Although she did like Peter, she was attracted to Ryan in a way that she could not explain. She had a feeling that something connected the two of them.

Avery began to board her bus. "I'll see you tomorrow, Lucy."

"Think about Thursday, okay? Colleges always want to see students who are involved with school activities."

"Okay, okay." Avery laughed. "You are relentless!"

Avery got off the bus, walked up the driveway, and punched in the code to the automatic garage. She dropped her book bag onto the laundry room floor and followed the delicious smell that was making her stomach rumble. "Mom! I'm home. What are you cooking? I am starving." She knew her mom would be in the kitchen getting dinner ready.

Avery froze in her tracks. Sitting next to her mother at the table was Ryan. Avery's mom was still wearing her oven mitt while she talked animatedly to him. Ryan, sensing that they were being watched, turned his head and met her gaze. His look was unsettling.

Just then, Avery's mom followed Ryan's gaze and stood up. "Oh, honey, your friend Ryan just stopped by. He was hoping that you had the chem notes since he wasn't in school today." Avery's mom walked to the oven. She opened the door and pulled out a tray of chocolate chip cookies.

"I don't have any notes," said Avery. "So, I guess you can go now." Avery could not bear to look at him. She could feel her crystal getting hot.

"Avery! That's not how we treat guests in our home." Talia pulled off the oven mitt. "I am sorry, Ryan. Would you like to stay for some cookies?"

Ryan's eyes darted to the crystal ring on her pinky, and he could feel the currents in his body increasing.

Steady, he thought. "Sure, thanks, er, Mrs.--"

"You can call me Talia."

Avery rolled her eyes at him. *Sure, sucking up to the mom,* she thought.

"You know what, Ryan?" Avery blurted out. "I do have those chem notes. Come on; I'll get them for you. Mom, I guess Ryan will have to take a rain check on the cookies."

"Thanks anyway, Talia. I think Avery wants to get rid of me as quickly as possible," he laughed.

Avery pulled him into the hallway. "What are you doing here?"

"Like I told your mom, I need the chem notes."

Avery searched in her backpack for her notebook. "Well, here, take them. You can give it back to me tomorrow. Just don't forget." She extended the notebook to him to take, but instead, he grabbed her hand. He pulled her close. She struggled. It was too late. In a flash, Avery felt electricity coursing through her body. Sparks flew out of her crystal. "Who are you?" she whispered. Ryan ran his hand down her throat. His eyes were the darkest green, and the flecks looked like strands of gold thread. Instead of answering, he kissed her throat and left tiny blazing imprints.

Avery gasped. Her hands flew to her throat. "Please, go. Now!"

Ryan looked at her. "Avery, you know that our bond is too strong to resist. Please don't try. It will only make things so much worse for all of us."

"All of us? Who is all of us?"

He took the notebook and smiled. "I'll see you tomorrow." He rubbed his hand slightly and turned to leave. "I'll see you *every* day, Avery." He walked out the door, and in an instant, was nowhere in sight.

The remnants of the electricity that both he and Avery created made it easy for him to get home in less than one minute. "Dad? Where are you? I saw her today. Talia. I was at the house, standing in her own kitchen. Can you believe it?"

Alec rushed into the room. His face was hard. Creases lined his forehead. "You shouldn't have gone over to that house, and you are forbidden to go back. It is much too dangerous. Talia has extremely potent powers."

"I was careful."

Alec grabbed his son by the shoulders and shook him hard. The veins in this neck pulsated, and his breathing was labored. "You will not ever step foot in that house again, do you hear me?" He dug his fingers into his son's shoulders. His rage consumed him.

Ryan tried to free himself, but his father's grip was unyielding. "Dad, you are hurting me. You need to let go. Now!"

Alec continued to restrain him in a viselike grip. Suddenly, Ryan felt the powers overcoming him. His palm started to quiver. He felt the heat burning, and soon, he knew, his powers would be released.

"Noo!" he shouted. But it was too late. Alec flew back and hit the wall. He crumpled to the floor. Scraggly lines of gold current crackled on the wall. Ryan could hear his father's shoulders sizzle, and he ran to him. "I am so sorry! I didn't mean to hurt you, but you wouldn't let go."

Alec looked at his son. "Do you see what your powers did to me when your emotions took hold?" Alec grimaced. "I can bet that Talia's powers are strong, and I am sure Avery's are even stronger. Like yours. If they sense danger, they will use those powers. You must get Avery alone and catch her at her weakest moment. That is the only way you will overpower her and get our revenge."

Ryan helped his father up and led him to the couch. Overcome with guilt; he whispered to his dad, "I promise I will be more careful. And I won't let you down."

"Mom, why did you let *him* in the house? You are always telling me not to open the door to strangers."

"I didn't think it was a big deal. He said you were in class together." Avery's mom looked down at her and said softly, "You know, you're right. I should not have let a stranger into the house. It won't happen again. I promise."

"Especially him, Mom," Avery muttered.

"What do you have against him? He seems like a nice kid."

Avery plopped down on the couch. She kicked off her sneakers. "I don't know; something about him makes the hair on my neck stand straight up. I mean, he *is* sexy, uh, I mean cute, but he makes me edgy when he's around." There was no way that Avery was going to tell her what happened when Ryan grabbed her. That's all she needed.

"Maybe it's just a bad crush." Talia smiled at her daughter. "You two do look cute together, with the black hair and green eyes and all."

"Okay, that's a little too weird, Mom. I'm going upstairs to study. Oh, by the way. What do you think of me trying out for the volleyball team? I was told I have good limbs."

Talia laughed. "I think it's a great idea." Talia's smile faded. "What will happen when the ball hits your crystal? What if the impact sends off sparks, and you lose control? What if--"

Avery kissed her mom's cheek. "I promise I will be careful. I will have everything under control."

Talia watched Avery head upstairs. She loved seeing her daughter finally happy. *I hope so, Avery, I really hope so.*

Ryan kicked back on his bed. He opened his laptop and began copying the chem notes that Avery had given him. He thought about what his father had said... the only way to seek our revenge. *Why does it have to be ours?* He thought. He was torn. He thought of Avery way too often. This should be his father's battle, not his. But then he felt like he was betraying his father. He logged on to Stanton High's Facebook page. He scrolled down through all its members, looking for Avery. His heart raced just looking at her name. He clicked on her, and her profile picture popped up. It was of Lucy and her at the football game. Her head was tilted towards

Lucy's, and she had the widest smile. Her eyes were bright, her cheeks glowing. Ryan couldn't stop staring at it. Avery shares only part of her profile with everyone, it said under her picture. Send her a message or add her as a friend.

Ryan clicked the Message icon and typed, "Avery, I'm sorry I stopped over at your house today. I needed the notes. Okay, who am I kidding? I wanted to see you."

Before he could stop himself, he hit send. *Was this part of his and his dad's plan? Or did he really want to see her?*

Avery was lying on her bed, trying to study. But every thought kept rushing back to Ryan. Her Facebook was minimized just in case her mom or dad decided to come into her room. She knew how they felt about her being on the computer when she had a test to study for the next day. She barely used Facebook lately and only kept it loaded on her computer so she could be updated about events going on in her high school. Lucy had sent her the picture of the two of them at the football game, and Avery made it her new profile pic. She heard the sound that indicated she had a message. Avery clicked on the Facebook icon at the bottom of her computer and opened the message. She read it over and over, her palm getting hotter each time. Peter and Lucy's warnings rang in her ears... *Choose your friends wisely...* he *made me feel uncomfortable.*

But something pulled her to him. She wrote back, "I guess it was sort of nice seeing you, too." Avery hit the send button, and in an instant, another message was waiting for her.

"Can I see you now?"

Was he crazy? Now? As in right now? Her mom would be calling her down to dinner soon, she thought. She typed, "I have to eat in about a half hour, so I don't think now is a very good time."

Just then, Avery heard a series of taps at her window. She jumped and ran to the window, and there he was, balancing precariously on the trellis that leaned against the house, bangs hanging in that one eye, hands still dug deep into his pockets.

Avery gasped and pushed up on the window. "How did you get here so quickly?" She softly called out to him.

"Where there's a will, there's a way."

Avery heard her mom call from downstairs, "Dinner is ready."

"I have to go."

"I'll wait. Meet me outside in an hour."

Avery knew this was crazy. "I can't, my mom won't--"

"I will be waiting for you. Now don't keep your mom waiting, or she will know something is up." Then he was gone.

Avery's mom and dad made a big deal about eating dinner together. They always ate in the dining room, making it feel special. It was often the only time that the three of them were together, and Avery looked forward to sharing her day with her parents. But tonight....

Ryan looked through the window. He could see the three of them laughing. He missed his mother so much. He could not remember the last time when he and his father had a home-cooked meal together.

If only his mother was still alive. The realization that he and his father had slowly killed her with their selfishness and greed, made him sick to his stomach.

"Why do you keep looking at your watch?" Avery's mom asked her.

"No reason. I just have a ton of studying to do."

"Okay. I get the hint," Talia said. "You are sprung."

Avery grabbed her dishes and brought them into the kitchen. Quickly, she slipped out the back door. Her heart was pounding.

"Hey," Avery came around the corner of the house to where Ryan was standing. "I only have a few minutes. My parents think I am upstairs—-"

Avery looked at him. Something was wrong.

Ryan smiled. "I was watching the three of you having dinner. It brought back memories of my mom, dad, and me sitting at the dinner table together."

Looking at Ryan's face filled with sadness, Avery experienced something that she hadn't ever felt before. It wasn't electricity or a current or even a bolt of lightning that sometimes coursed through her body. It was a tug at her heart. It was the deepest pull of empathy. "What happened to your mom?"

Ryan shrugged. "She died."

"Oh, I'm so sorry." Before she could stop herself, she was hugging him tightly. She could feel his heart beating.

Ryan leaned back and touched Avery's cheek. He trailed his finger down until it rested on her lips.

Avery gently kissed Ryan's finger. She could feel him shudder, and it sent sparks flying through her body. She removed his finger and brought her lips up to his. She kissed him tenderly at first, then more deeply.

"Who are you?" she whispered. She removed his right hand from her cheek and held it. She touched the sizzling crystal and traced it with her finger. "I know we are connected. It isn't every day that you see another person with a crystal in their hand."

He lifted her left hand. The crystal shone in the dark. He nuzzled her neck. "We are connected. More than you know."

But Ryan knew she wouldn't hear what he had just said to her. He had used his powers to freeze her before he did anything to sabotage his father's plan. She would not remember the crystal in his hand or even the way she told him that they were connected. The only thing she would remember was the kiss, the kiss that left him hungering for more. He ran his fingers through her hair and sent gold sparks flying. And then, with his crystal, he unfroze her and disappeared.

Avery was back in her room with her book propped up in her lap. She touched her lips. They felt hot. How did she get back upstairs? Her last memory was of kissing Ryan. "Oh, my god!" she whispered. "What did I do?"

The vibration of her cell phone unnerved her even more. "Hello?"

"Hey, Avery, this is Peter. I wanted to know if you wanted to grab dinner and a movie Friday night?"

Avery's head was spinning. "Um, I have to ask my parents if it's okay." She felt like such a dork saying that, but she also knew her parents were super protective of her. She didn't know how her parents would feel about her going out on a date. "Can I let you know tomorrow?"

"Sure, no problem. I hope your parents say it's okay. I'll come over if they want to meet me. I know they will fall in love with my good looks and winning personality."

Avery laughed. "I have no doubt. I'll let you know tomorrow, okay? I need to finish studying. Major calculus test on Friday."

"Talk to you tomorrow. Good luck on that test."

Avery ended the call, but before she was able to prop the book back onto her lap, she heard the familiar buzzing that indicated she had an incoming text.

"DON'T GO," it said. The capital letters sent her into a panic. She looked to see who had sent it, but there was no name or number. Buzz. She hit the text icon. "YOU WILL REGRET IT." Avery dropped the phone. She grabbed her computer and sent Ryan a Facebook message. "Is that you?" she typed.

In an instant, Ryan responded. "What are you talking about?"

"Are you sending me text messages on my phone?"

"I don't even have your cell number."

"Oh, okay, well, bye." Avery turned off both her cell and computer. She grabbed her book and willed herself to study.

Ryan rubbed the crystal in his palm. Its heat made his hand ache. He was using his powers too much lately, but he knew that it was necessary. Peter. He had to get Peter out of the picture. He felt bad about sending Avery those messages, but he needed to shake her up a bit. It worked. He could feel the tenseness in her voice.

Again, guilt washed over him. He was so torn. He liked her more and more every day, but his father was relentless.

Ryan closed his eyes. He had a pounding headache from overusing his crystal. A year before, he only used the crystal for selfish, childish reasons. Now he knew that the crystal was being abused for destructive and evil purposes. It was a heavy weight placed upon him by his father. He thought about his mom and could remember her pleading for him to stop. He tried to convince himself that part of the revenge was also for her. He tried so hard to believe that.

Chapter 13

The ground on the mountain of Oros shook violently. A howling sound, so deafening that even the crows took cover, filled the air. The sun and the moon collided. Instantly the soil cracked into two, and sparks of light illuminated the sky. The small grave in which Korinna lay split open, sending debris flying.

Korinna's eyes flew open. *I am alive! But how can this be? She thought.* Her hand ached as she raised her pinky ring toward the sky. The sun and the moon spilled their rays into her crystal. She struggled to lift herself out of the small grave. The air was now still, and the only light was that of her crystal in the small, delicate ring. She did not know where she was. She only knew that something was not right. Something had made her use her powers to bring her back from the dead. She looked around at the great expanse of land covered with graves. She walked slowly to each. Bending down, she read the tiny markers.

Her hands flew to her mouth. She knew where she was! But why? Why would she be at the top of Oros Mountain? She knew about the feud between her clan and the Leirion clan and remembered hearing how the Leirion had sought refuge on Oros Mountain. She walked on. There was no life. What happened to all the other clan members?

Korinna made her way back to her own grave. She had told her son and husband that it was her time and that she needed for them to let her go. But now, something stronger pulled at her and urged her to exercise her power.

The air was cool, and Korinna wrapped her arms around her body. She took a deep breath, marveling at how crisp and fragrant the air smelled. Out of the corner of her eye, she saw a headstone that she had not noticed earlier. Sparks shot out of her crystal. It looked like a spectacular display of fireworks as they arced and landed in the direction of the grave. The sparks gained intensity, and her hand was on fire, but she continued to walk until she arrived at her destination.

Korinna crouched down and examined the date. He was only fifteen when he died. Who was he, and why had she been buried close to him when there was so much land on the mountain? She bent closer to read the tiny inscription etched into the stone. Darius Lagos, beloved son to Alaceus and Demetria, brother to Alec.

Alec? Her Alec? "It can't be," Korinna whispered. "It can't be."

Korinna placed her palms over the grave. Images of Alec and his twin brother when they were toddlers flashed in front of her. She had visions of the twins' mother and father hugging the boys, the circle of clan members clasping hands and bestowing their gratefulness during their morning ritual... a young girl, looking much like the twins, throwing her head back in laughter and chasing them around the mountain's edge. Images of her sons, Ryan and Peter, and her first husband, Ben came to her. She smiled at those happy memories.

At once, she reeled back in agony. Now, horrific words and pictures seared through her body. The ground shook. She wanted the pain to stop but knew that this was the only way to get answers. She suddenly grimaced. There, in front of her eyes, were images of Alec and Darius forcing this young girl to the ground. She could see the struggle. She could taste the bitterness of the drunken words they slurred at her.

The grave heaved and buckled, but she willed herself to continue. She could hear the boys forcing her to choose one of them, and finally, she watched in horror as the young girl used the crystal in her ring to send them crashing into the stone wall. Korinna covered her nose. She could smell the acrid scent of the silvery liquid that oozed out of them.

She squeezed her eyes shut. She wanted to stop, but she needed to know the truth. Then the image of this young girl turning her back on the village, her parents, and everything she knew and loved to leave the mountain forever flashed in front of her. She saw this beautiful girl throw a kiss of sparks toward the direction of her home and descend the mountain.

That last image was so utterly sad. A wave of melancholy tugged at Korinna's heart. She closed her eyes. Tears flowed down her cheeks, her thoughts racing out of control. *Who really was my husband, Alec? Why didn't he tell me that he was a warlock? Where was his crystal?* It was far too much for her to take in all at once. She laid her head down on the hard soil and willed sleep to come and lessen the pain.

Korinna awoke to the repulsive smell of death. Images of Alec lying over his dead brother flashed in front of her. He saw him screaming at what appeared to be the young girl's mother, imploring her to bring his brother back from the dead. She heard the words, "You know I can't do that, Alec." She saw Alec's ravaged face screaming at her. "Your daughter will rot in hell!"

Korinna watched the images race across her eyes. She saw the plants wither, the sheep lose their wool, the cattle starve to death, and the cows' milk dry up. She witnessed the younger clan members descend the mountain, powerless, leaving the older ones to face their next life. *This is how Alec lost his powers*, she thought. *Who is this woman, and where is she now?*

Fixated upon Darius' grave, Korinna watched as more images illuminated in front of her. Pure evil, and she felt every nerve ending explode with electricity. Korinna gasped as she saw Alec stalking a young woman, watching her every move. She sobbed uncontrollably when she saw how she herself had been used by him, and she held her breath when she realized how Alec exerted his "fatherly" influence over Ryan to persuade him to avenge his brother's death. A girl appeared in Korinna's visions. She looked to be about the same age as her sons, Ryan and Peter. And then an enormous surge shot through her. Peter! He was in danger.

Korinna moaned. She doubled over, and her body shook in spasms. Knowing Peter was in danger left her almost incapacitated.

She struggled to her feet. She raised her pinky ring, closed her eyes, and felt the electricity flow through her entire body. When she reopened her eyes, she found herself at the bottom of the mountain. She wasn't sure where to go or what to do next. Her crystal had now weakened from overuse. But what she did know was that Peter was in imminent danger, and Ryan was destined to destroy himself and those around him.

Chapter 14

"Avery, wait up!" Peter called to her as she was leaving her locker.

"Hey, Peter." Avery smiled at him. *He sure was easy to look at. His eyes were so blue.* "How are you?" *Don't go. You will regret it.* The words had echoed in her head all night, and now they pounded against her eardrums.

"Great, now. Did you get a chance to ask your parents about Friday night?"

Avery was not going to let one stupid text message make her feel out of control. She did have her powers, after all. "My parents said I could go, but they do want to meet you first." Avery rolled her eyes. "They are so overprotective. Do you want to come over after school and stay for dinner?"

"Sure, I'll see you around four o'clock." Peter took her hand, held it for a second, and then gently let go. "See you later."

"Definitely," replied Avery. She looked down at her hand that Peter had just held and smiled.

"You sure have become the popular one, haven't you?" Avery spun around and saw Charlotte staring at her. Her hands were on her hips, and her eyes did not look like she wanted to make friends.

"What are you talking about?" Avery asked. She sure was not going to back down to her. If she wanted to be nasty, let her.

"First Ryan and now Peter. What is it about you that draws the guys in? Now Brandon can't stop talking about you. You might want to watch out, though. Rumors can ruin someone's life." Charlotte shot Avery a dirty look. "See ya around."

Avery lifted her hand slightly and aimed the crystal at Charlotte's books. Just a tiny current, she decided. The electricity left her palm and shot toward Charlotte. The girl's books flew out of her hands and scattered all over the floor. Papers were strewn everywhere. Charlotte let out a cry. No one seemed to notice as they stepped over her things to get to class. *That will teach you.* Avery hurried to her class. The last thing she wanted was to get in trouble.

"Nice move," Ryan chuckled to her as he took his seat behind her in chemistry class.

Avery turned. "I have no idea what you mean," she said as her pulse quickened. He knew everything about her. Ryan had been nowhere in sight when Charlotte's books crashed to the floor.

Ryan smiled. "Have fun with Peter Friday night."

"Don't worry, I will." Avery faced front. She hated how his mere presence invaded her thoughts and actions, but at the same time, she could not get him out of her mind.

Chapter 15

Something gnawed at Talia, but she could not place what it was. She stood in her shop and looked at all the unique findings she had collected over the years. There was a porcelain doll dating back to the eighteenth century, a bench that was used in a Roman cathedral, and a stunning Venetian glass mirror that she had found at an antique store going out of business.

Talia touched each piece with the same care she used when wrapping up the crystal chandelier so many years before. She shuddered. *Why do I always find myself remembering that day? It should have been forgotten,* she thought. But something about it had unsettled her. *That, man, Adam. He looked so familiar. And to think of it, so does Avery's friend, Ryan. In fact, all four of us look very similar--black hair and green eyes with flecks of gold.* Her thoughts were running wild. Talia let out a little chuckle. "Okay, that seems to account for two-thirds of the people living in this town," she said out loud.

She shook herself free of bad feelings and continued to work. It was an hour later when she heard the chime signaling that someone was at the front door of the main house. It must be Avery forgetting her key again. When they moved in, she had the electrician install some kind of "watch dog" system inside her shop so that she could keep track of the main house when she was working. She locked the shop's door and walked around to the house.

"Avery, you need to remember your key," Talia called to her daughter as she rounded the corner of the house. But instead of her daughter at the front door, a woman with light blond hair blowing in the breeze was staring at her. "I am so sorry to bother you. I just moved into the house down the street, and I hit my hand while trying to hang some pictures." I don't know if I broke anything, but it's swelling, and I think I need to see a doctor. Would you happen to have the name of one?" Korinna tried to sound convincing, but inside, her body trembled. She showed Talia her bandaged fingers. Her three fingers on her right hand had white gauze wrapped tightly around them, making sure her crystal pinky ring was hidden from view.

Talia moved toward her. She immediately felt a sense of kinship with this woman. Maybe it was because she was injured or that Talia had not made any friends since they moved to Willowdale, but she felt as if she had known her all her life. "Oh dear, let me try to unwrap your fingers to see if I need to get you to the emergency room. You wouldn't want them to swell up like grapefruits." Talia reached out for Korinna's hand.

"No!" cried Korinna. "I mean, it just really hurts, but I will be okay. If you have the doctor's number, I will be on my way. I appreciate it greatly."

"Why don't you come inside while I get the number of the doctor my daughter's high school guidance counselor recommended to use when we moved to Willowdale. I will make you a cup of tea."

"That's very gracious of you, uh…"

"Talia."

"My name is Korinna. Thank you so much, Talia."

"Which house did you say you bought?" asked Talia. She did not remember seeing any "For Sale" signs on her street.

Korinna quickly let her powers create a mental picture of one of the houses in the neighborhood. "Oh, it's the small white ranch with the blue shutters. Actually, it's around the corner on Grove."

"Well, welcome to the neighborhood. I just wish we would have met under better circumstances."

Korinna followed Talia into the house. She felt deceitful, but she also knew it was the only way to protect her sons. She needed to befriend this woman if it meant saving them. Korinna sat at the kitchen table while Talia was in the other room locating the number.

The kettle began to whistle. Not thinking, Korinna walked over to lift it off the burner with her bandaged hand. "Oh no!" Korinna cried. She had lost her grip, and the kettle began to fall.

Talia, hearing her cry, rushed in. She knew she shouldn't, but she had no choice. In a flash, Talia aimed her crystal at the kettle. Sparks leaped out and righted the kettle onto the burner.

Korinna whipped around; her eyes wide. So many emotions were surging through her body. The intensity of Talia's powers both awed and terrified her. She was grateful that Talia saved her from the scalding water. But she also felt a trace of animosity toward her. She wanted to blame Talia for her sons being put in danger.

Talia's hand went up to her mouth to stifle the gasp that was gurgling inside. She closed her eyes and directed the crystal's energy toward Korinna's head. "Close your eyes, Korinna, and forget everything," she whispered.

Korinna knew that she must not let on who she was. She knew that she had her own powers to reject the trance that Talia was placing upon her. Instead, she closed her eyes and let Talia's powers take over.

A moment later, Talia took a deep breath and began to pour the tea for Korinna. Her heart was pounding, but she knew that she had to stay calm. "So, here is the number to the doctor in town. But you really might be better off going to the ER."

"Thank you so much. I hope that we can meet again under better circumstances." Korinna finished her tea quickly; she wanted to be anywhere else but in that kitchen.

"Mom, are you decent? I brought someone over to meet you," called Avery from the foyer.

"I'm in the kitchen."

Avery walked in, and Korinna tried to stifle a small gasp. Standing next to Avery was her beautiful baby boy, Peter. When Ben left with him, he was just a baby, but now he was a handsome young man. He stood so close to Avery, and she knew right then by the way that he looked at her he was crazy for her.

She realized that Alec never gave her that look. It was more like a manic stare; something desperate in his eyes that she mistook for love. Her first husband, she knew, had deeply loved her.

Korinna felt frozen in the chair. She finally stood up and faced her son directly. She wanted to see if he remembered her, but his gaze did not show any recollection.

"Oh, sorry, Mom, I didn't mean to interrupt you," Avery apologized.

"Avery, I want you to meet Mrs.--"

"You can call me Korinna."

"Nice to meet you," Avery said, extending her hand. "Mom and Korinna, this is my friend, Peter."

Peter strode over to them. Korinna could not grasp just how handsome he had become. He looked more like her husband than herself, but he had her blond hair and crystal-blue eyes. "Nice to meet you both," he said.

"Ah, so you're the Burger Stop guy." Talia laughed. "Nice to meet you. Dinner is going to be a little delayed, so why don't the two of you head out back to my shop, and you can show Peter around." Avery took Peter by the hand, and Korinna caught sight of the tiny crystal glinting in the palm of her hand. She knew that Peter could not have seen it, for it was just a speck. But she knew where to look. Korinna could feel the heat radiating from the crystal, and she knew then that, in some way, Avery was also involved. The sight of it and knowing how much danger her sons were in left her hyperventilating.

"Are you okay?" asked Talia as she rushed over to Korinna.

"My hand hurts more than I let on," she murmured as she tried to compose herself. "I should get going. I left all my insurance information at my house. Again, thank you so much, Talia." Korinna looked into her eyes. They were kind and gentle and the same green of Alec and Ryan's eyes.

She turned. Her heart and head ached, and she had to leave immediately. Korinna rushed to the door and hurried out. She had nowhere to go. She was all alone.

Avery led Peter around the cramped aisles. The shop was so tiny and so packed with "treasures" that each time the two turned a corner, they bumped into each other. Avery could feel tiny sparks running down her body, but they were nowhere as strong as when she was with Ryan. *Peter's the nice guy*, she kept telling herself. *Stick with the nice guy.* She was just about to lead him outside when Peter's eyes settled on a black-and-white picture in a gold-leafed frame. His blue eyes suddenly darkened, and his jaw tightened. "Where did your mother get this?" he asked, his voice strained.

Avery turned to see what it was that Peter was looking at so intensely. The frame housed a small photo of a mountain in the background, and in the foreground stood two women, each holding an infant in her arms. Avery gingerly lifted the frame off her mother's desk.

Peter stood frozen. The veins in his neck pulsated. "How long have you had it?"

Avery looked at him strangely. He seemed different--not like the Peter she was used to talking to.

"It's a picture of my great-grandmother, Helene holding my grandmother. I don't know who the other woman is, or the baby for that matter, but I do know that it is the only picture that my mom has of them." Avery traced her fingers up and down the smeared glass. "Doesn't my mom look so much like her grandmother?"

But Peter wasn't listening. He just kept staring at the photo.

"Peter, what is wrong? It looks like you have seen a ghost."

Peter took the frame out of Avery's hands. He held it closely. "My father had the same picture and frame on the mantel of our fireplace. I remember when I was ten years old, I asked him who was in the photo. My father mumbled something about distant relatives. I didn't think anything about it, but now I realize that since that day, the photo has been missing. Avery, it is the *exact* frame and photo."

"It can't be! We had this from as far back as I can remember. No matter where we moved to, it always found its place in a special spot."

Peter turned to face Avery. His eyes were lighter now, but his face was still strained. He seemed to Avery to have aged in those few moments. "Please ask your mother who the other woman is. This is important. I have to know." Peter pulled her close. "This is weird. I know that we have only known each other a short time, but

I feel like we have known each other forever. I feel connected to you."

That word again. Connected. Avery pulled herself from him. "Umm, I think dinner must be about ready." Avery replaced the frame on her mother's desk, led Peter out of the shop, and locked the door behind her.

"So, I hear you are quite the football star," Avery's dad said to Peter.

Oh my god, Avery thought. *Nothing like my dad embarrassing the hell out of me.*

"Since it's just my dad and me, he focused all of his attention on making me a good athlete, like he was in his day," Peter said, laughing.

"Okay, enough of the grilling, Dad. By the way, Mom, you know the photo of your grandmother holding your mother in front of the mountain. Do you know who the other woman is in the photo? Peter could swear that his dad had the same photo."

The cup of coffee that Talia was drinking dropped out of her hand, spilled all over her, and smashed to the floor. The shards flew everywhere. Avery, Peter, and Steve jumped up to help.

"I am so sorry! I have been a little clumsy lately." She and Steve exchanged worried looks.

Avery sensed that something was up. She knew her mother's expressions down cold, and this one said, "Change the subject now!"

"Well, I think it's time for me to go," Peter said, sensing the tension. "Thank you for dinner." He stood up and shook hands with Talia and Steve.

"Come on. I'll walk you out," Avery said. She led him to the front door. "I do need to rest up for the big volleyball tryouts tomorrow." She rolled her eyes and smiled. "I can't believe Samantha coerced me into doing this. I am such a klutz. I know I am going to make a fool out of myself." Avery looked up at Peter and saw that he was staring at her. She blushed. So many emotions poured out of her. Ryan, Peter; she liked both, but in different ways. She knew that she was going to have to make a choice eventually, but for now, she was going to try to ignore their feelings and hers as well.

"You'll do great, Avery. Just watch the ball. It's as easy as that."

"Easy for you to say, Mr. Jock." Avery laughed. The mood felt lighter now, and for that, she was glad.

"So, did I pass the test?"

Avery looked at him, puzzled.

"You know, the 'Am I a good enough guy to take my daughter out on Friday?' test."

Avery smiled. "Yeah, I guess you did. I'll see you tomorrow."

Peter leaned in and kissed Avery lightly on the lips. "See you tomorrow."

Avery walked into the dining room. Her father had just finished sweeping the last pieces of glass into the dustpan.

"Where's Mom? What is going on?"

Steve looked at his daughter with pain in his eyes. "I think *she* should tell you." She's upstairs changing. She'll be down in a few minutes."

Avery looked at her dad. He was doing everything but looking at her. What was going on?

Her mom came downstairs and led her into the family room.

"Mom, this has something to do with the photo, doesn't it?"

"Let me talk. Please." Her green eyes were dark. "You are right. What happened tonight does have to do with the photograph. The other woman is my grandmother's best friend, Eva, and she was holding her baby, Sophia. Your great-grandmother Helene and her friend shared some very happy days, but after my mother and Sophia were born, things went spiraling out of control and ultimately led to great devastation.

"What happened to them? And how did Peter's father end up with the same photo?"

Talia suddenly felt all the memories weighing her down. She needed to sit. It was so painful to talk about, even to think about, but she knew that she needed to tell her daughter what had happened. "I don't know how the photo ended up in his house. That is very weird. Maybe it's not the same photo. He could have been wrong. But I will tell you what I know. She guided Avery into the overstuffed chair that sat next to the fireplace. Talia sat next to her and stroked her daughter's silky hair.

"My grandparents grew up in Greece. They were part of the Leirion clan and had the same powers that we do. My grandmother, I was told, was a robust, beautiful woman. She was the clan's midwife and was always on call to assist with the young mothers' births. She was wise and gentle and was even known for sporting a pint of whiskey to ease their pain." Avery's eyes widened. "That was before epidurals, my dear," she laughed gently. "Others came to her for medical advice, and she was forever cooking up potions to cure any type of ailment. Although my grandmother was a witch, she rarely used her powers. Like the rest of the Leirion, they believed in letting things take their natural course. Helene and Eva became pregnant at the same time and were excited to raise their babies to be best friends like they were. Eva was from another clan called Sethos, and for many years the two clans lived in harmony. When your grandmother Ria finally made her way into this world, everyone gasped at her beauty. She had eyes like emeralds with golden flecks." Talia smiled at her daughter. "Just like ours. Sophia, born only ten minutes later, also was a rare beauty, but with eyes as crystal blue as the Caribbean Sea."

Avery leaned in closer. Her mother was speaking so softly, it was almost impossible to hear her.

"Your great-grandmother Helene married a very kind man. He was also one of the four chiefs of the Leirion. He had unvanquished powers but only used them when necessary. Her friend married a much different man. He was also a chief, but a Sethos. He used his powers for all the wrong reasons. The women tried not to let their husbands' differences tarnish their friendship, but even after the first year of their marriages, it was apparent that they married men with opposing beliefs."

Talia paused. She closed her eyes, reliving the moment as if it had happened to her. She was not even born at the time, but the pain felt real to her now. "When Ria and Sophia were three years old, something devastating and tragic happened. It was late at night when Helene heard a banging on the door. When your great-grandmother opened the door, she saw Eva standing there, battered and bruised. Sophia was cowering next to her. Helene scooped the toddler into her arms and led her friend into the house. Eva told my grandmother the horrific story of how her husband abused her every night because she could not give him another child. He used his powers on her and sent currents of electricity surging through her body. But, to no avail, she could not become pregnant. Finally, on that very last night that Eva was beaten and electrocuted, she grabbed her Sophia and ran."

"I remember my mother telling me how my grandmother was racked with guilt for not knowing that her best friend was being tormented," said Talia.

"That's so horrible," Avery said. She hated seeing the anguish in her mom's eyes. "What happened next?" She asked softly.

Talia took a deep breath and continued. "My grandmother's husband came down the stairs. He took my grandmother into the next room and told her Eva could not stay there--she had to go back to her husband. However unfair it was, that was the rule of the two clans. One must never interfere with anyone else's marriage. He went into the other room to tell her, leaving my grandmother with Sophia." Tears rolled down Talia's face, and Avery reached up to wipe them away.

"My grandmother heard screaming in the next room. She rushed in and found her best friend lying in a pool of silver liquid.

In her hands, she held the knitting needles from my grandmother's sewing basket. Helene yelled at her husband for not using his powers to bring Eva back, but he only shook his head and told her that it was in the Leirion's decree to allow nature to take its course. My grandmother begged him, but he stood his ground."

"When they heard the pounding on the door, they knew it could only be one person. Eva's husband barreled in, demanding to see his wife and child. Out of the corner of his eye, he saw the river of silver liquid and his wife lying there. The man rushed over to her, screaming her name in anguish and promising the gods never to lay a hand on her again. He aimed his crystal at his wife and sent the same electricity he used to torment her now to save her, but nothing happened. She was gone forever. Sophia ran into the room and saw her mama lying on the floor. She began to scream. Her father picked her up and left. That was the last time my grandparents ever saw them. My grandmother buried her best friend outside on a beautiful mossy mound, and every year she would place a bouquet of wildflowers on her grave.

Talia stopped. She needed to take a break. Her head felt like it was exploding. She knew what that meant. The electricity in her body generated from all the tension was creating sparks.

Now it was Avery's time to be the mother. "Mom, we can stop. Take a break, and we will talk later."

"No, I need to finish this." Talia curled her legs up under her. "Shortly after what happened, the clans started to feud. The Sethos blamed my grandparents for what had happened. No one had known the truth. My grandparents vowed that they would never defame Eva's character, so they kept the truth to themselves. The feud intensified, ultimately forcing the Leirion to leave the village and find their way to the top of Oros Mountain. That is where my grandparents raised my mother, your grandmother Ria. I was born there and loved it. It was the most peaceful place. My mother said she always wondered what had happened to that little girl who would have grown up with her. She often thought about trying to locate her but knew that it was probably for the best not to. Too many bad memories would have been unearthed, causing so much pain."

Avery leaned her head into her mom's. "That is such a sad story. I feel so badly for my great-grandmother even though I never met her."

Talia kissed the top of her daughter's head. "It   was, especially, I think, for my grandmother. My mother was just a little girl, but my grandmother lost her best friend to suicide. She and my grandfather were blamed unmercifully and had to leave the village they called home. Although they did eventually adapt and learn to love their new life and began to make lasting friendships, they always felt a tiny part in their hearts was missing."

"Did you ever try to find Sophia?" Avery asked.

"No. But I sometimes think about her. If she married and had children, her kids would probably be roughly the same age as I. The women in the clans did not wait long to get married and have children. They thought of children as the most special gift from the gods."

"Why can't you search for them? Maybe if you Googled them, their names would come up."

Talia spoke softly. "The Leirion were private people. And remember, they had a special gift. Most mortals are not like your dad and would never understand or accept their powers. And many would try to use them for evil purposes. They would never risk being exposed."

"But don't you miss your parents?" Avery blurted. "What happened that I haven't even met them? They probably don't even know I exist."

Talia's back went rigid. She knew that this conversation was eventually going to resurface. Avery was only five when she first asked, and Talia could make up some excuse, but now her daughter was older and smarter. She could not change the subject as she had done so many times before.

Talia could feel the tiny sparks snapping at her skin. But she knew that today she would have to tell her daughter the truth. She owed her that. And so, with all the strength she could muster, she pulled her daughter even closer and began to unravel the hideous tale.

"That is why I can never go back up that mountain and why my parents would never come looking for me."

But Avery didn't hear the last part. All she could think of was her mother getting mauled by those two arrogant, disgusting boys. They were the ones responsible for the one brother dying and for her mother having to leave the mountain and never seeing her parents again.

Hot anger rose in her body. Her eyes started to flicker furiously. She could feel the currents race through her body. The hair on her arms was starting to singe, but she didn't care. Tears, which ran wildly down her face, were leaving stinging marks.

Talia looked at Avery in horror. She could see that it was too much for her daughter. She was starting to burn herself to death. Talia threw herself onto her daughter's body and tried to stamp out the sparks that were shooting out all over. Avery's screams were deafening, and Talia began to absorb the electricity until her own body was on fire. Avery was shouting at her to let her alone. She did not want her mom to have to go through any more pain than she had already suffered. But Talia continued. Finally, the screaming subsided, as did the sparks. The two lay there. "I am so sorry, Mom.

I did not mean for this to happen. I just added more misery to your memories."

Talia rubbed her daughter's arms. "Avery, you are the most important thing in my life. I could not imagine life without you. Please, never be sorry for me trying to protect you. That is what a mother does. If I hadn't been naïve and scared, I would have woken my own parents up and let them handle the situation that terrible night. But that can't be changed. I want you to know that you can come to me with anything."

Avery curled up into her mother's arms, and in an instant, she was asleep.

The school day seemed to last forever. Avery was nervous about the tryouts, and she kept looking at her watch, wishing she were already home in bed. She was grateful that her mom had intervened last night. Her body and face looked normal, no burns anywhere. She was walking to her second to last period of the day when she heard someone call her name.

"I hear you are trying out for the volleyball team." Ryan was by her side.

"Yeah, how did you know?" Avery was trying not to look at him. Every time she did, she could feel her heart pound.

"Don't you remember what I told you? We are connected. I know everything about you." Ryan walked by her side. He sniffed and said, "You smell a little like a smoldering fire. So, what happened last night?"

Avery whipped around to face him. "I don't know, Ryan. If we are so connected, why don't you tell me." Her face felt hot, and she wanted to get away from him.

Ryan grabbed her left hand. "I'll tell you what happened; something so horrible that your body started to burn." Avery tried to free herself from him and continued to her class, but he pulled her to a stop. He held on to her hand. With his thumb, he rubbed the tiny speck of crystal embedded into her palm.

Avery froze. How could he know it was there? It was so tiny, no one should be able to find it. No one, except one of them.

"I need to go to class," she snapped. "You are making me late." She tried to walk past, but he held her.

"Let her go. Now." Peter was standing next to them. The veins in his neck were pulsating, and his eyes were ice-blue marbles.

Ryan dropped Avery's hand. He looked at Peter and, in a seething voice, said, "Watch your back, Peter. You never know when you might wake up to a day of hell. As for Avery, forget her. She's not your type."

Before Peter could say anything, Ryan was gone.

"Are you okay? You're shaking." Peter said. He took her hand and held it for a moment. Avery noticed that the crystal was invisible to him. He could not feel it, so how could Ryan?

Avery shook her head. "I'll be fine. Thanks." They continued to walk down the hallway until they got to her class.

"Good luck today, Avery." He turned to leave and then suddenly stopped. "You smell great." A faint blush rose from his neck to his face. "Vanilla, right?" Avery nodded. "Well, anyway, I am really looking forward to tomorrow night."

Avery smiled, something she had not done in what seemed to be forever. "I am, too." *I really am*, she thought and opened the classroom door.

The last bell rang, and Avery headed toward the gym. Sam called out to her to wait, and the two walked there together. "You are going to be great," Sam reassured her. "How could you not, with those giraffe legs," she laughed.

"You're so funny." She swung open the locker room door. Avery recognized some of the girls. Sam introduced her to most of them, and already she felt a little more relaxed. She found an open locker and started putting her things into it when she heard that same annoying, whiny voice that she knew so well.

"Of course, you are trying out. Why wouldn't 'Miss Popular with the Boys' try out for the sport where you get to wear tiny gym shorts and tops that rise up when you spike the ball?" Charlotte looked like she was going on a date to a beach party. Her shorts were skintight, and her shirt revealed too much skin.

Avery stared down at her. She had about four inches on Charlotte, and that made her feel, to her satisfaction, a tad superior. She looked her up and down. "Well, now I know why you're trying out, Charlotte. I just hope you shaved the hair on the small of your back."

Avery walked away, but not before she could see Charlotte twisting to see what Avery was talking about.

What a witch with a capital B, Avery thought. There were always girls like that, but until Avery's makeover, she never had to deal with them. She didn't know what was worse, this kind of attention or the taunting she used to receive when she dressed Goth. She walked into the gym.

"Listen up, girls," Coach Matthews blew her whistle. The girls walked over to the center of the court. "I am going to divide you into four teams of six. The first two groups will play, and then the next two teams get a chance. By the end of today, all of you will have played at least once. If I ask someone to leave the court to have another player come in, please don't think you are not playing well. I want to see how you interact. Having the right mix of players is crucial. I will post the cuts tomorrow outside the lunchroom by your student ID number, and for those who have made it, I will see you here the same time tomorrow." The first teams were selected, and Avery was not in either one. She silently breathed a sigh of relief. She was very nervous now. She watched the players whack the ball over the net. She was amazed at how much strength these girls had. Some of the players ran to get the ball without setting it up for the others. It was all about them, and Avery knew that the proper way was setting up the ball so a teammate could ultimately hit it over the net.

The coach blew her whistle and signaled the end of the first game. She called Avery's and eleven other girls' names. *Oh, my god,* she thought. *This is it.* She felt like she was going to throw up. At first, she played timidly. She knew that a lot of the other girls had more experience from the middle-school team or out-of-school leagues, so unless the ball was directly in front of her and she knew that she could hit it successfully, she let them go for the ball. She didn't want anyone blaming her for losing the point.

Coach Williams blew her whistle. "Avery Weston, step off the court, please. Tara Henke, take her place."

Avery could feel her face get hot. She was so embarrassed. She knew that the coach had said earlier that it didn't mean that they were playing badly, but she *knew* how horribly she was doing.

"So, I guess this is it," she said to Sam. "The end of my volleyball career. And they said it wouldn't last."

Sam nudged her. "You're just nervous. Coach Williams knows who has never played. She's pretty fair, so I wouldn't worry yet."

They watched the game. There were so many great players; Avery knew that the probability of her making the team was slim. The whistle blared again. "Avery Weston, Samantha Lewis, Charlotte Meyers...."

Avery moaned. "I can't believe that I have to play against her. I so dislike that girl."

"That makes the two of us. Come on. We're on the same team. Let's make her eat dirt." Sam grabbed Avery's arm, and they strode on to the court. The game started out with several great volleys between the two teams. Avery was feeling more confident and began setting the ball up more and more often for her teammates. She even had some successful shots over the net where the opposing team member could not return the ball.

"You're doing great!" Sam called to her. At that moment, Avery felt a whoosh of air rush at her, and the ball smack her in the face. Stars danced in front of her. The whistle blew. Charlotte sneered at her, her hands resting on her hips.

Avery's hands flew up to her nose. She knew that she was bleeding, and it would not be red blood that flowed out of her nose. She could feel the silvery liquid begin to gurgle, and her hands were beginning to feel slick from the liquid. From the corner of her eye, she could see Coach Williams and Sam running up to her. Panic gripped her. She lifted her left palm and turned it toward the sky. Huge currents flew out, and in a split second, everyone in the gym was frozen. Then she rubbed her palm to her face, and the nosebleed was gone.

Not a soul in the gym would remember anything. She hated to use her powers; she promised her parents that she wouldn't, but this time it was necessary. The panic that pulsated in her body subsided, and the last thing she did, although she knew that it was so wrong, was to save one small current to back up time and replay what had happened. She curled her fingers into a fist, and the currents ceased.

Once again, the ball was flying toward Avery. She saw Charlotte sneering at her. She knew that it was meant for her face. Avery hunkered down, sprang back up, and spiked the ball over the net. The ball soared, increasing speed as it landed on the other team's court. Charlotte, determined to send it back over, reached up to save the ball, but instead, she landed on her butt. The ball slammed into the floor, landing with a thud, deflated. Everyone stared in amazement. Coach Williams blew her whistle. "That's the winning point. Nice shot, Avery."

Sam lightly punched Avery in the arm. "Welcome to the team."

Avery laughed. "Hopefully, I get to see you tomorrow. That was really fun." Avery walked out of the locker room to catch the late bus. She finally felt like she belonged. She had the slightest twinge of guilt for how she had sent that ball flying over the net. She promised herself that she wouldn't use her powers again and that she would practice hard to become a great player.

"Nice spike." The voice had an edge to it, and she knew who it was. She continued to walk across the parking lot toward the bus. "I thought you promised your parents, but then, a girl's gotta do what a girl's gotta do, right?"

Avery spun around. "What do you want, Ryan? Stop stalking me, or I will tell my parents and Principal Stone." She quickened her pace. *I'm almost to the bus*, she thought. *Just get me onto that bus, and I don't have to deal with him.* He brought out so many feelings in her. Those feelings kept her up at night; sometimes, all night that she woke up with dark circles under her eyes. Her mother would ask her what was wrong, and she would answer that she was just nervous about a test she was taking that day. *Five feet, and I'm home free.*

"Avery, I was thinking. Wouldn't it be a shame if Peter broke something during the last football game of the season? Say an arm or a leg? Who knows for sure? Now that would really suck. He probably would be carried off on a stretcher like a hero but think of the excruciating pain! If you ask me, it would be unnecessary pain that could have been avoided. Don't you think?"

That was it. She came to a stop. She could feel his smug grin. "You leave him alone, understand? I am warning you, Ryan. If you do anything to Peter--."

He grabbed her hand. "What, Avery?" He roughly pried open her fingers and found the tiny crystal embedded in her palm. "Are you going to use this against me?" She struggled to get free, but he held her tightly. He placed his palm against hers. She could feel the tiny sparks coursing through her palm and up her arms. He pressed harder. "Don't you see? We are the same. You and me. Whether you like it or not." Finally, he released his hold, and his voice became gentle. "Listen, Avery. I don't want to be the bad guy but understand I can't let you out of my life. I just can't."

Avery stared into his green eyes, identical to her own. "What do you want from me? You seem to know everything about me."

Looking into her intense green eyes, Ryan felt overwhelming guilt. *Why did she have to be so smart, so beautiful, so tough and gentle at the same time?* If she was just some ordinary girl, it would be easy to fulfill his father's wishes for revenge. But Avery, she was the one. The one he knew that he could spend the rest of his life with. Even at seventeen, he knew. He led her over to the curb. The bus had taken off without her.

"I know who you are. You are a Leirion. Your ancestors lived on the mountaintop of Oros. Your powers come from the crystal in your left hand, just as mine come from the crystal in my right palm." He raised his palm, and the tiny crystal sparkled in the sunlight. "So, you see, we will be together forever."

Avery continued to stare at him. She had so many questions, but she did not want to ruin the moment. Ryan was sitting so close to her; it was as if their hearts were beating as one.

Finally, she spoke. "Ryan, you haven't answered my question. What do you want from me? And why are you so bent on hurting Peter?"

"He isn't right for you. We are the same. Peter is not like us. Don't you see? You would be doing him harm. It's too hard of a life for a mortal to live with someone from a clan."

Avery stood up. Her hands were on her hips now, and she looked at Ryan defiantly. "Don't talk like that, Ryan. My father is a mortal, and he and my mother have a great marriage. They have told me time and time again that it made no difference if I was born a Leirion or a mortal. Being born healthy was all that mattered to them. How many of us are here in this town? Is it just a coincidence that you are living in the same town as I, or is there a motive?"

"I promise this is a coincidence. I realized that you were one of us when I could feel the energy in your body. I don't think there are any more of us living here."

"What about your dad? Is he a warlock or a mortal?"

Ryan knew that this question was going to be inevitable. Guilt washed over him. It was bad enough that he lied about it being purely coincidental that they both lived in the same town, but what he was about to tell her crossed the line. Furiously his brain tried to sort out his devotions, but he knew that family came first.

"My dad was a twin. Both of his parents were from the Leirion clan and had the powers. When my dad's brother was born, they could see the small crystal ring on his left pinky. It was tiny, but the sign that he would carry on the powers. When my dad was born two minutes later, there was no ring. No one could explain how he could have been born a mortal since both his parents were not.

"Wait. If your dad is a mortal, then how do you have the crystal, and why is it in your right palm if your uncle and grandparents were Leirion?" Avery asked.

"My mother was from a different clan, and the crystal was in a pinky ring on their right hand. Like you, our generation also had the crystal embedded into our right palm."

Ryan continued, "As the years went on, the jealousy between my father and his brother increased. My dad's brother always felt that because my dad was mortal, and to compensate for his lack of powers, their parents loved him more. Clan members were forbidden to use their powers for selfish reasons. But my uncle tried everything to bring my father down. One night, my father was with the love of his life, about to declare his undying love for her, when my uncle came upon them. He, too, was in love with this woman, but she only was in love with one man, my father.

"My dad and uncle got into a huge fight. My uncle was on top of my father. He looked at the woman and, with menacing eyes, told her that if she did not give her heart to him, he would kill my father. She sent huge currents of electricity into my uncle's body. He was electrocuted instantly. My father was so overcome with grief and guilt over the death of his brother he went into a severe depression. The woman was shunned by the clan, even her parents, for such a horrendous use of her powers that she left the mountain never to return."

Ryan looked at Avery. Her eyes were dark green, and flecks of gold sent off minute sparks. Most of what he had told her was the truth; it was what his father had told him. He could not get himself to tell her that he was there to seek revenge for his uncle and mother's death. It made him sick to his stomach to think about inflicting pain upon Avery. He took her hand and touched her crystal. It was scalding. "Avery, that woman was your mother."

"Liar!"

Ryan reeled backward. The shock that surged through his body felt like a jolt of lightning.

"That's not how it happened!" she screamed. "Take it back, Ryan. Take it back, or I will hurt you more!" She aimed her palm at him. He knew that her powers were much stronger than his own.

He had no choice. He yelled at her, "Okay, I take it back!"

Ryan stood up. Avery was sobbing. He tried to put his arms around her, but she violently shook them off. "That is not how it happened," she continued to murmur repeatedly through her tears. And then, regaining her composure, she looked at him hard. "On that dark and terrible night, your father and uncle were trying to force her into making a decision!"

Ryan was listening to her now. He did not know what to believe. Would his father lie to him? Ryan's head was pounding. This was too much to take in. "She killed my uncle. He is still dead and gone. Nothing you say can change that."

"*Your uncle.*" Avery hissed. "It was your uncle and father that tried to hurt my mother. Can't you get that through that thick head of yours? My mother was protecting herself. She did not mean for him to die. She used her powers to get them off her. Your uncle hit the wall. My mother has lived with that guilt for all these years. She was just protecting herself."

Avery's voice sounded tinny; her shoulders slumped. "At least you can get to see your grandparents if you want. I will never get that chance, and it's all because of your father and uncle!" Avery started to run. She had to get away from him. It was all just too much for her.

Ryan ran after her. He grabbed her by the shoulders. His eyes were dark, and the golden flecks looked like tiny fireworks going off. "Avery, no one is there anymore. The mountain, it's barren except for those who have passed on into the afterlife."

"What do you mean?"

"After your mother left, the grief became unbearable. Allegiances were made, and the members divided. The thick veil of despair took its toll on all, and it caused the Leirion to lose their powers. They had to leave Oros Mountain to rebuild their lives." Ryan stopped talking. He did not dare mention how his father only cared about revenge toward Avery's mother. He had to gain her trust if he were to follow his father's wishes.

"So, my grandparents could be anywhere, and all that is left of Oros are some scattered graves?"

Ryan clenched his jaw. She sounded so callous, but she could not know, he told himself, that his sweet and beautiful mother lay next to his uncle beneath the hard, cold dirt. Not an hour went by when he did not think of her or the part that he played in her death. "My uncle is buried there."

I don't care, Avery thought. *My mother's life was torn apart because of him. He deserves to be dead.*

Sparks bounced off Ryan. "Don't think that! Such cruel thoughts will only hurt you in the end." *He could read her mind!* Ryan tried to control himself. He felt his body burn. He had to get out of there.

"I hate you, Ryan! Leave my family and me alone for good. What you told me will never leave my lips. I will never make my mother's life more horrible than that night, and I warn you that if you try to hurt my family, you will be sorry!"

With those final words, she raised her palm and sent red-hot sparks shooting onto the ground. The tar between them melted away, leaving a huge gash in the street. It looked like molten rock oozing and gurgling. Avery turned and took off, the ground rumbling underneath her.

Avery opened the door to her mom's shop. "I'm home," she called to her mom. She forced herself to keep calm and not let her mom see the fire still blazing in her eyes.

"So, are you going to be the next Gabrielle Reece?"

"Let's just say that I am pretty sure I am going to make the first cut." Avery strolled to the back, where her mom was completing some paperwork. She passed the photograph. "Mom, can I keep this in my room? It would make me feel closer to my great-grandmother and grandmother."

"Absolutely. You are very sweet."

Guilt washed over her. She hated lying to her mother, but she was doing just that.

Peter had texted her. He wanted her to look through some boxes with him in the attic to see if he could find the photograph. He was sure that it was the same picture. His father was at work until eight, and that would give them plenty of time.

"Mom, can Peter pick me up after dinner tonight so we could go to the library for a couple of hours?" *Lies, again.* "He had chemistry last year and said he would go over my study review sheet with me. I should be back around eight."

"Just make sure that you buckle up. This is a huge deal that I am letting you drive with someone other than your father or me."

"I promise." She tucked the frame under her arm. Her mother was too busy to realize that she was not going back inside to put it in her room before she left. Instead, she placed it into her book bag that was lying by the door.

Avery plopped down in the front seat. "I hate lying to my mom, Peter. That is all I have been doing lately. Between you and Ry--" Avery stopped herself.

"Between me and Ryan, right?"

Avery blushed.

"It's okay. I know that you like both of us. Ryan's the bad boy, and I am the good boy. Right? But don't worry. Bad boys never win in the end."

"Um, isn't the saying 'Good guys always finish last'?" Avery said with a laugh.

"Not in this case."

Peter pulled his car into the garage. The door closed with a heavy clang, and Avery suddenly felt like she was suffocating. She did not feel right about being there, but it was too late. Although she trusted Peter, she knew what she was doing was wrong on so many levels. She was lying to her mom, at a boy's house without anyone home and going through someone else's belongings without permission. She did not like who she was turning into. As if reading her mind, Peter came around her side and opened the door. "There's something to be said about the good guy," he laughed softly, as if to ease her nerves. He held his hand out for her to grab onto and whispered, "It's going to be alright, Avery. I promise." His eyes were warm, and she knew there was not a menacing bone in his body.

"I believe you," she said and followed him into the house.

"Welcome to the bachelors' pad," Peter joked. The house was laid out pretty much the same as Avery's, but a cozy house, it was not. There was barely any furniture, and smack in the middle of the room stood a massive 82-inch television. Clothes were scattered everywhere, and the dishes were still strewn on the table.

"My father would kill me if he knew we had a guest here without us cleaning up. But this is how it is pretty much every day with just the two of us. My father doesn't date, even though I beg him to, and you're the first girl I have brought here. It's rough growing up without a mom. You are very lucky that you have both parents to care about you." Peter cleared his throat.

Avery felt her heart go out to him.

The attic was a million times worse. Boxes took over almost the entire floor space. Cobwebs hung low, and dust covered every surface. Avery, look out for the bat!" Peter shouted. Avery ducked, her hands waving wildly in front.

"Just kidding; I needed something to lighten the mood."

"So funny I forgot to laugh." She stood up. "You do know what they say about paybacks, don't you?"

Peter laughed. "Can't wait."

Avery's eyes stung, and she started to cough. "It looks like no one has been up here in years."

"My dad shoved the boxes he didn't need up here when we moved in, and I don't think he has been here since." He stopped and looked at her. "I guess it was kind of stupid for me to think that the photograph might be up here. Come on, let's go. Your eyes look like they are starting to swell."

Avery found herself liking Peter more and more. True, there *was* that unbreakable tie between Ryan and her, but he was trouble. She started to follow Peter out when suddenly she stopped short. There on the floor was a thin path. The dust had been cleared away. "Peter, look. Your dad must be going up here. See? This is the only spot where there's no dust."

They followed the path until they came to the very end. One solitary box was propped up against the wall. The air suddenly became much thicker, and it was not from all the dust. "It didn't get here by accident," Peter said quietly. "It was brought back here on purpose."

"Maybe we shouldn't. I feel like we are intruding. These are your father's personal things."

He turned around to face her. He was so close that she could see the hurt in his eyes. "I feel like something in that box will help me learn why my mother left us. Don't you think that makes them my things, too?"

Taking his hand, she pulled him in close. She touched his face tenderly and let her crystal graze his skin ever so slightly. Peter let out a small shudder. Avery could sense that he felt the tiny current pass through his body. She brought her lips up to his and kissed him gently. Kissing him felt like she was in heaven. His lips were warm and soft. It did not last long, but it was enough to know that they, too, were connected, but in a totally different way. She led him over to the box. "Let's see what's inside," she said quietly.

Sitting next to him, barely breathing, Avery watched Peter use his car key to rip open the tape that sealed the box. There were two strips, indicating that it had been resealed.

"Ready?" Avery said.

He shook his head. The contents were covered by a beautiful blanket. Small squares of different shades of blue, with a tiny, small circle of silver in the middle of each one, were crocheted together. At the bottom, also in silver wool, was the name *Peter*. Avery gingerly lifted the blanket out of the box. She placed it on Peter's lap. "This must be your baby blanket. Your mother must have crocheted it for you before you were born. It's beautiful. It looks like it took her a long time."

Peter shrugged. The hurt in his eyes turned them dark blue, and Avery found herself aching for him just as much as he was clearly aching for the mother he never knew. "You sure you want to continue?"

Peter nodded, but this time it was he who reached into the box. He pulled out a small silver teething ring engraved with his initials and birth date and a stuffed bunny. Its cloth ears were matted, and it looked like it had been washed repeatedly. The stuffing had sunk to the bottom.

"It looks like how I feel after a tough football game."

Avery could see that underneath his joking exterior, he was trying hard to keep it together. Peter gently placed the items next to the baby blanket.

"And for my next trick, what will it be? A rabbit, perhaps?" There were more baby toys and a small silver box with an angel on top. "I guess this was intended for the first tooth I lost." He shook it, expecting to hear nothing. But instead, a tiny sound echoed through the silver interior. "Well, I guess my dad must have been the Tooth Fairy, after all." He laughed quietly. He took another look in the box. "It must have been really hard on my dad after my mom left." Looking at the floor, he said, "How could a mother leave her child?" Tears filled Peter's eyes.

Avery threw her arms around him. She held him close, the two of them entwined in his grief. "I am sure it's not what you think," she whispered in his ear. "She must have had her reasons; I am sure of it."

"I'm glad you're here with me."

"I am, too. Come on. Let's put this stuff back. I have to be home in an hour, and what if your dad comes home early?" She picked up the rabbit and placed it at the bottom of the box, smoothing out its tattered ears. "Sleep tight," she murmured to it.

Suddenly, she felt something sharp catch her finger. At the bottom of the box, was a tiny incision etched into the cardboard. It looked like someone had added another layer to the box and then set it back in place. "Peter! Quick, give me your key."

He leaned over to see what she was doing. Avery pried the layer off, leaving in its place a space about six inches deep.

Peter lifted the gilded frame out of the box. He blew the dust off the glass and stared at the photograph gazing back at him. "I told you! I knew it was the same photograph."

Avery gasped. She pulled the photograph out of her book bag. They were identical. "I don't understand. How did your father end up with this?"

He shook his head. "I don't know, but what I do know is that my father went to great lengths to hide it from me. Who are they, Avery? Who are these women and babies in the picture?"

"There's no time now. Your father is going to be home soon, and my mom is expecting me at exactly eight. Put everything back in the box except for the frame. I'll tell you everything I know tomorrow night."

Grabbing hold of her waist, Peter leaned in. "That is going to make for one intense first date. Are you sure you want to do it then?"

Feeling herself totally succumbing to him, she laughed softly. "I think we are way beyond a first date, Peter." He kissed her one last time before they took a final glance around the attic.

I wonder what other secrets are lurking up here, he thought, and then with one swift gesture, flicked off the lights.

Talia had been thinking about Korinna all day. She felt badly that all she did was get her a phone number. But then again, it appeared that Korinna could not wait to get out of the house, especially when Avery came home with Peter.

Having an hour or so before Avery came home, she wanted to check on how her new neighbor was doing. She packed up the casserole she had made for her and drove to her home. She was hoping they could become friends.

Talia pulled up to the house and parked. Juggling the casserole dish and a bottle of white wine that she grabbed from the fridge, she walked up the path to the front door. She pressed the bell and waited. She was just about to press again when an older-looking man opened the door. "May I help you?" he inquired, staring at the dish and bottle of wine.

Talia stammered, "Uh, is Korinna here?" She felt like a schoolgirl ringing the door of her friend's house for the first time. "I knew that she probably wouldn't be up to making dinner with just having moved in, especially with a bandaged hand." *I guess she's not alone,* she thought. *Either this is her father, or she is really into older men.* Talia suppressed a giggle.

The man continued to stare at her. "I am sorry dear, but no one by the name of Korinna lives here," the man said to her apologetically.

"Oh, I must have the wrong address. I am sorry to bother you."

"What address are you looking for? I have been living here forever with my wife. I know this neighborhood."

"Twenty-seven Grove Street," Talia said.

"Well, that's this house. Maybe you wrote the address down incorrectly. Good luck finding your friend."

Talia got back into the car. She set the dish and bottle of wine on the passenger seat and fished the address out of her purse. *Maybe I transposed the numbers,* she thought. But there, clearly written on the notepad, was 27 Grove Street, white ranch, blue shutters, around the corner and down the street.

This is so weird. She let out a sigh and headed home. *So much for my new friend.*

"How was your study review? I hope chemistry was the only thing you two were studying," Avery's mom said with a chuckle.

"Eww. That's really weird coming from my mom." But Avery blushed, and it certainly did not go unnoticed by Talia.

"I see the way he looks at you--the same way that other boy, Ryan, looked at you the day he came over the house."

"Mom! Stop! You are really starting to creep me out."

"Just be careful, Avery. I know that these feelings are inevitable. After all, you are beautiful, smart, and funny. You also have an obligation to withhold. And that is to never make your powers known. One day you will fall in love forever. When that day finally arrives--and trust me, you will be absolutely sure--only then will you be able to disclose your powers to him."

Strange how her mom was not able to read her mind, but Ryan could. Guilt stabbed at Avery's heart. She desperately wanted to tell her mom about Ryan and her and Peter's discovery, but it wasn't the right time.

"I understand, Mom. Well, I am going upstairs to finish studying. Good night."

"Sleep tight, honey. Don't stay up too late." Talia kissed her daughter on the cheek. "Oh, before you go up, the weirdest thing happened to me tonight while you were out. I went to visit that woman Korinna who came to our house yesterday. But when I got to the house, no one by that name lived there. Weird, huh? I guess your mom is getting old, and senility is finally setting in. Well, goodnight, sweetie. Love you."

"Love you, too."

Avery went upstairs and collapsed on her bed, her emotions twisting inside her, making her feel so utterly exhausted. She sought sleep desperately, but it evaded her. Finally, still in her clothes, she sank into a deep slumber.

Chapter 16

Avery was exhausted the next morning, but she was anxious to get to school. She knew that the list of the team's members was going to be posted outside the cafeteria. She scoured it for her ID number.

"Why are you even looking?" Sam teased. "You know you made the first cut."

"There were a lot of good players. I don't want to take anything for granted." Her eyes scanned the list. She wished the names were listed instead of the numbers. She was praying that Charlotte's ID number was not posted. She was such a nasty person, and Avery was fed up with her. Avery finally found her number, and with a squeal of delight, shouted, "Sam, I made it! Now, there's only one more tryout to go."

"Sam, I made it!" said a mocking voice.

"What do you want, Charlotte?" Avery had enough of her yesterday, and it was taking every ounce of perseverance not to use her powers to knock her on her ass.

"Well, let's see. I also made the cut, so I don't want your spot. I'm way prettier than you, so I don't want your looks. Hmmm, what is it that I want?"

Avery could see the hatred flaring in Charlotte's eyes. Charlotte moved in closer. "What I want, Avery, is for you to take your freakish self and leave. You may have Ryan and Peter under your trance, but you don't fool me." Charlotte spat her words like they were venom. She turned to leave, but Avery caught her by the wrist. Avery could feel her powers letting loose. She took deep breaths to calm herself. Charlotte's eyes turned to fear. "You're hurting me!" She tried to twist out of Avery's hold, but the more she struggled, the stronger the shocks became. "Everyone around you can now see you for the freak you really are!" Charlotte looked around. The hallway was empty. "Where is Sam? Where is everyone?"

Avery had used her powers to create an opaque veil that prevented Charlotte from seeing anyone. They were also frozen and would remember nothing.

Avery leaned in close. "Listen very carefully. When I release my hand on your wrist, you will remember nothing. In fact, you are going to become my best friend. You are going to trail after me like a puppy dog. It will get somewhat annoying on my end, but I will learn to live with it. And one last thing--my friend Ryan, the one with the dark green eyes and sexy smile, really, really likes you. Pursue him like you've never pursued another guy before. Don't worry about Brandon. When I let go, he will hate your guts. Come to think of it, everyone except for me will despise you. And it will be my best friend 'obligation' to get them to reconsider."

She released Charlotte's hand, and the girl collapsed to the floor. The veil disappeared, and everyone unfroze. "Here, let me help you up." Avery held her hand out for Charlotte.

"Thanks so much, Avery. You are the best friend anyone could ever have. I can't believe I tripped over my own two feet like that. I am so clumsy."

"Yeah, it's too bad you didn't make the first cut. Charlotte ran back to the door only to see her ID not listed. Confusion crossed her face. "You know what they say... better luck next year." Avery tossed her hair back. "Come on, Sam, let's get to class." She walked over to Sam.

"Why were you even talking to that disgusting girl, Avery? Everyone hates her."

In the sincerest tone that she could muster, she said, "I know, but someone has to feel sorry for her."

Chapter 17

Korinna had nowhere to go. She felt out of place and needed to be somewhere where she could find a morsel of comfort. She was exhausted and needed time to work out her own plan. *What am I going to do?* She wondered. Seeing Peter and not having him recognize her was unbearable, but the thought that he was in danger was worse. She had to stop Ryan from destroying his life just to keep his allegiance with his father. Warped allegiance. Alec had done everything in his evil powers to make Ryan believe that he was to blame for her death. Korinna found herself using her powers to return to Oros. The day was warm, and the ground felt soothing beneath her. She sat by her grave and stared at the inscription. She *was* a beloved mother, but the part that read beloved wife, well, that was just a mockery. Alec never loved her; he used her, and she, in all her loneliness and desperation, had fallen for it.

She awoke to terrible pains shooting through her body. The air on Oros Mountain was filled with electricity. The sky was ominous. The ground shook, and she could see a trio of hawks circling overhead. She shuddered. The hawks landed next to Korinna. Panic filled her as they began to surround her. She backed up against the stone wall and covered her face as she forced the powers out of her body. The pains were increasing, but Korinna focused. Bolts of currents shot out as she aimed them at the hawks. *Concentrate,* she thought to herself. *Let my powers penetrate their bodies.* They screeched, and feathers flew, but they were not dying. There were no flames. She could smell singed feathers, but they kept flying toward her. Suddenly, the air was still, the sky lighter, and her pains gone. Gone, too, were the hawks, and in their place, were three figures standing over her.

The figures looked identical. They wore simple black pants and turtlenecks. Fastened to their turtlenecks was a small crystal pin. At first, they looked normal enough to Korinna, except when she looked at their faces, she gasped. Their eyes were crystal clear, and minuscule waves of silver flickered through them. There were two men and one woman. Their pure-white hair was cropped close with what looked like silken threads of silver running through it. Their faces were pale, and their lips glistened. Korinna covered her mouth. She did not want to appear frightened. Their powers were strong; she knew that from having seen them in hawk form. Trying to use her own powers would be futile.

The woman walked over and extended her hand. Still against the stone wall, Korinna grasped the woman's bony, pale hand and let herself be pulled to her feet.

The woman held on to Korinna. Tiny currents ran through her like sharp knives. Finally, she let go.

Korinna struggled to appear brave, but intense fear overcame her when she surveyed the woman's face. Her body went rigid.

One of the men stepped forward. "Do not be frightened, my darling Korinna. We are here to help you if you help us. We have been waiting for you for a very long time. What do the mortals say? Patience is a virtue. Well, we are the most virtuous bunch around." His hoarse laugh curdled Korinna's insides. He motioned to the other man who was standing behind him. They used their powers in their crystals that lay embedded in their pinky rings to form a solid barrier around Korinna. Their eyes were brilliant. The flecks of silver crackled and sizzled feverously.

The woman entered the circle and embraced Korinna. Her body was ice, numbing Korinna's spine. "Don't be afraid. We will not harm you. You must know that I am not your enemy." A hint of recollection flashed through Korinna's mind, causing her to become dizzy and nauseous. But the woman's soft whispers lulled Korinna into a state of complete surrender. The woman let go and faced the two men. "It is time."

Chapter 18

"Rough night? You look like crap."

Avery kept walking. "Leave me alone, Ryan. Go stalk someone else. How about Charlotte? I heard she has the hots for you."

"Yeah, I wanted to thank you for my gift, Avery. Charlotte and I really hit it off last night. It's amazing how she idolizes me. A guy can really get used to that."

Feelings of disgust and jealousy swept over her. She despised that she still had the overwhelming attraction to him. "After the things you said about my mother, don't ever talk to me or even look my way again. I am serious, Ryan. Make it like I am invisible to you. Go about your life and leave me out of it."

I can't do that," he said with humility. "I wish I could. Really." He took her hand. "Believe it or not, I do care for you. And that's what makes this so torturous for me." He turned and walked away.

Tears welled up in her eyes, and she fought them back. She was so torn. Part of her wanted to run after him and tell him how she thought about him day and night, the other part detested him and still had feelings for Peter. It was all so confusing. She took a deep breath and headed for her last class.

The last bell of the day rang, and Avery felt a strong sense of relief. It was as if a vise that had been squeezing all the energy out of her finally released. She hated all the chaos in her life between Ryan and Peter. She always wanted to be "wanted," but getting what she desired felt overwhelming.

"Avery!" Peter walked up to her. "I'll pick you up at seven. Don't forget the photograph."

And just like that, Avery felt the pressure again. She wanted the truth, but she also wanted to go on a "normal" date. This was going to be far from that. "I have it in my book bag. Don't forget yours."

He leaned in close. As if sensing her thoughts, he whispered, "I promise that this won't be too weird." His warm breath made her skin tingle. "I am really looking forward to spending time with you."

She felt herself relax. "Me, too."

He walked her to volleyball practice.

Peter squeezed her hand gently. "Have fun. I'll see you in a few hours." As he turned to leave, he came face to face with Ryan, Charlotte by his side.

"I told you to leave her alone, Peter," Ryan said. His eyes were blazing, his body rigid.

"Ryan, let's just go. He's not worth it," Charlotte whined. She tried to grab Ryan's hand, but he roughly shook it away.

"Shut up, Charlotte!" he snapped.

Charlotte looked like a stray dog that had been kicked a few too many times. She cowered behind him and hung her head. "Anything you say, Ryan."

Peter looked at her strangely. This was not the obnoxious conceited Charlotte he knew. His eyes met Ryan's.

"This is the work of your girlfriend, Peter. Why don't you ask her about it?"

"Listen, Ryan. I don't know what you think you and Avery have, but she makes her own decisions on whom to or not to date."

Ryan raised his hand and sent a current into Charlotte's body, freezing her for the moment. Peter's body slammed into the floor, his right knee bone jutting outward. "I am not going to tell you again, Peter. Leave Avery alone!" He grabbed Charlotte's hand and practically dragged her down the hall.

Peter's agonizing screams brought all the volleyball players out into the hallway. Avery ran up to him. "Oh, my God, what happened?"

Before he could open his mouth, Avery's coach was leaning beside him, calling 911.

"Who did this to you, Peter?" Avery whispered to him, knowing deep down, she already had the answer. She knew he could not hear her; the pain had rendered him unconscious.

Avery looked around. She saw no one. Then she saw it; the text that was flashing on his phone--the text that she knew was meant for her. "I warned you…."

Chapter 19

Peter's pain shot through Korinna's body. She jerked forward and screamed. Confusion racked her brain.

"There, there, Korinna," the woman whispered into her ear. She crouched beside Korinna, embracing her tightly. "I know how difficult it must be to see your sons despise each other so much. And poor Peter's leg; how horrible!"

Through her sobs, Korinna tried to escape the woman's hold, but she was too weak and powerless to do so.

She sprang to her feet and pulled Korinna up. "Let's start at the beginning. I am now called Anastasia," the woman purred. "My Master gave me the name." Her words were smooth as honey, but Korinna could detect evil in them. Korinna felt her heart tighten around her chest and begin to pound thunderously. Her breathing became laborious, and she shrieked, "Noo!"

She felt them then--the stabbing pains of history enter her body, like knives cutting through secrets that lay buried for what seemed an eternity. Korinna now knew for sure who Anastasia was.

Anastasia knelt beside Korinna. Her hands were bone cold as she placed them on Korinna's shoulders. "You do remember me, don't you?" Korinna nodded, slumped in defeat.

"But why now?" Korinna asked Anastasia. "After all these years, why did you return?"

Anastasia's eyes were crystal clear. Korinna felt as if she could see deep into her soul, exposing motives of pure evil.

Anastasia laughed, her voice coarse and icy. "And leave my sister by herself with all this misery going on in her life?"

Korinna cringed. The word sister brought back horrifying memories, resurfacing to wreak more havoc on her life.

"You have no business here, Celine," Korinna replied softly. "Please, for everyone's sake, go back from where you came."

"My name is Anastasia! Never call me by my birth name again!" She touched Korinna's hair. "You look so much like our mother. It's almost frightening." She laughed, her head thrown back, exposing her throat.

Korinna gasped. "Your neck!"

Anastasia's eyes formed into tiny slits, and she touched her long fingers to her neck. "Oh, this little thing," she spat with sarcasm in her voice. "This was a present from my Master. Isn't he the most generous person in the world?" Anastasia pulled the rest of the turtleneck down, exposing a dozen more one-inch raised marks. They each formed an oval, and inside of each was the letter

D. "These, my dear sister, were my gifts from him when I tried to escape one dark night."

Korinna's eyes fixated on her sister's neck. The scars looked like someone had burned the skin and then branded the letter *D.* Her skin puckered around each one.

"I am so sorry this horrific thing happened, but our parents warned you over and over not to leave. They begged you to stay with the Sethos. They insisted that abiding by our rules was less difficult than life outside." Korinna lowered her eyes and murmured, "And, clearly, less tortuous."

The laugh that erupted from Anastasia sent spine-tingling chills down Korinna's back. This was not the sister she had played with when they were young. Korinna's memories flashed back to them playing tag in the lush green valley they called home. Her sister would pretend to look for Korinna, calling out her name when, in fact, Korinna learned a couple of years later she had known where she was all along. Korinna loved her big sister, and seeing her this way broke her heart.

"What's done is done. I have a duty to fulfill, and that is where you come into play. You will do this for me, Korinna. You have no choice."

Korinna began to protest, but sharp pains pierced her head.

"Make them stop!" she screamed.

"In time, my dear baby sister. In time."

The pounding sensation in Korinna's head finally ceased. All that was left was a dull ache and a ringing in her ears. Once again, Anastasia extended her hand to Korinna. But instead of expecting to be yanked and pushed, her sister gingerly helped her up and then placed her arms around her.

"I need you to listen to me, Korinna," Anastasia whispered, her voice so low that she had to move her face in close. "Please, don't pull away, even if I start to scream at you or try to hurt you again." Something in Anastasia's eyes revealed the tenderness and warmth of who was once Korinna's beloved sister. "Just nod to show me that you understand," she continued. Korinna nodded, confused at what was now happening. "I have her under my control now," she said to the men. "You may now return and wait for my arrival." The men bowed to Anastasia. They turned, clasped their hands together and with bolts of light streaking the sky, they were gone.

Korinna's mouth flew open. She could not comprehend the power those men had. It was incredible and terrifying at the same time. But she also understood that they seemed to be under her sister's control. The only question was, why?

Chapter 20

Ryan slammed the front door. "Damn it," he muttered. He had gone too far. "Damn it, Dad!" He now screamed at the top of his lungs. He blamed him for all of this. *Why couldn't he just get over it and get on with his life?* He hated that his father was using him for revenge.

He had no idea what the truth was after he had spoken to Avery that day. All of this was too much for him. His head was pounding. He had used his powers to get home, leaving Charlotte standing in the parking lot, confused and dazed.

The instant after he stupidly sent the text message, he regretted it. Avery knew he had done that awful thing to Peter, and she would never forgive him. It was unclear to him whether he had hurt Peter out of pure jealousy, or if he just wanted to get him out of the picture so that he could get to Avery and avenge his uncle's death. Everything seemed to be a blur; his life was spiraling out of control.

His hand ached, and the crystal was blazing hot to the touch. Pure hate permeated his body. He hated himself, his father, his powers, and the way he could feel the sadness and the tension in Avery's body. He hated his life. But he could not hate Avery. She was all he could think of, and he was certain that, ultimately, they would be together.

"Well, I told you that our date wouldn't be boring," Peter sighed, his eyes half open.

"Shh, don't talk. I am here, and I will stay with you. The nurses will physically have to restrain me to try to get me to leave." Avery sat at the edge of the hospital bed. Peter had just come out of recovery from a two-hour surgery on his knee. He looked beaten up, and Avery had to force back the tears. *It's all my fault*; she chastised herself. *If I had just taken Ryan's threats seriously, Peter would not be here.*

"No, save the restraining part for me when I am feeling a little more like myself," he smiled.

Avery felt that a lifetime had passed in the five hours since she had called her mom and explained to her what had happened at school. Her mom picked her up and drove her to the hospital. Peter's father, Ben, was already waiting for the ambulance to arrive. Shaking, Avery introduced herself and explained that she did not know who would have wanted to do this to Peter. Her face felt hot, and she hated herself for lying to him. She could not tell him the truth--not without telling Peter everything first. She owed Peter that much.

"Mom, I am going to stay here until visiting hours are over. Can you pick me up later?"

"Just text me. Either your father or I will come."

"Thanks, Mom," Avery murmured. "I really do love you."

"It was really cool of your dad to let me spend some time with you," Avery said. She knew she was blushing when Ben told her that he would wait outside for a bit.

"Um, I only mentioned you about a thousand times this week," Peter said sheepishly.

Avery moved closer to him. She leaned down and touched her lips to his. He felt so cold, and she let a bit of her powers release to warm his body. "I am so sorry this happened to you." Tears came and spilled down her cheeks, wetting Peter's face.

Peter's fingers caressed her face. His lips found hers. Afraid that she might hurt him, Avery pulled back, but Peter just pulled her in closer. It felt so right, so perfect, and everything that was troubling Avery seemed to melt away.

The door opened, and Ben walked in. "Ahem, you two might want to come up for some air before the nurses come running in due to Peter's heart monitor going crazy. I guess you're feeling a little better," he chuckled.

Avery felt her face redden again. She flew off the bed. "Um, I guess I better let you get some rest," she said, stumbling over her words in embarrassment.

"Wait, Avery," Peter called after her. "Dad, can you give us two more minutes, please? I promise I'll sleep after," he said groggily.

"Two minutes, and then I am calling Nurse Ratchet," his father replied, smiling.

"Nurse Ratchet?" Avery questioned.

"Yeah, she is a character from my dad's all-time favorite movie, *One Flew over the Cuckoo's Nest*; it's a classic. We'll have to make a date real soon to watch it together," he said, patting the indented space where she had been only moments before. He took her hand and held it in his. "Listen, Avery. I know that you have a lot to tell me. And I know that Ryan, you, and *I* are tied together in a bizarre way. The photographs, the flashes of heat that I feel running through my body when I kiss you, my busted knee... I know all these things are related."

Avery flinched. She tried to move away, but Peter held on.

"But we will sort of all this out together, and nothing that you can say to me will change the way that I feel about you." He let go, his energy spent. Avery leaned in to kiss him, but he seemed to be sleeping. She turned to leave, but not before she heard him murmur, "I love you, Avery."

"Thanks for letting me go with you to pick Peter up, Mr. Saunders," Avery said.

"Call me Ben. And are you kidding me, Avery? You are the only one Peter talks about. If I *didn't* bring you, he probably would have hated me for the rest of his life."

Avery smiled. She liked Peter's dad, and feeling her cheeks flush, she thought, *and I really like Peter.* As soon as the thought entered her brain, another thought chased after it. Ryan. Damn him. He was always in her mind, even when she willed herself not to think about him.

Peter's good leg was tapping impatiently against the side of the bed when the two arrived. "I thought you'd never get here," he said to his dad.

Avery walked over to the bed. She kissed Peter tenderly on the cheek and, with her fingers closed into a little fist, gently knocked on his cast.

"Wow! That sure is solid."

"Six weeks, and I'll be good as new," Peter replied. "But till then, I *am* going to need some attention."

"Okay, that's enough, Casanova." Ben laughed. "I'll call the nurse and get this show on the road. Will you stay for dinner, Avery? I am making Peter's favorite from when he was a little boy--roast beef and mashed potatoes. Peter loved to make a small indentation in the potatoes and pour the gravy into it, pretending that it was a volcano about to erupt."

"Come on, Dad. Show me some mercy," Peter joked.

But Avery could see the tinge of sadness that crept into his face. She knew that he was missing the mother he never got to know.

"That would be great, Mr. Saunders, uh, I mean Ben. Let me just call my mom to make sure it's okay." Avery stepped out into the hallway to dial her mom's number. As the phone powered up, Avery saw five text messages glaring at her. They were from *him,* and each one said the same thing: "Call me. We need to talk." Avery deleted them and dialed her mom.

The wheelchair was a requirement for leaving the hospital, and Peter tried to put on a macho front, but Avery could see that he was embarrassed. Walking alongside, she casually took his hand and gave it a little squeeze. Peter smiled, grateful at Avery for somehow always reading his mind and knowing what to do.

Dinner seemed to take forever. Peter and Avery could not stop looking at each other. They both knew what lay ahead of them. It was the conversation that never occurred, the conversation that bound them, the conversation that centered on two photographs of two women, each holding an infant in her arms.

"Thanks for keeping Peter company, Avery," Ben said as he and Avery were loading the dishwasher. "He is a great kid. Sometimes he gets a little withdrawn, but I guess that just comes with the territory of not having a mom around."

"He thinks you are the greatest dad in the world," Avery said tenderly.

Ben cleared his throat. "Thanks for saying that, Avery. It means so much to me to hear those words. There have really been some rough times during all these years of him not having a mom." Avery could not bear to look at Ben. She knew that he was trying to control his emotions. She could not imagine her mom not being there for her, even if she sometimes drove her nuts.

"Well, that's the last of them," Ben said as he tried to squeeze the last dirty plate into the dishwasher.

Avery laughed. "That is something my dad would do. He never washes them the way my mom does... " She caught her words and looked empathically at Peter's dad. "I'm really sorry."

"Don't say that. You should be able to talk about your family without feeling guilty. Peter told me how nice they were to him. You are a lucky girl, and Peter is lucky to have you for his friend."

Avery blushed. She knew they were both thinking that they were more than just pals.

They heard a loud thumping. They both ran into the family room. "Hello? Did you forget me?" Peter was banging his crutch against the floor.

"This is going to be a long six weeks," Ben groaned with a smile on his face. Avery smiled back and nudged herself onto the couch next to Peter. "Well, I guess this is my cue to head upstairs. Avery, thanks for everything. Peter, don't be too much of a pain. Good night, kids."

"I thought he would never leave," Peter said with a mischievous grin.

Avery nudged closer. "Your dad is really sweet."

"Yeah, I know. Everyone tells me that." He laughed, clearly proud of his father. "But now, it's my time with you." Peter reached out his arms and drew Avery in closer. She was exhausted, and it felt amazing to be so close to him. She could feel her body emanating tiny sparks, and it warmed her to the core. Peter's eyes locked onto hers. She knew that he could feel them too.

Self-conscious, Avery pulled away from his embrace. "Do you want to talk about the photographs, or are you too tired? We are also going to have to wait until your father is at work to go back through all the boxes in the attic. I am going to have to bring them downstairs. There's no way you are going to be able to hobble up those narrow steps." She knew she was blabbering, anything to get her mind and his off what was really going on between them. The attraction was getting stronger and stronger, and at that point, Ryan was just a faint thought in the back of her mind.

Peter used his arms to prop himself up into a half-sitting position. He reached out to Avery again and brought her in closer. His hands felt her lips, eyes, and nose, his fingers touching every inch of her perfect face. He pressed her closer against him, their breathing in synch. "Um, I don't want to hurt you," Avery mumbled.

"Shh," Peter whispered as he placed his lips against hers and kissed her gently. His hands roamed her body as his kisses became stronger. "I feel them, Avery," he murmured softly into her ear as the sparks lightly sent hot flashes through his body. "I know that you are different; I knew that from the day I saw your beautiful green eyes. And I know that we were meant to be together."

Hearing those words from Peter's mouth, his breath, sweet and warm on her face sounded so different than when Ryan said them. Avery succumbed to Peter's embrace.

Chapter 21

Ryan slammed his hand against the kitchen table. He knew what went on at Peter's. He could feel their electricity in his own body all night long, and he felt rage and disgust. *Peter is winning. He cannot win. I will not let him win.*

Alec looked up from his newspaper. "Rough morning?" he asked sarcastically.

Ryan began to feel sheer hatred mounting toward his father. He cared about only one thing, revenge. For Ryan, it was more than that, and all his feelings made his insides twist into a tight knot. He was falling in love with Avery, and Peter was getting in the way. Jealousy of their closeness when he felt the heat between them was tormenting him. He had tried to block the images of them cuddled together on the couch by pressing the crystal in his palm as hard as he could, but everything remained clear, and it made him sick.

"Why can't you drop this vendetta, Dad, and get on with your life? This hatred toward Avery's mom is unhealthy."

"I told you not to get attached, Ryan. I warned you!"

Ryan stared at his father. Alec's eyes were dark stones. His breathing was rapid, and his nostrils flared when he exhaled.

"You are a fool to think she will fall for you! She is like her mother, deceitful and conceited, and she will never give you a second thought. She killed your uncle and your mother! Don't ever forget that."

Ryan never despised his father more than he did at that moment. Looking at his twisted face revolted him. "I'm late for school," he muttered. But before he walked out of the kitchen, he turned to his father and said in a low, barely audible voice, "Just remember, Dad, who has the powers in this house."

Alec heard the front door slam shut. He looked out the window and saw Ryan peel down the street. Grabbing the bat propped up in the corner by the front door, he walked into the dining room and pummeled it into the chandelier. Shards of crystal rained down, creating pinpoint cuts in his skin. The pain fueled his vengeance that much more. Alec watched what was left of the chandelier sway, casting hundreds of exquisite rainbows around the room. He laughed bitterly. His life was anything but puppy dogs and rainbows. Everything was falling apart. His son was turning against him, and he could not let that happen. Alec dropped the bat and walked over to the mirror. He stared at his reflection. He had razor-sharp pieces of crystal embedded all over his body. Silver liquid flowed freely. Alec threw back his head and howled like a madman. *The blood of a warlock, but not the powers,* he thought. He stood frozen and silently cursed Talia for all the pain she had caused him and his family. Mesmerized by the jagged crystals protruding from his body, he began to feel a savage rage mounting in his body. The hundreds of crystals glinting in the mirror mocked him, as if chanting, "You are lacking the one crystal that really matters."

Yes, Talia had destroyed that. Alec removed one of the biggest pieces of glass from his arm. The pain just seemed to escalate the revenge he sought. The tip was covered in blood. Alec raised it to the mirror, and with manic strokes, he etched into the glass the bloody message for Ryan to see and remember. He stood back and watched as the metallic silver filled his gashes.

Alec knew it was too late for Ryan and him to reconcile. So much had been destroyed. Those he loved and cared for had died. And now, as much as it killed him to fathom the horrible fate his son would have to endure created by his own hands, he knew it was inevitable. His insatiable need for revenge overtook everything. "Forgive me, Ryan," he whispered into dead air.

Chapter 22

Talia tossed and turned the entire night and willed the minutes on the alarm clock to move more quickly. At the first sight of sunrise, she finally decided to get up and make herself a cup of tea. She passed Avery's door. It was opened a crack. She could see the blankets twisted and balled up in a knot. Avery's left leg dangled off the side of the bed, her hair splayed all over the pillow, and of course, her cell phone, beside her. *How many times have I told her about radiation?* Talia tiptoed to the bed and placed the phone on the nightstand. The movement of the phone made it light up and Talia saw the texts. "Avery, you need to call me, please." "Avery, I am sorry for what happened to Peter. Please call me." "Avery, you have to listen to my side of the story." "Avery, you…" Talia let out a gasp so loud that Avery sat up in bed.

"Jeez, Mom, you scared me half to death!" Avery looked down and saw her mother holding the phone, staring at the illuminated words.

"What is going on here?" Talia whispered to her daughter.

"Why are you touching my things?" Avery yelled back. She went to grab the phone away from her but felt a sharp stinging sensation in her arm. "What--"

"Avery, you listen to me now!" her mother replied, pulling her daughter to her feet. The last thing I would want to do is use my powers on my daughter. But you must tell me everything that has been going on. What have you been keeping from me? What have you done?"

Avery started to sob. Hot tears of shame for keeping secrets from her mom slid down her cheeks.

"Okay, calm down and let's start from the beginning," her mom softly said as she stroked her daughter's bed head hair.

Avery told her everything; the connections she felt with Ryan and Peter, the trance she had placed on Charlotte, Peter's "accident," and the story Ryan had told her.

"I am so sorry for keeping all of this from you! But I know how you wanted us to be a 'normal' family. I know how you didn't want me relying on my powers to make things go my way." Avery paused and stared at her mom. Talia was twisting her ring around and around. Her eyes were flashing.

"I knew we should have gone somewhere far away. I could have home-schooled you. You would have been safe. Your dad and I should not have put you in this danger. Avery, do you understand what is going on? Do you grasp how dire this situation is?"

Avery nodded, guilt wracking her body.

"We need to wake your father up and tell him everything. We need to pack and figure out a way to leave here without a trace."

"Mom, I don't want to go anywhere. It'll be okay, I promise."

Suddenly Talia's eyes grew wide. She now pictured the man in her shop all those years ago, and how he had given her the creeps. And the woman Korinna, who had given her a fake address. They must have come here for a purpose. She remembered something, something even her daughter had forgotten to mention. "The picture," she whispered. "Go get the picture."

"I forgot to tell you one more thing," Avery said. "The night I was supposed to be 'studying' with Peter——well, we were actually at his house looking for the photograph he claimed was the same as ours."

Talia stared at her daughter.

"We found it in a box, and it was identical! The way it was hidden, someone did not want it to be discovered. Peter now has it."

Avery unzipped her backpack, pulled out the photograph, and handed it to her mom. Staring at the photograph, Talia suddenly knew why Korinna looked so familiar to her. She traced her fingers over the picture, murmuring softly to herself.

Avery knew it was better to let her mom continue the conversation when she was ready, and so she watched intently as her mom took the photograph and hugged it close to her heart. "Avery, the woman who came here the other day with her hand all bandaged--I just know she must be related to the women in this picture." Now Talia could be barely heard, for her voice was a mere whisper. "Remember I told you about Sophia, the little girl who was taken away by her father after her mother, Eva, killed herself? The girl I never had the chance to meet. I think Korinna must be Sophia's daughter!"

"Are you sure?" Avery asked while she continued to stare at the photograph that her mom held onto so tightly. "How can you be sure from a photo that is so old and faded?"

"I have this feeling, Avery. I used to get them often when I was much younger. They started when I was about your age. I would lapse into this acute state of consciousness where I knew that something terrible was about to occur. It is hard to explain, but a sense of foreboding would creep into my body, and the feeling would linger there until, eventually, the bad thing that was going to happen, did. Sometimes it was a minor feeling, and the next day I would find myself bleeding from a cut I made while shaving my legs. Other times, my body would remain in this state for days--two, three, sometimes even four. It was horrible. I never knew when the inevitable was going to happen; I was just certain that it would."

Talia's eyes lowered, her voice becoming barely audible. "One time, it lasted for two weeks. I felt like a zombie, going through the motions of the day. Every morning I would try to use my powers to get rid of the feeling. I would send currents of electricity coursing through my body as if the scalding heat would burn the feeling out of me. But it never went away, until that is, that horrible night with Darius and Alec."

Just thinking about that night made Avery want to hurt Ryan and his father. She could feel tiny synapses of electricity bouncing off her skin. The heat intensified so quickly that it even caught her off-guard. Sparks scorched the walls and sent tiny balls of fire landing on the carpet. The room was ablaze. Talia's eyes grew wide. "No, Avery!" She grabbed her daughter's hand, but Avery just shook it away. The sizzling was deafening, and the flames licked their lips around them.

"We are going to burn to death!" Talia screamed at her daughter. Her own powers were useless. The power embedded in her daughter's crystal was much stronger.

Choking on the smoke, Talia watched in horror as the curtains in Avery's room caught on fire. Steve lay sleeping in bed, undoubtedly in a trance by her daughter. The smoke detectors and sprinkler system were silent.

Then, just as quickly as the electricity poured out of Avery's crystal, it ceased. The flames subsided, and all that was left was the crinkling of ashes. The smell was acrid.

Avery looked around and surveyed the destruction. She then placed her palm against the curtains, and instantly they were restored. She continued until the room looked as if nothing had happened. She faced her mom, a smirk on her face. "See? No harm done."

Talia's rage surged. She slapped Avery across the face. Avery cried out. "No harm done? Avery, you could have killed us!"

"Mom, I wanted to show you how powerful I am. We do not have to move. I will never let anyone or anything hurt our family again."

"Avery, I realize that you wanted to show me that moving again was not the solution, but you acted recklessly. Your dad and I have told you repeatedly that using your powers for selfish means is not permitted in this family-ever! I understand your need to protect us, but I will not condone it."

"One month--no television, cell phone, or going out," Avery groaned to Peter, who was hobbling along on crutches, the bright yellow cast covering his leg. "Oh, and by the way, what is with that color cast?"

"With these crowded hallways--I just wanted to make sure I didn't get run over."

Avery laughed. It felt good. So much rage was pent up inside her.

"Thanks again for helping me out with my book bag, but I am sure your back is killing you from carrying both."

Peter was right. She *was* in pain. She desperately wanted to use her crystal to make the weight more bearable, but she still felt the guilt from seeing her mom so terrified.

"What did you do that rendered such a harsh punishment upon the perfect little Avery?" Peter nudged her playfully in the ribs that almost sent her reeling face-first onto the disgusting linoleum-tiled floor.

"Hey, watch it, or you'll be falling right along with me," Avery joked.

Peter stopped and looked into Avery's eyes. "Too late. I've already fallen." He loved watching Avery's face turn the tiniest shade of pink. In fact, he loved watching everything about her. Cutting her a break from her embarrassment, Peter asked again, "Really, what did you do? Your parents don't seem like the type to be issuing such a harsh punishment."

Although she and Peter had a deep bond, she knew that now was not the time to admit she had set her bedroom on fire by using a tiny crystal that had been embedded in her hand since birth. And then she used it once more to make everything tidy and new again. Instead, she shrugged her heavily laden shoulders and said, "You know, just mother-daughter stuff."

Peter took that as a cue to change the subject. "Well, at least I get to see you at school, being that you are my personal assistant."

"You're just so funny, Peter. And I will be sure to send you my chiropractic bills," she teased. Avery gave him a playful jab.

He tried to tell Avery that she did not have to lug his bag, but she insisted. He knew she felt guilty for what had happened between Ryan and him. *Ryan.* Even his name left a bitter taste in his mouth. But as strange as it seemed, Peter was a little grateful for Ryan's violence. It had made Avery and him closer.

Stopping to adjust his crutches--his armpits were bruised and raw from the constant pressure--Peter touched Avery gently on her shoulder. He lifted the padded book bag strap and began to slowly massage the area. His fingers were strong, and he pressed into the sore spot with tenderness and strength.

Peter lifted the second strap and worked on her other shoulder. Avery felt the tension releasing from her body. "Mm," she moaned softly, her eyes half closed. Suddenly sensing that they were being watched, Avery's eyes flew open. She abruptly straightened her back, almost sending Peter to the floor.

"Here, let me help you." Ryan held out his hand to steady Peter. "It must be tough getting used to those." He pointed at the crutches, now firmly planted under Peter's arms.

Avery stiffened. All the tension surged back into her body, and this time it had nothing to do with Peter's book bag. Her eyes locked on to Ryan's, and for a split second, she felt that familiar rush of excitement that she always experienced when she was around him. But she knew that; however, he made her feel he was no good for her. In fact, he was no good for anyone. "Don't come near us, Ryan." She moved in front of Peter, as if shielding him from the powers that she knew had caused the accident in the first place.

Peter's face reddened. He loved that Avery wanted to protect him, but he was not going to let Ryan think he was a wimp. He witnessed the intense pull between Ryan and Avery, and he was not going to let that ruin the relationship he was forming with her. Moving Avery gently aside, Peter faced Ryan. The crutches dropped to the floor. The sound was loud enough that people in the hallway turned around to stare. Peter moved in close. His eyes were ice blue, and the veins throbbed in his neck. He saw that Avery was trying to step in, but he shot her a look that made her stop cold. A crowd gathered. Everyone waited to see what would happen next.

The two locked eyes and Peter clenched his fingers into a fist and swung hard and fast. The sudden contact sent Ryan crashing to the ground. The hallway swarmed with students shouting encouragement to both Ryan and Peter.

Avery turned her hand over. She froze time and aimed her crystal at Peter. The intense sparks sent him crashing into the wall. Using her powers against Peter killed her, but she knew that there was no other choice.

"Get up!" she shouted at Ryan. The power from her crystal surrounded him. The electrical charges were stinging his body. *Not enough to kill him*, she thought. *But enough to hurt him, like he had hurt Peter.*

Ryan struggled to stand, but tiny jolts of electricity continued to singe every part of his body, the hair on his arms burning. His own crystal was no match for Avery's. Plus, she had debilitated him before he had a chance to use it. *Would he have even tried to use it on her?*

Avery took a deep breath and finally let the power within her crystal subside. "Get up! she shouted at him again. She held out her arm and yanked him up. Her strength was formidable, and it sent him reeling into her arms.

Avery found herself having difficulty breathing. Ryan wrapped his arms around her waist. The feeling was so powerful she knew that even the crystal in her palm could not break the bond that sealed them together.

Lips that were as hot as smoldering embers met hers. His hands moved up and down her body, exploring and touching places that he only had dreamed about. At the mercy of some unknown force, Avery's hands roamed up and down Ryan's body. She could feel his excitement and felt powerful that she could cause such a reaction. He pressed into her while their eyes remained open. They could both see the tiny flecks of energy that seemed to dance in each other's emerald-green irises.

And then she remembered. She broke away from him with such force that, once again sent Ryan reeling, except this time it was onto the floor.

"Don't ever touch me again!" Avery shouted with such turmoil in her voice that Ryan could not bear to look at her. "You are evil! Everything you and your father touch, everything you both say is destructive."

"I know that you think I am evil, but you can't deny that I am your soul mate." Ryan slowly stood up and began to walk toward Avery. He stopped a few feet in front of her. "And as much as you want to force that idea out of your head, we both know that it is the truth."

Avery lifted her palm and aimed at Ryan. She was already exhausted from all the energy that had been released from the crystal, but she was prepared to muster up every bit of strength that she could if it meant stopping Ryan from coming closer.

He continued to walk toward her. Something made her resist using the crystal. She hated herself, hated that she was putting her feelings for Ryan in front of what she felt for Peter. Shoulders sagging in defeat, Avery slumped to the ground. "Why can't you leave us alone?" she sobbed.

Ryan knelt and wrapped his arms around her so gently that she felt safe with him.

"I need to tell you something," Ryan said softly. He dreaded those words that would come out of his mouth but knew that he had to tell the truth; it was the love that he felt toward Avery that ultimately tore apart that pact that he had made with his father. It was the most dangerous decision that he was ever going to have to make in his life. But whatever the outcome, Ryan had no choice.

Avery looked up at him, her eyes half closed. She looked like a wilted flower. Ryan took her face in his hands and lifted her chin up slightly, so she would focus on what he was about to say.

Avery's eyes opened and, at that instant, dreaded what she was about to hear.

"Do you remember that horrible day when I accused your mother of killing my uncle?" Ryan's hands were sweating, and Avery felt him losing his grip. She knew that it was her chance to pull away, but something about the way he looked at her caused her to remain still. Ryan cleared his throat. Avery could not believe that he was nervous, and she lowered her face into the palm of his hand, rubbing her cheek against his moist fingers.

"You have to tell me what you know, Ryan," pleaded Avery.

Ryan paused. He began to doubt that he had the courage to turn Avery's world into a hellish turmoil.

"Please, Ryan. If you really care about me, then you'll tell me now."

Stroking her cheek, Ryan spoke so softly that Avery had to strain to hear him. "I believe you, Avery. I know now that everything my father told me about how your mother had some vendetta against my family was a lie." His words became louder as his omission became known. "You were right. My father and uncle did try to rape your mother." Ryan looked deep into Avery's eyes. He could see tiny sparks flashing. "I believe it when you said your mother was trying to protect herself from the two monsters that I am ashamed to call my father and uncle. I promised my father that I would avenge his brother's death by destroying you and, as a result, destroy your mother. I believed him, Avery. He's my father,"

Ryan admitted. "I knew that he had a temper and that his vengeance was out of control, but still, he is my dad. I begged him to let go of this horrific grudge against your mom, but I believed she killed my uncle and ruined my family's life. My mother died because of his bloodthirsty need for revenge. And because of that, because you have a mom and I do not, I went along with his plan."

Avery remained still. This was just too much information to process. Her whole world was being turned upside down. She did not know what to think anymore, who to trust or what to do. She looked at Ryan. He seemed ravaged by this information he gave her. Then she turned to look at Peter, still in a frozen state. *Oh, my god!* she thought. *Poor Peter!* She had never wanted him to be involved in this, but now it was too late. Her thoughts returned to last night. She thought about her mother holding the photograph and insisting that Peter was somehow connected to them.

Avery stood up and walked over to Peter. "I am waking him up now," she said to Ryan. "If you think about hurting him again or coming between us, think long and hard. Your powers are no match for mine, and I wouldn't like to have to bring you down."

"Avery, there's more. I forgot my gym clothes, so I had to go back to the house. My father was gone. He left a message for me. It was written in his own blood! It read, 'Talia and Avery will die!' You and your mom are in imminent danger. We need to—"

"Shut the hell up!" Avery screamed. "I heard everything! The three of us are going to figure something out."

Staring at her as if she had two heads, Ryan shook his head. "Are you crazy? Peter can't know about our powers!"

"I am waking him up now," repeated Avery, her voice firm. She knelt beside Peter, and with her palm turned towards his body. She let out the tiniest stream of electrical currents. She wanted him to awake feeling refreshed, not remembering anything that had happened.

The halls were filled with students rushing to their classes. Everything was back to normal. *Normal. Ha! What is that?* She thought.

"You're still here?" Peter said to Ryan with irritation in his voice.

Taking a deep breath, Ryan walked over to Peter. He knew that he was going to have to play by Avery's rules. He cared about her too much to let anything happen to her or her family, even if it meant being nice to the one person standing in his way. "We need to talk, Peter," Ryan said in the sincerest voice he could muster.

"We have nothing to say to each other! Leave me and Avery alone." Peter kept his voice low. He did not want to attract attention. He reached for Avery's hand, but something made him stop. Her eyes. He saw it then. Something had happened between her and Ryan. He did not know how he knew. It was a feeling. It was like venom. Peter turned on his crutches. He had to get away. Now.

Avery stepped out in front of him to block his way.

"Avery, please. Don't make things worse."

"But you don't understand!"

"But I do."

"Please, I can explain everything. All three of us need to talk." And then, with a voice barely audible, she murmured, "My family's fate depends on it."

Chapter 23

Alec stood hidden behind the antique shop. He watched the lights go off, and Talia appear in the doorway. She made sure the door was locked and began to walk toward the house but stopped.

He held his breath, realizing that she sensed something. All members of the Leirion had that power. She stood motionless for a minute and then continued.

As he watched her enter, he thought about his old life and how he, too, had been happy. He was taking a huge chance by watching her in broad daylight, but the danger excited him and fueled the flames of hatred.

Alec glanced at his watch. Avery would be home soon, and then Steve. The porch lights would turn on, and the family would sit down for dinner. *Their safe, perfect family*, he thought. *But not for long.*

Alec was just about to leave when he heard voices. They were getting louder, and he knew that whoever they belonged to were coming towards him. He had just enough time to duck behind a tall evergreen when he saw the kids walk up to the house. He sucked in his breath. He knew if he moved even the tiniest muscle, his anger would explode, and rage would take over. He saw her.

Avery. *My God, she looks just like her mother*, he thought. *No wonder Ryan has fallen in love with her.*

He saw Ryan walking next to her and next to him, a boy about the same age. He looked familiar but could not place the face. Alec could see the cast on his leg and the scowl on his face. Then, as quick as lightning, it came to him. *It can't be,* he told himself. He stared at his face. His eyes. They were identical to hers. Alec stifled a sob. Still, buried deep inside of that cold heart of his, he thought of Korinna. What started as a ploy to father a child with her for the sole purpose of seeking revenge became a marriage with real love. But that, too, Alec managed to destroy. This was just too coincidental; something or someone had to be the puppeteer in this deadly game.

"I hope this is quick," Peter grumbled.

Avery knew how painful this was for him. Seeing her with Ryan was killing him. She could not look at him in the face. It was destroying her to know that he was hurting. She tried to help him up the walk, but he pulled his arm away. "I am capable of walking by myself, Avery."

The abruptness of his voice made her body stiffen. It was all her fault. *Everything lately is my fault,* she thought. Avery cast a sideways glance at Ryan, who at least was not interfering with Peter and her. He lagged a few steps behind them, and for that, she was grateful. She used her key, and the three of them walked inside.

"Mom, are you home?" Avery called out.

"In the kitchen, getting dinner started. I thought you and dad might like lasagna. We haven't had it in a while. And I remembered that you are on this vegetarian kick ever since we watched *Bambi* again on TV."

Ryan and Peter both turned to her and let out a laugh. It was the first time that the two agreed on something.

"Hey, it was a mommy-daughter bonding session, and that was my favorite movie when I was little. Uh, Mom, we have some company."

Talia walked out of the kitchen. Avery could see her mother's eyebrows rise in confusion at the sight of both Ryan and Peter, but she quickly recovered. "Hi, boys," she said simply.

The boys shifted uncomfortably and waited for someone to save them. Avery, sensing their mood, finally broke the silence. "Mom, we need to talk with you about something really important. Is Dad home yet? I think at this point it would be better to leave him out of what we need to discuss with you."

"Avery!" Talia said sharply. "I have never kept secrets from your father, and I do not expect to start now."

"But--"

"No. This is not open to discussion."

Avery could see that her mother was fuming and that tiny sparks were beginning to shoot off her skin.

"Mom!" Avery screamed. But before she could do anything more, Ryan reached out and placed his hand on Talia's left shoulder.

"Don't touch her!" Avery rushed over but felt a sudden impact of force hitting her straight in the chest. It was not strong enough to hurt, but it stopped her in her tracks. Mesmerized, she stood watching as Ryan slowly pressed down on Talia's shoulder, causing the sparks to subside.

Talia, realizing what had just occurred, broke away from Ryan's hold. She looked up at him. They were the same, the same emerald green eyes that she and Avery had. Something else was familiar. Ryan's features. Why didn't she see this the first time she met him? Talia gasped and slumped to the floor.

Avery rushed to her mom. "What did you do to her?" she screamed at Ryan.

For the second time, Ryan placed his hand on Talia. She began to stir.

Talia slowly sat up and looked at her daughter and the two boys. "Ryan and Peter, you both look like fine, strong men. How about you help a damsel in distress get to that comfy chair in the corner?" Peter stood, transfixed on what had just happened. Ryan nudged him in the arm, and they helped Talia into the chair. "Avery, why don't you set the table? Your father should be coming home any minute now, and after we all eat dinner, the five of us can have a good heart-to-heart."

Dinnertime was quiet. Steve looked at the four faces in front of him and wondered to himself just what was going on. He knew that Avery really liked Peter, but he knew nothing about this other boy, Ryan. The weird thing was he had this uncanny resemblance to his wife and daughter. "So, are the three of you working on some kind of school project that I am now going to be suckered into helping by building some kind of six-foot wooden structure?" he joked, trying to lighten the mood.

Avery looked at her dad like he was the biggest dork she had ever seen but remained quiet.

Talia cleared her voice. "Steve, the boys and Avery have something very important to discuss with us. After we eat and clear the table, let's all go into the family room."

After the last plate was neatly loaded into the dishwasher, Talia led them into the family room. "Well, I am guessing this is a good time to get started," she said. "Who wants to begin?"

Steve listened to every detail about the two identical photographs. They all agreed the two families were somehow connected. Talia looked at Peter and said tenderly, "Do you remember anything about your mother?"

"My mother left my dad and me. Why would I want to remember anything about her?" he countered. The second the words left his mouth, Peter blushed. "I'm sorry, Mrs. Weston. I didn't mean to talk like that to you."

Talia walked over to where he was sitting. "I know, honey," she said with such empathy that Peter's emptiness felt unbearable. "But try to remember something, anything at all. You and Avery found the photograph hidden in the attic. What else was there?"

Peter shrugged. "Just some stuffed animals and a blanket with my initials embroidered on it."

Avery stood up. "Wait, Peter, remember that tiny box? Something was in it. Remember how we talked about your father being the Tooth Fairy?"

Peter smiled. His posture had relaxed a bit.

Ryan cleared his throat. Jealously was getting the better of him, and now was not the time to feel the effect of the Green-eyed Monster coursing through his veins.

Avery turned to her mom. "Do you think something important was in that box?"

Talia shook her head. "I don't know, but I think you two have to go back to Peter's house and look in the attic again. Peter, I think you should tell your dad what is going on. He has a right to know."

"Mrs. Weston, if my dad hid those things, he did so with a good reason. How am I going to tell him that I was snooping around in his stuff?"

Steve turned toward Peter. "He would want to know. Do not underestimate your dad, Peter. I saw how he acted when you were in the hospital. You are the most important thing in his life."

Ryan shifted uncomfortably in his seat. The mention of Peter's accident--the accident that *he* had caused--set his energy in motion. Sparks started to fly.

Now it was Avery's turn to get even. She turned her palm upwards and aimed it right toward the sparks that began shooting out of Ryan's body. In one swift movement, the currents retracted and surged back into his veins. Ryan let out low moans of pain. It felt as if someone had lit a match to his entire body. There was nothing he could do; Avery's powers were so much stronger. And even if he could do something, he knew that it was her turn for revenge. He deserved every ounce of pain that she was now inflicting upon him.

"Avery!" Talia screamed at her daughter. "Stop!" Talia lifted her pinky, and the ring's crystal blazed with color. She aimed it at her daughter. She knew that she had to be careful and send just the right amount of electricity to stop her daughter, but not hurt her.

"I deserve this, Mrs. Weston," Ryan groaned. "I deserve to feel all the pain that I have imposed on everyone in this room." His breaths were heavy, his words barely audible.

Talia knew that her daughter had so much vengeance stored up in her body that she surely could kill him. She could not let that happen.

But before she could act, Avery lowered her arm. The sparks ceased. Ryan lay writhing in pain. Talia rushed up to him and gently cradled his head. Peter stood immobilized. Nothing made sense to him. Nothing seemed real at that moment. He always knew something was different about Avery. And now, looking at Ryan, he could feel that bond between the two of them.

Before Talia could open her mouth to say anything, Avery stormed upstairs. The walls shook as she slammed the door. Steve stood there. He had seen his wife's and Avery's powers before, but this was different. The room still sizzled with electricity. He didn't know if it was the sparks or the tension that stood between the two boys, but the air was suffocating him.

"Um, I am going upstairs to see if Avery is all right," he said softly.

Talia looked at the two boys, one with such blond hair and blue eyes, the other with black hair and green eyes. Their appearance was so strikingly different, but she knew a "sameness" tied them. She also knew that it was not going to be easy telling them the truth.

"I know this is going to be extremely difficult for you to understand what I am about to say, but you must listen very carefully." Talia cleared her throat. The words felt like globs of molasses, and she found it almost impossible to get them out. "Peter, I believe that you are the son of a woman who came to visit me not long ago. She looked familiar, actually *felt* familiar, but I ignored the feeling."

Peter was now staring at Talia. His muscles were twitching, and his body shook. "Here, come sit down," Talia said in a motherly tone.

It made Peter almost want to reach out and cling to her. His heart ached, and he could feel tears begin to form. But he was damned if he was going to let Ryan see them. Just the thought of his mother being so close and not wanting to see him made him angry and so deeply sad at the same time. He took a deep breath and let himself be led to the couch.

"I think we need to get Avery downstairs to hear what I am about to say."

"I am right here, Mom," Avery said softly. "It's weird, but I felt all of your emotions."

Talia looked at Peter. "This woman who came to me, her name is Korinna. Does that name mean anything to you?"

Before Peter could even open his mouth, Ryan jumped up. His eyes flashed. "Korinna?" he asked, the words almost choking him.

Talia nodded.

In a voice that sounded like a wounded animal, he wailed, "That was my mother's name."

Everyone in the room stared at him. Avery jumped up and ran over to where Ryan was standing. She could feel his anguish, and it crushed her heart. She took him into her arms and held him tightly. At that moment, she did not care what anyone thought--not her mom, not even Peter. They stood, clutching each other until Avery could sense that he was ready to speak. She did not want to let go. Every nerve in her body was on fire, and at that instant, she knew that Ryan *was* her soul mate. As much as she was struggling internally with that realization, she knew it was inevitable. She looked into Ryan's eyes, and the world just seemed to stop.

Talia cleared her throat. Avery pulled away. Peter was staring at the two of them, his face showing no emotion. Avery felt horrible.

"Ryan, tell us about your mother," Talia said gently, getting up and leading him to the couch next to where she had been sitting.

Ryan looked straight at Talia. He was trying to avoid Avery's gaze because he knew he would fall apart. "My mother is dead," he whispered. "My father and I buried her on Oros Mountain next to my dad's brother, Darius."

Ryan looked at Talia's beautiful face. Avery looked just like her mother. He could see why his father and uncle had fallen for her. But her beauty did not excuse their forcing themselves on her. Shame filled his body. He felt sick to his stomach when he thought of how he tried to force Avery into liking him. It was not to the extent of what they had done to Talia, but he was no better than them.

Steve rose to his feet. "What is going on, Talia? What is Ryan talking about? What revenge?" Steve's face was hard.

"I was going to tell you. I was just trying to process all the information myself before I--."

"We don't keep secrets, Talia," he said sharply.

"I didn't want to upset you until I knew what was going on. This has been a crazy couple of days."

Talia took Ryan's hand and firmly pressed on the crystal that was embedded into his palm. "I also need to know whose side you are on. You made a promise to your father, Ryan, but it can have no happy ending."

Ryan felt the crystal get hot. Talia's powers were very strong. She could have destroyed him right there, but she continued to press. The bloody mirror flashed in his mind. The name of the woman sitting next to him was spelled out in blood. He cringed. His father had turned into a monster. He had loved his father, but their relationship always had a "catch" to it.

Ryan flash-backed to all the times his father had said to him, "If you love me, Ryan, then you will do this one thing for me." But it was never just "one thing." Alec was constantly demanding him to use his powers for greed and destruction. Repeatedly, he would blame his lack of powers on Talia, continuously reinforcing how imperative it was to destroy her. His dear mother had died as a result.

Ryan looked deeply into Talia's eyes. He realized how they looked so much alike. "I have no father, Talia. He is now dead to me." The tears rolled down his cheeks.

Talia's heart broke for him. Even though his intentions had been to destroy her and her family, she knew that he was just serving his father. How a father could do that to his son, she had no idea. There wasn't an ounce of goodness in Alec's soul. She also knew Ryan must come to terms with this.

Talia went to Peter; her heart also breaking for him. She understood the feelings that he had for her daughter.

"Peter, please call your father and ask him to come over. It is extremely important that we all discuss this together."

"He doesn't need to know," Peter insisted. "I am not going to involve my father." Peter hoisted himself up. "I need someone to take me home now. Mr. Weston, do you think you can give me a ride?"

Ryan got up and gently placed a hand on Peter's shoulders. Avery could see Peter recoil.

"Peter," Ryan said. "We both care for Avery, so for her and her mom, call your dad and let's try to unravel this mess."

"Fine. But I am only doing this for you, Mrs. Weston." Peter glared at Avery, then turned to Ryan. "Now get your damn hand off of me!"

They waited for Ben to arrive. As Talia and Steve began to unravel their tale, he was at first in disbelief, and it took Talia and

Steve's gentle explaining to finally make him understand that the three families were undoubtedly connected.

Ryan turned to Ben. "Please tell me what you know about my mother. I sense that you are holding some information from us."

"Don't talk to my father like that--."

Ben looked at his son. "There *is* something I need to say to you. In fact, I have something to say to all of you. Peter, your mother did not leave us. We left her."

"What?" Peter's voice was now rising to panic mode. "You have been lying to me! You pretended it was her fault!"

"Please, let me explain," Ben said weakly.

"I don't want to hear!" Peter grabbed his crutches and left the room.

Avery ran out of the room behind him.

"What do you want? Haven't you done enough?"

"Please come back inside. You should hear what your father has to say."

Peter glared at her. The blue in his eyes looked like a torrent of ocean waves. They seemed to fill his entire eyes. "You know, life was good before I met you. My dad and I, we were good. I was a popular football player, and I had no trouble getting girls. But then you came along and ruined everything!"

Stricken, Avery shut her eyes for a second and then reached out to Peter. "Come back to the family room and let your father talk to you."

"Listen carefully. Do not ever talk to me again. We are not boyfriend and girlfriend. We are not friends. We are not anything! Do you hear what I am saying?" Peter grabbed her by the shoulders.

"Stop! You are hurting me!"

"Good," he replied. "You finally understand how it feels."

Peter hobbled back into the room and took a seat next to Talia. He felt a closeness with her and did not mind when she took his hand. He didn't dare look at his father. "So, let's hear what you have to say."

Ben took a seat next to Steve. "I met your mother and instantly fell in love with her. Her beauty was intoxicating. She had the eyes the color of the bluest robin's egg, and they would often flash little specks of silver. I loved how she would play with her hair, twisting it into one giant tangle when she was nervous." Ben's voice grew faint. "I loved everything about her, including her powers." Ben got up and walked over to his son. "Your mother was an amazing person. Her laugh was contagious, and we spent many days just touring Matas and having an incredible time."

Talia motioned to Ben to take her place next to his son.

Before Peter could protest, Talia took Peter's hand and held it tightly. "Let him. Your father loves you very much. And I know that you love him very much, too. It is important that he tells you what happened." Peter clenched his jaw to hold back the tears and nodded for his father to sit and continue.

"And that is everything. I hope you can understand why I took you and left," Ben said.

Peter jumped up, almost knocking over his father. "I don't understand! You said we were fine!" he yelled. "You promised her that you would never let her go!" Ben reached out, but Peter withdrew.

Talia reached out for Peter and, with her warm embrace, coaxed him into the spot beside her. "Peter, you need to know how powerful our crystals can be. Even when we do not intend to hurt someone, it can happen. You mustn't blame your mother or father."

"You must know that you are the best thing that ever happened to us. Your mom lived for you. She would spend hours rocking you and singing these sweet songs. She delighted in your every move--from your first coo to the first time you rolled over. She loved you more than life itself," Ben said quietly. "Call me a coward, but I thought it was what she would have wanted." Ben bowed his head as if in prayer. The room was still. Finally, he cleared his throat and said, "If I had to do it over again, I would have held on to your mother tightly and never let go."

The sound of a slammed door broke the conversation. Peter noticed Ryan was gone. "I'll go talk to him."

"Are you sure that's a good idea at this moment?" asked Steve.

Peter grappled with his jealousy. "I *have* to go. If the two of us are really connected in some twisted sort of fate, then it's time to deal with it."

He walked out onto the driveway and saw Ryan sitting on the curb. He sat down next to him. "This is pretty messed up, isn't it?" Peter said, trying to loosen the tension.

"Yeah, just slightly."

The two sat in silence.

"Listen," Peter said, "I know that what you're hearing in there is difficult for you. It is for me, too. I blamed my mom for leaving. And now, you drop the bomb that your mother's name was Korinna."

"Yeah, with everything that is happening, it just seems too strange to be a coincidence." Ryan knocked his knuckles against Peter's cast. "About that..."

"It's over with," Peter replied.

"Why didn't you tell your father that it was me who broke your leg? You could have gotten me expelled from school and had Avery all to yourself."

"Ryan, as much as I dislike you, I know that Avery does not. And I would never bring more hurt to her."

"Well, I am sorry. I didn't mean to hurt you so badly."

"'All's fair in love and war,'" Peter tried to joke, but the words seemed hollow.

Ryan cleared his throat. "We both have feelings for Avery. And she has feelings for both of us."

"Well, how can she not? We are the two studliest guys in the school," Peter replied lightly.

"'Studliest'? I don't even think that is a word, but yeah, we are." He laughed.

Their mood grew somber again. All Peter could think about, and he was certain Ryan was doing the same, was, *What if they were brothers?*

Avery watched Peter and Ryan enter the room. There were no visible bruises, bloody noses, or broken bones, but from the grim look on their faces, she could sense that they were still having a rough time.

Peter again sat down next to Talia. He felt that she understood everything he was experiencing. She was an amazing mother to Avery, and he was envious of their solid bond. Ryan searched the room for a spot to sit as well. Ben was sitting next to Steve, which meant the only free spot was...

Avery could feel it starting. It was like every nerve ending in her body was beginning to twitch. The mere thought of Ryan sitting next to her made her body hot.

Ryan could feel it, too, and with a mischievous smile, he plopped himself down next to her, just a little too close for comfort. Ryan grazed the palm of his hand gently against Avery's, their two crystals barely touching.

Avery felt the tingling spreading through her body. *Oh, my god! I can read his thoughts. He can't wait to kiss me!* The sensation was over in a flash when Ryan removed his hand from hers, but Avery could feel her face burning.

"Ahem, can we continue, or do you two want to continue with your PDAs?" Peter said through clenched teeth.

Peter turned to Ryan. "How and when did your dad meet our mom? His eyes then traveled to his father. "And since Ryan and I are not even a year apart, it must not have taken her long to get over us, Dad," he said sardonically. Peter could see the hurt in his father's eyes, but he was hurting just as badly, and it felt good to be able to vent his anger.

"My father obviously concocted a twisted plan to father a son quickly," Ryan said. "He knew that he needed a woman with powers since his had been destroyed the second he deserted the mountain. My dad is an expert at preying on people's weaknesses and playing with their emotions." Ryan walked over to Peter. "He poked his nose around the village and found out all he could about recently divorced or widowed women." And then, in a soft murmur, he added, "We both know how beautiful she...."

Peter choked up. "I don't know anything about her. I was a baby." He shot an accusatory glance in his father's direction. "We didn't talk about her. She was a forbidden subject."

"I thought I was doing the right thing, Peter," Ben said. "I thought it was for the best. It would be just the two of us, and the less you heard about your mom or saw pictures of her, the better. I thought I would be sparing you pain. Now I know that wasn't the answer. I'm so sorry I didn't share with you all the amazing qualities that your mom possessed."

"I know you were trying to protect me, but my heart finds it hard to accept what you did." Peter turned to Ryan. "How old were you when you learned about your father's plan?"

"Not until our mom had passed away." He gazed over at Avery. "I didn't know what had happened on the mountain that night, but Avery filled me in on the details. I didn't want to believe that my dad and his brother would try to rape someone with the sick notion that she would fall in love with one of them, but Avery convinced me that it was true." Ryan extended his hand to Talia and kneeled in front of her. "My father told me that you had ruined his and his brother's life. His mantra was that you had destroyed everything that was dear to him, and for that, you would pay. I was to fall in love with Avery, and then after she had gained my trust, I would destroy her. It was his perfect plan to get back at you." Tears streamed down his face. "I am so, so sorry, to all of you," he motioned to Avery and her father. "He was my dad, and I was supposed to believe anything he told me."

His sobs were getting louder, and all the toughness that usually seemed to exude from his body, vanished. Avery walked over and took his hand, and squeezed it gently.

"Shh, it's going to be okay," Talia said, stroking his hair.

"Avery, I hope you can forgive me. I thought that it would be easy to abide by my father's wishes. I trusted him. But in the process, I *did* fall in love with you. You are the best thing that has ever happened to me."

Peter shifted uncomfortably in his seat. He hated watching them together, but he could not deny that they were in love.

"How did Korinna die?" Talia quietly asked.

"I am positive it was from my father's obsession with her crystal and its powers. He was always forcing her to use it against her will. My dad never held down a job. Why should he, when he had my mother using every ounce of energy in her crystal to provide him with all his desires?" Ryan clenched his jaw. "Can you imagine what that did to her body? He persisted until her death. My father and I fought constantly. I must admit that many times I was no better than he. I enjoyed having it all, too." He lowered his head. "I am just as guilty. I am also to blame for my mother's death."

"This is not your fault," whispered Avery. "A father is not supposed to 'use' his child the way your father did to you."

"I should have stopped it! I loved my mother. I should have seen what it was doing to her and stopped it instead of making it worse. I destroyed her!"

"You were just a kid; it's not your fault," Peter said quietly. "You may be a lot of things, but you are *not* a killer."

Talia cleared her throat. Her hands were trembling, and she had to clasp them tightly together to keep them still. She also had to concentrate on not releasing her powers. She knew that whenever she became nervous or agitated, there was always the chance that sparks would fly. "The woman who came to me that day with her hand bandaged must have been your mother, boys. So, the question is... how in God's name did she rise from the dead, and where is she now?"

Chapter 24

Alec finally let out his breath and quickly sprinted down the street to his awaiting car. He had no idea what was up, but he swore to himself that he would find out. He called a taxi and headed straight for the airport. There was only one place he now knew he had to be.

The plane ride seemed to last an eternity, and once again, Alec cursed Talia for ruining his powers. He had not been to the mountain since he buried Korinna. He had nothing left to lose. Ryan would now do everything to protect Avery and her mom. Alec was on his own, and that was the way he now wanted it.

The plane touched down at six in the evening. Alec hailed a cab and told the driver his destination.

"There is nothing left, sir. The mountaintop village is deserted," said the driver.

"Just do what I say," snapped Alec. "Unless you don't need my money--"

"We will be there in an hour."

Alec closed his eyes, hoping that sleep would come and block out the nightmarish thoughts pervading his head.

The cab dropped Alec in the middle of nowhere. The fare was substantial, and from the backseat, Alec pulled out a wad of Euros from his wallet. He peeled back fifty Euros and added ten more for a tip. He knew the driver was hesitant about taking him here.

"They say this village is cursed."

Alec looked into the driver's eyes. "Why don't you tell me about it."

"The people of the nearby villages blame the curse on that mountain in front of us."

Alec looked up at majestic Oros. It was once his home, and he marveled how it towered in the distance. It would look menacing to anyone who did not know what it was like to be born and raised there. Alec cleared his throat, indicating that the driver should continue.

The driver turned around to face him. "There's no business here for you. Come, I will take you back. That mountain is evil, I tell you, and no good will come from staying here."

Alec willed himself not to show any emotion. *It is so distasteful that a mere mortal should be talking about my home like this*, he thought. An acidic taste rose in his mouth. He opened the door and stepped out into the darkness. "I don't believe in curses. I believe you make your own destiny."

Chapter 25

Sophia was the perfect mother to her children, Celine and Korinna, and the village where the Sethos lived was the ideal setting for Sophia to raise them. Korinna and Celine were only eighteen months apart. At first, the two acted like twins. They were rarely seen apart. Sophia's children were her pride and joy, and their closeness warmed her heart immensely. But as the girls entered their preteens, things began to change. Celine would test her mother and push her to the limit, and Korinna would often find herself playing mediator between the two. Celine would sneak out of the house and return when the sun was just beginning to emerge through the darkness.

Knowing that her powers were stronger than her mother's and father's, Celine would often place a spell over them that would prevent them from feeling her actions. Only poor Korinna would have to lie awake at night sick with worry about her sister. Although they had grown apart over the years, Korinna loved her sister with all her heart and agonized over Celine's rebellions.

Sophia did not know exactly what Celine was doing, but she could not deny the dramatic shift in her personality. Defiance, disrespect, and apathy now ruled her daughter, and it was getting worse every day. Sophia tried to use her powers to lull Celine into submission, but Celine's powers were too strong. She begged her daughter to change her ways and to be "more like Korinna," but Celine would ignore her pleas and cast accusatory glances at her sister.

It killed Korinna to be hated by her sister, and she resented her mother for comparing them again and again. But seeing how much strife Celine caused the family, Korinna vowed to remain compliant. She also silently declared that she would never use her powers for evil and desired a mortal life.

When Celine turned fourteen and Korinna was twelve, the family was viciously torn apart. The night was clear, the air pure and crisp. The family had finished a late supper and was getting ready for bed. The house was secured for the night, and Korinna and Celine lay in their beds in the room they shared. The room was pitch black, except for the silvery slice of light that the moon cast through their small window.

The light always comforted Korinna, and that night was no exception. Her eyes were almost closed when she felt the first small shock. Sitting up in bed, she saw her sister haphazardly stuffing clothes into a bag.

"Where are you going?"

Celine ignored her and continued to pack at a hurried speed. "Celine, please stop!" pleaded Korinna. "Just tell me what is going on."

Celine placed her cool hand on Korinna's cheek and let it rest there. "Close your eyes and go back to bed. Please do not get involved. I love you too much to see you hurt."

"I don't understand, Celine. Why are you leaving us? Why are you leaving me?" Korinna's cries started to escalate, and Celine abruptly clamped her other hand over her sister's mouth. Korinna's eyes grew wide.

"Stop, or you'll wake Mother and Father," Celine hissed. "I must go. Life will be better without me. You will be better off. Please, Korinna, if you love me, do not ask questions. Celine grabbed her bag and faced the opened window. "I'll always love you."

Chapter 26

"You can relax now, my dear sister." With her sister's soothing words, Korinna crumpled to the floor. Sobs wracked her body. She looked up at Anastasia with a mix of fear and confusion. She had no idea what was happening. Anastasia knelt beside her and continued to whisper into her ear, while at the same time, she began hugging her tightly. She could feel Korinna's whole body stiffen as her arms encircled her. She did not blame her and would not take it personally. What had just occurred was horrifying. How could she expect her sister to trust her now? "Korinna, you must trust me. I know that all that you just encountered with my men and me might make it almost impossible, but you must."

Korinna's body relaxed a tiny bit. Her sister's eyes were crystal clear, and Korinna felt that she could now see deep into her sister's soul. What Korinna saw, pained her almost as deeply as the pain inflicted upon her moments before. Sadness, terror, and extreme loneliness welled up within her sister, with each emotion competing to take hold of her body. "What has happened to you, Celine, since the night you left through our bedroom window? What unimaginable things have you encountered?"

Anastasia collapsed and began to sob. Her cries intensified and became so deafening that flocks of birds scattered in the sky.

The earth under them shook, and Korinna feared that they might become the victims of an earthquake. Finally, her sobs quieted, and Anastasia lay spent. Her eyes now looked vacant, her body limp. The gruesome scars on her neck throbbed and pulsated, casting a reddish tint. Korinna bent down and reached her hand out to touch them.

"No!" Anastasia screamed. Her body went rigid. Her eyes now blazed, and the scars began to ooze with a silvery liquid.

Korinna watched her sister with terror.

"Don't ever touch them! They are evil and a constant reminder of how I sold my soul so many years ago. Promise me, Korinna, that you will never try to touch them again."

Korinna nodded. She watched as Anastasia's body relaxed. The pulsating abated, and the silvery liquid instantly dried. The two of them huddled together. "I have missed you so much," Korinna said to her sister. "I need to know everything."

Korinna clasped her sister's hand tightly and urged her to commence her story. "So much time has passed, and it is finally time that we both share our stories."

Anastasia closed her eyes. "Korinna, I know everything about you. I have traced your every step; I have been a part of every dream, every nightmare of yours. I have seen all your delights and miseries. It was all part of *His* plan; the man that I thought I was in love with, only to find out that he used me like a pawn."

"I don't understand what you are saying to me," Korinna said softly. "You have known where I have been all along, and you didn't try to see me, to help me, to save me?" The betrayal she felt was mounting. Korinna got to her feet. "I have lost my two sons and both husbands! I am going now, Celine, and I do not want you to follow me. What a fool I have been, feeling sorry for you and thinking that we can reseal the bond that we used to have." Korinna turned to leave but felt a stab of electricity hit her body. She fell to the floor.

Anastasia immediately erased any pain from her sister and cradled her in her arms. "Please, you can't go anywhere until I tell my story. Our lives, your sons' lives, depend upon it. Do you remember when the village next to ours had that huge carnival?" Anastasia asked her sister.

Korinna nodded and then smiled. She recalled hearing the music and how she had used the crystal in her pinky ring to see the festivities. It was the children who made her smile the most. Their hands, sticky from cotton candy, clung to the shiny polished brass poles of the carousel horses. Their parents stood next to them as they rode the horses up and down. She could hear their giddy laughter and could almost feel the warmth of their bodies. Korinna yearned to be one of them, at least just for the day. But she knew the rules. If you left Matas, you could never return. The panic of never seeing her family again kept Korinna's feet planted firmly on her village's soil, even if in her heart she was somewhere else.

Finally, as if reality had reached out its hand and cruelly snapped her back into the present time, Korinna said, "I remember."

"That day, I did something that went against all that our clan believed in. I used my powers and went to the carnival." Sensing the hostility that rose in Korinna's body, Anastasia murmured, "Korinna, we were both just kids. I also wanted to experience what was going on at a 'normal' village, you know, where the mortals lived. Like you, I heard the music that day, but I broke the rules.

"When I was at the carnival, I met someone. He was sixteen, and I was fourteen. He did not come up to me right away. He kept his distance, watching my every move. I could feel his eyes, though. I played some games, ate an ice cream cone, and then headed for the Ferris wheel. I was having so much fun--the most I'd ever had. As I waited in line, I heard someone call my name."

"Anastasia?" Korinna asked.

"Shh, what did I tell you about interrupting? No, he said my birth name, Celine. I turned around, and it was *him*. His eyes were flashing, and his mouth was turned up at the corners as if he were keeping some hilarious joke all to himself." Anastasia stretched out her legs. She lifted her arms and stretched those as well. "I am so tired, my dear sister. I am tired of playing this wretched game. I am tired of life."

Just as Korinna was about to open her mouth, Anastasia hushed her by bringing her fingers up to her sister's lips. "I must continue. He leaned in close to me. I could feel his hot breath down my neck. He smelled of freshly cut grass, and I wanted to reach out my hands to touch him. He was addicting, to say the least. 'I am Darius,' he whispered in my ear." Korinna gasped. Anastasia grabbed her sister and held her tightly before she collapsed.

She opened her eyes. She could feel Anastasia shaking her. "How long have I been out?"

"Just for a few moments, but we have to get out of here!" Anastasia seemed panicked. "I sense something very evil coming our way. We must..."

At that moment, they saw him. Anastasia gasped as Korinna's eyes grew wide with terror. Korinna and Anastasia clung to each other, using their powers to turn themselves into part of the stone wall that surrounded the mountain.

Alec was walking toward the two graves that stood in the far corner of the mountain. He bent over Korinna's and placed his hand on top of the cold ground. His mouth was moving. She tried to focus and channel the energy in her crystal ring to hear what he was saying. She pressed down on the crystal and let the sparks delve into her mind.

"My dear Korinna," Alec murmured. "I have nothing left. Even our son has turned against me. He promised that he would help me seek revenge against Talia and her daughter, Avery." Alec clasped his hands together and continued. "I must confess. You were part of my plan--a plan to ruin Talia's life."

Korinna felt herself beginning to scream. The words were daggers piercing her body. As if on cue, like she had done once before so many years ago, Anastasia clamped her hand hard against Korinna's mouth.

Alec continued. "It was all for Darius. Don't you see that? That woman, she ruined our lives. She killed my brother and destroyed my powers. I had to get back at her." Alec's voice was becoming almost hysterical, and Korinna had to strain to hear him. "When I came to your village, I noticed you right away. You were beautiful, Korinna. So beautiful that I felt guilty to use you for my plan. But I also saw the sadness in your eyes. I felt that you were living with your own misery, and so you became my choice. You were the one that I would woo, marry, and let bear my child."

With those last words, Korinna's body began to tingle. She knew that it was not long before every nerve ending would be on fire and sparks would start to fly. She could not let Alec see her.

Sensing her energy, Anastasia lifted her own crystal and sent out a stream of cool air that calmed her sister. Korinna nodded that she was okay, but she felt that her body would never turn into flesh again; it would remain cold, hard stone from the wounding words that Alec had just inflicted upon her.

"Remember that night when Ryan was created? The sky was dotted with a million stars. Do you remember when we both looked up and saw the same shooting star? We knew we had just made a baby. I knew it was going to be a boy."

Korinna felt tears pouring down her cheeks. It was still so vivid in her mind. It was a beautiful night. The shooting star was a marvelous sight, and she and Alec clung to each other, both knowing it was that instant when a tiny life was starting to grow inside her. She thought of all the times when Alec would feel her belly and talk to the baby. He would always call him Ryan, as if he knew all along that it would be a boy, a boy to follow out his warped and sick plan. Korinna touched her stomach. All she felt now was a repulsion that made her want to vomit.

"Korinna," Alec continued. "You have to know that I did love you. I loved you with all my heart. You must understand that it just was not enough. Inside me, was always a hatred that ultimately killed you and made our son despise me."

Alec suddenly rose. He walked over to his brother's grave. "Darius, everything I have done, is for you. I will continue until justice for your death has been served." He then turned and began his descent down the mountain.

Korinna and Anastasia remained part of the stone wall until Alec had finally reached the bottom. They leaned over the ridge and could see him walking toward the deserted village. "I hate him!" cried Korinna. She felt used and wanted nothing more than to destroy his life. She raised her crystal and aimed it in Alec's direction. One huge spark could blow up everything in his path, including him.

"Don't, Korinna!" Anastasia yelled. "If I wanted him dead, I would have killed him already."

"You would have killed him?" Korinna barked. "You don't know what he has put me through! My life with him has been a lie. My own son was part of his devious plan. And even after all that has happened to him, he continues to carry on this vendetta! You do not have the right to kill him. I do!"

Korinna began to sob. Her body shook. Her muscles were twisted in knots, her head pounding. What hurt more than anything, though, was her heart. It was broken into a million pieces. "Kill me now, Anastasia! Please, put me out of my misery! Bury me again in my same grave and use all your powers to make sure that I will never be able to resurface."

"Shh, I will do nothing of the sort." Anastasia wrapped her arms tightly around Korinna until the torment in her sister's body abated. "I am never going to lose you again." Korinna looked into her sister's clear eyes and knew that she meant it. "First, we need Alec alive. He might be useful to us later. Secondly, your sons need you. Lastly, I need you."

Korinna's eyes fixated on the spots where her sister's oozing scars pulsated. Now reaching for her sister's hands, she squeezed them firmly. "I need you to continue with your story. I need to know why and how Darius came to seek you out and what this warped plan of his is all about."

"First, let's get Alec home safe and sound. He will remember nothing about being on this mountain."

Korinna looked at her sister quizzically. "You sure you want to do that? Can't we just let him wander aimlessly?"

A tiny smile formed. "As tempting as that sounds, we must get him home."

Korinna and her sister clasped hands. They aimed their rings toward the small figure in the distance. They touched their crystals together and sent sparks of light shooting into Alec's back. In an instant, he disappeared.

"I can continue," Anastasia said. "I fell completely in love with Darius, and he knew it. He also knew that I would do anything he asked of me." Anastasia touched her neck. She placed a finger on one of the scars. "If I disappointed him in the slightest, this was my reward."

"Why didn't you leave? You have powers. It should have been easy for you." Korinna could not bear to see her sister touch her disfigured neck and thought how dreadful it must have been each time she was branded.

"You can't understand the power he had over me. It was stronger than anything either one of us could ever imagine."

But Korinna shook her head. "I still don't understand. How did Darius get to the carnival in the first place? He was dead; his brother and parents buried him. That is all Alec ever talked about for the first year we were married. I would often have to wake him from a nightmare. He would thrash so wildly that, at times, the crystal in my ring would be the only way to stop it. He would cry out Darius' name and Talia's. I did not know who she was, and when I asked him the next morning, he would yell about how the house was messy and how Ryan was not disciplined--anything to divert my attention."

Anastasia continued. "That night, when the village was quiet, Darius felt a slight beating of his heart. He had been buried alive! The crystal in his ring was still shooting tiny sparks, and Darius used the electricity to cut away at the dirt that encased him and create a tunnel. And with all the energy he could muster, he was able to climb out of the grave."

"Why didn't he wake up his family?" Korinna asked.

Pacing the ground, Anastasia shook her head. "Darius knew that if he went to his parents and brother, they would have thought that he had arisen from the dead. You know our clan's many superstitions? The Leirion had theirs as well. They would view Darius as the devil. And so, he fled."

"How long was he gone before you met him?" Korinna asked.

"Long enough to devise his plan to destroy everyone's lives. It was no coincidence that Darius pursued me. I was his 'chosen' one." Anastasia laughed bitterly. "I guess that should make me feel so special."

"Shh," Korinna whispered to her sister. "All we wanted was to be loved. There should be no harm in that."

"Look where it got us," she said bitterly.

Korinna continued to lull her sister into a calmer state of mind. "Everything is going to be okay." And as if she had to convince herself of her own words, she repeated them until the two sisters fell into a deep sleep.

Korinna opened her eyes. "Something strange is happening," she said groggily.

"I feel it, too."

The wind blew ferociously. The mountain started to rumble, and the two women struggled to hold on to each other.

"Something is very wrong," Anastasia said.

"What is happening?" Korinna gasped. She watched as Anastasia's scars began to ooze silver liquid.

"They are coming!"

"Who?" Korinna panicked. She flinched at the tiny sparks that began to surge out of her crystal and ricochet onto her skin. She willed herself to remain calm.

"Darius' lackeys. You saw them the other day."

"The two men that looked like you?"

Anastasia nodded. "That was Darius's idea."

"But why would he do th..."

"We are running out of time!" She grabbed Korinna's hand and touched her crystal to her sister's. In a split second, they found themselves down the mountain and in front of the Weston's' door.

Breathe, Korinna willed herself. "What are we doing here? It's too soon to meet."

"No, now is the time," her sister interrupted. "There is no turning back, Korinna. Darius' men will sense something is up. We must act quickly."

Before Korinna could protest, Anastasia rang the doorbell. Anastasia could hear voices inside, but no one came to the door. She rang again. Still nothing.

"Maybe we should leave." Korinna turned to go and pulled on her sister's arm to follow.

The door swung open. Talia was looking at them square in the eyes. "I've been expecting you," she said.

"How did you know we were coming?" asked Korinna.

"I could feel it. My heart started to race, and sparks shot out of my crystal. I covered my ring before the others could see."

Talia took Korinna's hand. "I need to tell you who is inside before we go in." Korinna did not want to think about who was in the house, but she knew. And now was the time to face her fears.

"But first, you need to tell me who this is?" Talia tried, with all her might, to avoid staring at Anastasia's oozing scars.

Everything about her was just so eerie, from her short silvery hair to her pale, almost see-through eyes. But the scars, they were the worst.

"This is my sister, Celi... um, no, Anastasia. Talia, I am deeply sorry I did not tell you who I was from the start. I knew that my boys were in danger, and something inside me shook me from my resting place to bring me here. I knew I needed to protect them."

Anastasia stepped forward. "We don't have much time to stay here. It's imperative that we go inside so I can tell my story. Everyone's safety is hanging on a thread at this moment."

A shudder went through Talia's body. She could not bear to think of her daughter and husband being in danger. She also felt immense guilt that it was her fault that all this was happening.

"This is not your fault, Talia."

Talia looked up at Anastasia with a puzzled look.

"I can read your mind." She looked directly into Talia's eyes. "We are all going to work together to ensure that no one's life will be at risk."

Grasping the doorknob, Talia said, "It's time."

Korinna walked into the room. Seeing her boys standing shoulder to shoulder made her cry out in relief. They were safe. She went to them and brought her hands to their faces. "Oh, how I missed the two of you!"

Peter took a step back. He examined his mother closely and could see the striking resemblance between them.

"But how?" Ryan asked incredulously. "How did you rise from the dead? Dad and I buried you ourselves." The mere mention of his father made him feel repulsed, but he needed to continue. "Dad dug out the grave, and I placed you in the hole and covered you with mountains of dirt. You were dead!" Ryan was losing it. His breathing was staggered. He tried to resist the realization that he might have buried his mother alive.

Nodding, Korinna tenderly touched his shoulder. "Ryan, I was dead. I do not remember anything about that day, so do not worry. You did not bury me alive. It was not until I felt a power so incredibly strong that the two of you were in danger that life came back to me. I don't know how to explain it. I knew I had to leave that mountain and Greece and make sure that you were safe."

"Wait, that was the day that Avery and I were in the kitchen, and Talia was talking about some woman who came to her with a bandaged arm, wasn't it?" Peter asked.

"Yes, it was. I remember seeing you for a split second and couldn't believe what a handsome young man you had turned into."

Anger now grabbed hold of Peter. He glanced at his father and shot him an accusatory look. "We could have still been a family if it wasn't for him. It was all his fault!"

It was at that moment when Korinna finally laid her eyes on Ben. He was standing in the room, immobilized.

Korinna walked over to him, tears flowing freely down her face. She placed her hand on his heart and murmured, "I am sorry." She glanced at Peter. It killed her to see him hurting so badly. "Peter, you cannot blame your father. It was a smart decision that he took you and left. I didn't want to cause harm to you and your father." She smiled at Ben. "I can see that you did an amazing job raising him. Thank you."

"What about *my* father?" Ryan spat out angrily. "How could you have ever loved a man so evil and cruel?" The anguish that filled every cavity in Ryan's body made her own body ache. She knew the guilt he felt for going along with his father's plan. *Damn that man. Damn him to hell!*

An awkward silence filled the air. How could she explain in front of Ben that despite all of Alec's devious motives, she had loved him immensely?

Talia, sensing Korinna's predicament, came to her rescue. "I think we need to save this discussion for later. Korinna and Anastasia came here to tell us something that will affect us all."

Korinna relaxed a bit, relieved that Talia had saved her. It saddened her to think that they could have been best friends, much like their grandmothers had been.

Talia took Steve's' hand. "Let's all have a seat and hear what they have to tell us. I'll put a pot of coffee on. It's going to be a long night."

Chapter 27

Rubbing his eyes, Alec did not know what to think. How did he get back here? Was it just a dream that he was traveling to Greece to see the graves of Korinna and Darius? He was standing in his own apartment, the mirror still smeared with the bloody promise that he had made to himself. He peered into Ryan's room. His bed was still unmade, the covers twisted into a pretzel. *He always did toss and turn like crazy in his sleep.* The thought of his son made Alec so deeply saddened that he knelt and buried his face in his hands. Ryan would never forgive him, and Alec could not blame him. He didn't even know where Ryan was; the dirty dishes were still stacked precariously in the sink, and crumbs dotted the table. Alec began picking up the shards of crystal strewn all over the floor. He brought a piece close to his neck, his veins bulging. It could be over in one swift cut. Ryan would be better off without him. His relentless vendetta would be over. He grazed the glass across his skin. A droplet of silvery liquid rolled down the front of his shirt. Just one more stroke; that's all it would take.

He stopped suddenly and walked over to his desk. He picked up a pen and paper and began to write.

Dear Ryan,

You must believe that I love you and your mother with all my heart. It was the promise, though, that I made to your uncle the day I buried him. I know that your mind is poisoned by now with Talia's own account of what happened, but please know that I was trying to honor my brother.

When you find this note, I will already be gone. I ask one last favor of you, my dear son. I will understand if you decide not to honor my last dying wish, and will still not love you any less. Please take my body back up the mountain where I may lie next to your mother and my brother. There, my tormented mind will finally be able rest.

Always and forever,

Father

Folding the note in half, Alec placed it on the kitchen table. He picked up the shard of crystal and with one ax like motion, brought his arm down.

Chapter 28

Darius' servants stood over the man, anxiously waiting for him to open his eyes. They had arrived just moments after Alec had sliced his neck open, exposing a gash from which silver liquid flowed freely. They immediately used their combined powers to seal the gash back up and put Alec into a sleeping state. For the past five hours, while he slept, they watched him grapple with his nightmares. Screams poured out of his mouth, and violent tremors shook him. They patiently waited, knowing that this was their job, their duty to their master.

They watched as his eyelids started to flutter. They could see movement under the lids and knew that he would awaken any moment. It was finally time to return. Standing up, they arched their backs and let the sparks flow from their crystals in their rings. Their semi-human forms disappeared, and in their place were huge, winged hawks. They let out their blood-curdling squawks and violently flapped their wings. They had done well, and their master would be quite pleased. They were back in an instant and once again turned into their human form.

They could hear the footsteps coming closer. They waited in anticipation for their master's approval. It was what they lived for. Their own lives depended upon it.

"Ahh, I see you have completed your mission. You have indeed made me proud, and for that, you will be rewarded handsomely."

The two bowed and murmured, "It is but our one goal in life to fulfill your orders."

With a grandiloquent gesture, he waved to his servants, the softness in his voice now replaced by a snarl. "It is now time for the second part, and by far the most crucial of your mission. Find Anastasia and Korinna and bring me the crystal. I don't care what it takes. Just do it!"

They bowed and chanted in unison, "Yes, Master," and turned to leave.

"Not so quickly," he growled. He grabbed the servants' hands that bore the crystal pinky rings and placed one against his heart, the other over his own hand.

"Now!" he said urgently.

The servants bowed their heads and allowed their energy to surge through the crystal in their rings and into the body of their master. Spasms shook the servants. The energy that their master demanded was too much for them to endure. It took every ounce of strength not to resist. The oozing holes in their necks were a constant reminder of what would happen if they tried. Acrid smell filled the air. Their bodies were on fire. Their master's form was illuminated. "I am the One!" he shouted into the heavens.

"Yes, *you* are the One," the servants echoed.

"Now go! And do not come back until you have found them! It was my mistake to let her alone. I should have known she would turn against me. But I will not allow them to ruin my plan!"

The servants bowed. Although exhausted by the transference of their powers, they mustered enough energy to turn themselves back into hawks and took off to find the women and crystal.

He knelt and gently placed his hand on Alec's chest. He watched as his hand moved up and down in a steady rhythm. He hated how peacefully Alec looked while he slept. Leaning in very closely, he began to whisper. "It is time, Alec. Time for you to wake up. It is I. Darius."

"Who is he, Papa?" the girl asked. She had been standing in the doorway watching her father lean over this strange man. She had never seen him before, but she instantly noticed the striking resemblance. Darius stood up and strode over to his daughter. It was the only time when his mood lightened. Leah was his world. "This is your uncle Alec. He is my twin brother."

Leah took her father's outstretched hand and walked over with him to where Alec lay. "But why hasn't he ever visited us before? I always hear you say that family is the most important thing to you."

Darius marveled over his daughter's innocence. Her light blue eyes twinkled even in the dim light, and her skin was so pale that it seemed translucent. Darius smiled. "You are right. I do always say that." He chuckled. "And now, you will meet him. I think that Alec will be spending some time with us, if that is okay with you."

Leah clapped her hands. "That would be splendid, just simply splendid." Darius again smiled. It always amused him that his daughter spoke with such properness. She was his princess, and he treated her like one.

"Why don't we wake him up together? I am sure he will be so incredibly surprised to see us both."

"Wait!" Leah cried. "Don't you think that we should gather Mother to be here when we wake him?"

Darius tried hard to hide the contempt in his voice. "No, my darling, your mother is not here at the moment."

Leah's crystal-blue eyes widened. A sense of fear grabbed ahold of her, and she started to tremble. "But... where is she,

Father? How am I ever going to have sweet dreams if she is not here to tuck me in tonight?"

"She will be back soon, my dear. She has taken a short trip. But for tonight, I shall tuck you in, and together, we will say our prayers."

Leah's troubled face softened. "My first prayer will be for Mother to have a safe and speedy return back to us."

She bent down and gently tapped her uncle on the shoulder. Alec's eyes fluttered, and finally, they opened.

He gazed at this beautiful young woman. "Talia, you have come back for me."

His head was pounding, creating a crushing sensation in his ears. Alec brought his hands to his head.

Leah looked at her father quizzically. "Father, who is Talia, and why does Uncle Alec think that I am her?"

"Ah, my darling. Talia was our childhood friend. Your uncle had a crush on her because she was so beautiful. But not as beautiful as you, dear." Darius would rather die before he would let his daughter in on his past and the consequences that led him here.

"Let's sit him up, Father. I think he needs something to drink."

"That is a wonderful idea. Would you please be a dutiful daughter and make your uncle some tea?"

Leah ran off, leaving the two men alone.

"Talia! Don't leave me!" Alec moaned loudly.

Darius looked down at his brother. Alec looked so pitiful lying there, and it gave Darius satisfaction to see him look so helpless. Alec always thought he was just a tad bit better than he was. When it came to sports, Alec always won and gloated about it. When it came to looks, Alec would make jabs at Darius that his jaw was just a little bit more defined and his nose just slightly straighter. And when it came to Talia, Alec believed that *he* was the one who should end up with her. So, watching his twin brother writhing in pain, while he himself was soon to have everything in the world that he so deserved, gave him an immense feeling of payback.

"Time to sit up," Darius said as he grasped Alec's arms.

Alec's eyes widened as he focused on his brother's face.

"No! It cannot be. You are dead! You are dead!"

Darius pulled Alec to his feet. Alec stared at his brother. He studied every feature and knew, without any doubt, that it was Darius. *But how?* He thought.

"It certainly has been a long time," Darius said. "Welcome to my home."

Alec's eyes surveyed the enormous room. Velvet draperies adorned the twenty-foot-high windows. Marble floors glistened, and crystal chandeliers hung from the ceiling. The furniture was expertly carved, and artwork hung from the walls. It was a magnificent room and Alec could only begin to imagine what the rest looked like. "Not bad for someone who was buried alive, eh, brother?"

Alec cringed at the thought. His back straightened, and his jaw tightened. "You were dead. We all saw you lying there with blood oozing out of you!"

"It's okay. Relax. I do not blame any of you. Not to worry. I am not known to hold a grudge." Darius let out a laugh that sent chills coursing through Alec's body.

"I wanted to help you. I begged Mother and Father to let me use my powers. I even pleaded with the chief. Alec looked at his brother's left hand. There, on his ring finger, was the crystal ring that he had also worn when they were children.

The door suddenly opened, and Alec watched as a girl, as beautiful as the lilies that had once grown so abundantly on their mountaintop, entered the room and came toward them. "Here you go, Uncle Alec. I am sure my special blend of teas will make you feel much better." Alec looked up at his brother. *Uncle Alec?*

Darius' mouth formed into a thin smile. He nodded to his brother. "We have much to talk about."

"This beautiful angel is my daughter, Leah," Darius said proudly. "Her mother and I don't know how we got so lucky to create this exquisite young woman." Leah blushed. "Now, honey. Why don't you run along and practice your violin? Your concert is only days away."

"Yes, Father. It was so nice to meet you. I hope we get the opportunity to visit again soon." Leah turned and left the room.

Alec got quiet. He could not believe how he had destroyed his relationship with his son. He knew that he was dead to Ryan, and he already had faced the reality that the only one to blame was himself.

Chapter 29

The tale that Anastasia began to unravel was extremely difficult for everyone in the room to grasp. "So, what you are telling us," Ryan said, shaking his head incredulously, "is that Darius, my uncle, has been alive for all these years and patiently waiting to gain control of us?"

Anastasia shook her head. "I wouldn't say patiently," as she placed her hand on her scars. "And I wouldn't say it's just us. Darius wants control over the universe. That is his goal."

Avery's eyes widened. "Over the universe? How is that possible?"

"Are you ready to hear everything? This is going to be very disturbing."

In unison, they murmured, "yes."

"From the moment Darius realized he was alive, he set his plan in motion. He knew he must find someone to fall madly in love with him, and quickly." Anastasia's face slightly reddened. "He was so handsome, so funny, so smart... so everything. How could I not fall in love with him?"

"You always have to remember, Anastasia, that you wanted to free yourself from our secluded life, and you thought that Darius was your ticket to freedom," Korinna said gently.

Anastasia shook her head. "You see how that turned out."

"Love can make people lose sight of reality," said Talia.

"Thank you for those kind words." She looked at Steve, sitting next to Avery. "You have such a wonderful family. It agonizes me to see that you are in peril."

With those words, Steve jumped up, nearly knocking Avery to the floor. "I will not let anything happen to my family!" he bellowed. "And I will not have to rely on my wife and daughter's powers to protect them. If anyone tries to hurt them, I will destroy him."

Anastasia placed her pale and cold hand on Steve's shoulder. "I understand how you feel, but you must listen to what I am going to say. Darius' powers are much too strong for anyone to retaliate against him, much less a mere mortal."

"Hey!" shouted Avery jumping up to her feet. "That is my father you are talking about!"

"It's okay, honey." Steve turned to Anastasia, "I know you are only trying to protect me from harm. And I do appreciate your concern."

"Promise me that you will not try to go against Darius or his servants."

"Yes, Steve! Promise her. If anything happened to you, I would never forgive myself," Talia said, clinging tightly to her husband.

Steve smiled. "Okay, okay, I promise. Jeez, women!" His jokingly chauvinistic comment seemed to lift the dark veil that was beginning to smother all of them.

"I think it's time for some coffee and snacks. Avery, will you help me in the kitchen, please?"

Avery knew her mom's "I need you *now*" look. "Sure, no problem," she said, following her into the next room.

"And I want you to promise that you will never use your powers against Darius or Alec," her mom said quietly so no one in the next room could hear them.

"But my powers are the strongest! You were the one that even told me that," Avery said. "I can destroy them both, like a two-for-one deal," she said jokingly.

Talia whipped around so quickly that Avery could feel a cool gust of air in her face.

"Whoa, Mom, take it easy. I was just kidding."

"This is not a joke, Avery! Do you even realize the catastrophic consequences of this hideous plan that Darius has concocted will have on everybody? And I am not even speaking solely about the people who are in the next room."

"But what plan? We don't even know what Darius has up his sleeve. For all we know, he could be some delusional guy that can't even work a remote."

"Avery! Are you blind? Are you deaf?" Talia was losing patience with her daughter. She could feel the slightest burning of her skin. "Didn't you see the oozing scars on Anastasia's body? Didn't you hear her speak of imminent danger? This is not a game. You need to stop acting like a spoiled brat and listen to what I have to say!"

The words stung Avery. She knew that her mother only wanted to protect her, but it still irritated her that she felt like she was being treated like a baby. "Okay, I got it," she said in a placating voice that she knew was going to tick her mom off.

Talia shook her head. "Good." Avery was waiting for another speech on how not to be disrespectful, but that was the only word that came out of her mother's mouth. It was at that moment when Avery could sense the extreme danger that they were in.

"I am sorry, Mom," Avery lowered her head apologetically.

Talia could never stay mad at her daughter for very long. "I know, sweetheart." She took Avery's hand, gave it a little squeeze, and led her back into the family room.

"Korinna, I think there is something that you need to disclose to everyone who is gathered with us," Anastasia said in a gentle voice to her sister.

For a split second, the group could see the bewilderment on Korinna's face, and then her face grew white. Korinna shook her head and began to sob.

"It is time. I know that you only did it out of love, but you must tell them now."

Ben stood up and faced her. He cupped her face in his hands and placed a gentle kiss on her lips. "I will be with you, and I am never ever going to let you go again," he murmured softly into her ear. "Whatever you must tell us, it will be okay because I will help you through it. I love you, Korinna. I have never stopped loving you."

Avery glanced at Ryan, who was looking down at the floor. She knew this was painful for him, but she had to resist the urge to go over and hug him. Peter was also shifting uncomfortably in his seat, and Avery knew that it was just as difficult for him. All these years without a mother, only to have her suddenly reappear, must be excruciating.

Korinna walked over to where Peter was sitting. She took hold of his hand and turned it over so that his palm was facing upward. "It *is* time," she said to the group.

Still holding Peter's right hand, Korinna touched her finger to a tiny scar in his palm. It was tiny, and Peter had thought it was one of the many creases that lined his palm. But now, with his mother's finger gently pressing on it, he realized that it was so much more. He pulled his hand back. "No!" he shouted.

Korinna looked as though she had been slapped in the face. She knew that it was going to be a shock to her son, but still, his violent reaction shook her to the core.

Ben held his son. "Peter, you need to hear what your mother has to tell you," he said gently.

"I am one of you, aren't I?" he whispered.

"Peter, I saw it the second you were born. It was barely visible, but I knew that it was already deeply embedded in your palm. I wanted to protect you. I didn't want you to have to go through life having to make decisions on whether to use your powers." Then looking at Ben, she continued. "I didn't want you to ever have to worry that one day your powers might take hold of you so tightly that you might hurt the ones you love. I made the decision to remove your crystal and let you live a mortal life."

Peter looked at his father. "Did you know? Did you also agree with this plan?" he demanded.

"No, Peter," Korinna replied. "I never gave your father the chance. I just couldn't bear to have you endure all the pain that comes with having powers."

Peter's eyes were transfixed on Talia. "Do you agree with my mother? If having powers causes such destruction, why didn't you remove Avery's crystal when she was born?"

Talia did not know how to respond to such a question. She knew, either way, she was going to hurt someone. All she could do was answer honestly. "I agree with your mother that having powers can be a burden. They are strong and must be used wisely." She pointed to Peter, Avery, and Ryan. "The three of you have to be even more fastidious, for your powers are much more potent than ours. But, on the other hand, they are also amazing. They make us unique."

Steve interposed. "Talia and I agreed that whether Avery was born a witch or a mortal, we would embrace it." Steve's voice grew stronger. He saw the pain that Korinna and Ben were going through and wanted to support them. "Peter, your mother was trying to protect you. She did what she thought was best for you."

The words fell on deaf ears. "Where is the crystal, Mom?" Peter shouted.

"Peter, you will not yell at your mother like that!"

"Why are you taking her side? Why, after all these years? We were fine without her!" Peter's voice began to quiver. "Where is the crystal?"

"Oh, my God!" Everyone in the room turned. Avery was on her feet. "The crystal, I know where it is! Your attic, Peter," Avery said excitedly. "Remember the box where we found the photograph?"

Peter did not want to remember that time with Avery. It was special; he had felt so close to her, and he knew that she felt it, too. But those feelings were stolen by Ryan. Peter hated that she cared for him more.

Unaware of how hurt he was feeling, Avery continued. "Peter, the little silver fairy box. You thought that your father put your tooth in there. It's not your tooth!"

"She is correct." Anastasia seemed to be speaking only to Peter. Her eyes were closed; her voice was whispery. "Your mother used the power from the crystal in her pinky ring to remove the crystal from your hand. She had to burn it out of your palm, and the pain it caused you nearly destroyed her." Anastasia's eyes remained shut, and the words that came out of her mouth were monotone and barely audible. "She then sealed the tiny incision with the heat from her crystal. All that remained is that minuscule scar." Peter examined his palm. "For days, your mother kept the crystal close to her. She stared at it every waking moment, praying that she had done the right thing. She kept it hidden under the mattress in your crib when your father was around but feared that it would only be a matter of time before he discovered it. When she received the tiny fairy box, she knew that it would become the crystal's forever home. Until now."

"Is all that true?" Peter turned his head in the direction where Korinna was sitting.

Korinna nodded slowly. Then the realization hit. "I never told anyone what I did." She looked at her sister. "How do you know?"

Anastasia turned to Korinna. "As per Darius' orders, I have followed your life down to the last second." She then faced the group. "I regret what I am telling all of you." Her hand moved up to her neck, where she touched one of the scars. Silver liquid began to ooze. "But you see, it was not by choice."

"So, what you are saying is that for all these years, Darius has been recharging his powers by relying on your own crystal?" Talia asked. Anastasia's story was excruciatingly painful to listen to. She could not even begin to fathom what torture she had endured.

Anastasia nodded. "I fear that what else I have to tell you may not be suitable for young ears."

Ryan rose to his feet. "This concerns all of us, and we need to hear what you have to say." Peter and Avery nodded their heads in agreement.

"Please, Mom? I am old enough, and Ryan is right. If what Korinna and Anastasia are saying is true, then we need to stay."

Talia smiled weakly. "My girl is growing up to be such a wise woman. You may stay, but it is up to Ben and Korinna if they want Peter and Ryan to be involved. Ryan began to object, but Talia cut him off. "She is your mother, Ryan," she said gently to him. "She gets to make the decision." As much as he wanted to seem independent, Ryan was glad to hear those words. He smiled at Talia. She knew him so well. It was agreed that they all should stay and wait in anticipation for Anastasia to continue.

"More than anything, Darius wanted a daughter. When I asked him why a daughter, he would begin to ramble on how it was part of his plan." Anastasia paused and looked at the three young adults. "Are you sure you want to hear everything?" They nodded. "When we first got married, life was great. Our lovemaking was passionate and easy."

Avery could feel her face get hot. She knew she was blushing. She could also feel the electricity stirring around Ryan.

She dug her nails into her palm to try and stop the sensation and focus on what Anastasia was saying.

"We made love morning, noon, and night. Darius would whisper in my ears the sweetest things, but the last whisper was always the same. *A daughter is what we will create.*"

"But what if you became pregnant and you found out it was a boy? What would Darius have done? I am sure he would have loved the baby once he held him in his arms," Talia said.

Anastasia smiled ruefully. "I never had that opportunity. For one solid year we tried, but no baby. Each month, Darius grew increasingly impatient with me. He called me worthless and barren. At this point, I would have done anything to create a baby with him. I just wanted him to love me. I know it sounds twisted now, but that is the truth."

"Why didn't you go to a doctor?" Korinna asked. "She could have helped you conceive."

"You should know the answer to that. How could I let a doctor examine me and see that I wasn't mortal? That was out of the question."

"What about using your powers? Couldn't you have done something with them to have a baby?" asked Avery.

"Avery! Your remark is out of line! You, of all people, to say that. You were taught that you do not use your powers for your own gratification. It would be inexcusable. Apologize right now."

"That is not necessary." Anastasia cast her eyes downward. "I am ashamed to say that is ultimately what I did. And that month, I became pregnant. I was desperate. The cruelty which Darius was imposing upon me was escalating. I know that you must all be thinking why didn't I leave? Why would I put up with all this torture? But it was not easy as you think," she continued. "Darius had his servant thugs with me at all times."

Korinna shook her head. "I encountered them, and they are not the friendliest pair of men. But I also heard them obey your orders. Why couldn't you order them to leave you alone so you could escape?"

"They only obeyed me when it came to certain orders. Darius told them exactly when they could listen to me. Darius also gained power from them. He used the powers in their crystal rings. You must remember that when he dug himself out of the grave, his powers were all but gone."

Peter knotted his hands together. "Too bad he wasn't really dead," he muttered.

Korinna went up to her son and gently placed her hand on his shoulder. She could feel his back tighten, and it silently killed her to think of all the pain she had caused him. "I know this is difficult for you, but Darius did do one good thing; he gave my sister a child. Peter and Ryan, you have a cousin. Anastasia, I cannot wait to meet my niece. I hope that day will come soon."

With those words, Anastasia dropped to her knees and quietly began to sob. "There is no child," she whispered in anguish.

"But you said that you used your powers to create a baby," insisted Avery.

"Avery!"

"It's okay, Talia. I like a woman who speaks her mind. Darius and I were so excited that I was pregnant. I loved the thought of being a mother, and Darius was treating me like a queen. Not once did he try to force my powers from me. He told me over and over, that I needed my energy to ensure that I had a healthy pregnancy and baby. The first two months were bliss. The horrible times that I had endured began to fade like distant memories, and in their place, new memories were being made. Darius would constantly place his hand on my belly and whisper to the baby. It was so touching that I began to forget the 'real' Darius. All I cared about was that we were going to have a baby and life would be great."

"You don't have to continue if this is too difficult. We can talk later," Korinna said.

"No, it is important to talk about this. It is crucial for you to know what my life was like in the beginning for you to understand how I got to this point." She hesitated and then said in a barely audible voice, "And how it is that all of you are in grave danger."

Talia sucked in her breath. Hearing those words always made her feel like she was being punched in the gut. She looked over at her family. It was hard to believe how their lives had turned upside down in such a short time.

"I was just completing my first trimester. Everything was perfect. The hardest part of the pregnancy was now over, and Darius and I could relax a bit." Anastasia closed her eyes. It seemed like she was in a trance. Silence permeated the room. Then she spoke in a low, dull voice. "I can remember like it was just yesterday. I had gone out shopping. I was so excited that I was beginning to show, and I wanted to pick out maternity clothes. I was gone for most of the day. When I came home, Darius called out to me to meet him in one of the guest rooms. What I saw almost brought me to my knees. The room was completely decorated as a nursery."

"But that should have made you happy; I know my mom said she and my dad decorated my room together. Is that why you were upset because you didn't do it together?" Avery babbled on. "Mom showed me pictures. They didn't know if I was a boy or a girl, so it was painted in this beautiful minty green color with splashes of yellow. My comforter had baby zoo animals, and the border matched. Even the curtains... Ouch!" A tiny spark hit Avery in the shoulder. Her mother again was staring at her with the look of death. Avery felt like a complete fool, a complete insensitive fool. *When am I ever going to learn to shut my mouth?* She thought.

"It wasn't the fact that we didn't decorate together. It was the fact that the entire nursery was decorated in pink. There was no question in mind that Darius would only accept this baby if it was a girl. I didn't know what he had up his sleeve at that moment, but I can still remember shuddering at the thought that having a girl was the only option. And from that moment on, my pregnancy took a turn for the worse. Every day seemed like torture to get out of bed. Passing that 'pink' room sent waves of nausea rumbling through my body. I began to resent the life that was growing inside of me. I am so ashamed to say that, but it was true."

"I know that it goes against our tradition to use our powers for our gratification, but couldn't you have used them just once more to find out the sex of the baby?" asked Talia softly.

"I was petrified to find out. What if it was a boy? Then what? Would I have to use my powers once again for something so hideous, like ending a baby's life? Even to this day, I am riddled with guilt to even have thought of such a notion. I did not know what to do, so I waited. Waited for six long months. Every night I would silently say my prayers and wish that the baby kicking inside of me was a girl."

"That must have been so horrible living each day with such despair. I am so sorry for you," Korinna said, as she hugged her sister tightly. "I wish you would have come to me."

"There was no way that I would have involved you in that horrible situation. Darius would have tried to destroy you. I could never put you in danger." She looked up at the group. "And I can't believe that I am standing here now with all of you and thinking that is exactly what I have done."

Chapter 30

"And so, you see, I wasn't completely dead. I used every ounce of my powers that I had left to dig myself out of the grave."

"But why didn't you come back to us? Why did you let us all think that you were dead?" Alec was getting mad. His life could have been entirely different.

"Mother and Father would have thought I was the devil coming back from Hell. They could never have come to terms with the fact that I was buried alive. I just thought that the best thing for me to do was leave and start a new life."

Alec glanced once more around the room. "Well, I certainly can see that's what you did," he said bitterly. "It was selfish what you did, Darius, and you know it. Mother and Father would have gotten over it. They would have seen that you were not the devil but the son they loved immensely. They would have you back home, and that was more important than any wise tale." Everything would have been fine.

The veins in Darius' neck began to bulge. Alec could see silvery sparks flickering in the whites of his eyes. Alec took a step back, but Darius lunged at him, grabbing him by the neck. "I could destroy you right now!" he hissed. "You will now listen to what I have to say and obey every instruction I give you. Do you understand?"

Alec's eyes moved about in a frenzied matter. He was running out of air as Darius' hold grew tighter.

"Do you?" Darius squeezed harder.

All Alec could do was nod. Darius released his grip. "Now then, let's continue."

"As you can see, I've created a fine life for myself here. I have a magnificent house, a beautiful and doting daughter, and all the riches that a person could ever desire." The arrogance spilled out of him like cascading water.

"You forgot to mention a wife," Alec said wearily. His neck was throbbing from Darius' vise-like grip, and he was having a difficult time getting the air back into his lungs.

"Ah, a wife," laughed Darius bitterly. "I have one of those, too." His laugh sent chills down Alec's spine. He was wondering who was more evil--himself or his brother?

"When do I get to meet your wife? She must be beautiful if she looks anything like your daughter."

With that, Darius sent a searing blow to Alec's stomach. Alec crumpled. "Do not mention my wife and daughter in the same breath!" he hissed, his eyes flashing.

Darius knelt close to him. Unable to catch his breath once more, Alec brought his hands up to his face. He could not bear another strike to his body. His brother had turned into a lunatic, and Alec feared for his life.

"Say it," he insisted. "Say that you will never mention their names together again! Say it now, or I will end your pitiful life!"

"I promise," Alec said in a choked whisper.

"Well, now that we agree on that, let me help you up." Darius grabbed Alec by the arm and yanked him to his feet. Alec felt like his arm was being torn from the socket, but he was terrified to utter a sound.

And as if nothing had happened, Darius continued to speak in a melodic voice that seemed unnatural and strange to Alec. "You want to know about my wife? Well, in a sense, you are related to her."

Alec looked at Darius. His brother was having a good time, and it was making him more furious by the moment. *If only I still had my powers*, he thought.

"Now, now, no nasty thoughts about me, Alec," Darius laughed. "I do have *my* powers."

"Just get on with it," Alec grumbled. Powerless or not he was losing his patience.

"You always were short-tempered. My wife is Korinna's sister."

"Celine?"

Darius clapped his hands together. "Ding, ding, ding! You have won the one-million-dollar prize!"

He was clearly losing it. His voice took on a hysterical tone.

"We call her Anastasia in this house. And now for double or nothing."

Alec stared at his brother. It was like watching a spoiled kid who wanted all the attention and had the means to obtain it. "Do you know why you picked Korinna out of all the available 'down on my luck' women in the Sethos clan?"

The mention of his wife in such a derogatory way sent Alec charging. He smashed his fist into Darius' nose.

Silvery liquid flowed freely out of his nostrils. Darius watched it form a pool at his feet. Electric currents flowed through his body to his nose. The liquid ceased, and his nose once again looked flawless. He gazed down at the floor. "Such a shame; I just had these marble floors polished. As I was saying before, you so rudely *tried* to prevent me from disgracing your wife. Do you know why you picked her? It's because *I* led you to Korinna--you have been my puppet all these years. Your plan for revenge on Talia through Ryan was all my doing. It's such a shame that the plan is backfiring. I guess we know who has more control, don't we?"

Alec knew he was being baited and willed himself to remain calm. "Whatever your grotesque plan is, I don't want any part of it. Use your powers and end my life now. I have nothing left to live for. My son despises me, and my wife is dead."

"That would be too easy." Darius shook his head. "This is going to be fun. I have waited all these years for my plan to finally come to fruition, and now who better to watch it with than my own twin brother? We are going to have a super time together. Just like the old days. By the way Alec, you look like hell. Why don't I show you your suite where you will be staying? Take a long relaxing bath and change into one of the many outfits that I have selected for you. Then we can talk some more. We have so much catching up to do."

Alec began to ascend the stairs. The staircase was made of mahogany, and the wood glistened in the dim light. Each step was agony for him. But he had no right to feel sorry for himself. He deserved every ounce of evil that was now being bestowed upon him. Before he reached the last step, he heard his name.

"Oh, and Alec, one more thing. Your wife, Korinna? She is alive and well. She wishes you dead, but all in all, she is doing just fine." Darius let out a childlike laugh and vanished from the room.

Chapter 31

The strands of Anastasia's silvery hair stood straight up and tiny sparks flicked off her body. "They are coming," she whispered.

"Who?" Steve demanded.

"Darius' servants. We must go to the attic and get the crystal!" she said urgently.

Peter jumped up. I will get it. I know where it is. Avery can come with me. After all, she *is* the one with the powers. I might need her protection," he said with a not-so-hidden trace of bitterness in his voice.

"No, Peter. It is safer if Ryan and Avery go. They both have powers."

Avery's heart ached for Peter. She tried not to look at him, but she knew that if jealousy were a poison, he would be dead. Regardless of her intense feelings for Ryan, she still cared deeply for him.

"Yeah. Sure. Whatever," Peter said.

"Peter." Avery walked over to him and tried to take his arm, but he shrugged it off.

"Don't try to make yourself feel better by placating me," he whispered menacingly. "Leave me the hell alone."

His words stung Avery, but she was jolted back into reality by Anastasia leading her and Ryan to the front door.

"Wait!" Steve blocked Anastasia. "I will not allow you to expose my daughter to danger."

Talia walked over to her husband and took his hand. The tiny crystal in her pinky ring flashed. "I know how you feel, but we must let them get the crystal. If Darius' servants get to it first, who knows how much more danger we will be facing? Avery and Ryan's powers are the strongest. They are our only hope."

"Ryan and Avery, you must go now. Be careful and use your powers wisely. You will need to have them at full potency if you face a crisis."

Talia and Korinna shuddered at the same time and grasped each other's hand for comfort.

Anastasia placed her arms around Avery and Ryan. "I will give you all my powers that I have stored at this moment. I just hope all of it combined is enough." She held them in a strong embrace.

Sparks of energy left Anastasia's pinky ring and flew into Ryan and Avery's crystals. Finally, she let go. Her body seemed weak, and Korinna ran to get her a chair while Ben gave Avery his house key.

They drove over to Peter's house to save their powers. Avery felt weird being at the house without Peter, and Ryan could sense what she was feeling. "Hey, I know that you like him, Avery. It's okay because I know that you *love* me."

Avery smacked him in the arm. She knew that he was just trying to lighten up her mood, but she also knew that there was truth to what Ryan had just said. She opened the door. It was dark, and she groped around to find a light.

"Well, I guess it's now or never." Avery said as she flipped the switch. "The attic door is to the left of the kitchen." They rounded the corner and stood in front of the closed door. Even though it was not that long ago when she and Peter had climbed those steps, she still felt her nerves getting the better of her. She remembered how rickety they were and how stuffy the air was up there. She took a deep breath and pulled on the string attached to the light bulb. The scent of mothballs wafted down to them.

"Ladies first," Ryan said.

"You are so charming," Avery shot back. She led the way.

"Nice view." He chuckled.

"Ryan, this is serious. Those goons could be here any moment."

"Okay, okay. Sorry. I'm nervous, too. I'm just trying hard to act like this is not affecting me."

Avery stepped onto the wooden floor and glanced around. "It doesn't look like anyone has been here since Peter, and I found the box. That's reassuring."

"But you're right. They could be on their way right now."

"Ryan! I am freaked out enough without you giving me more to worry about. We need to get the crystal quickly and get out of here."

Avery heard a crackle. She looked up and saw the flickering of the light bulb.

"Take my hand!" Ryan whispered to her. Avery seemed to be frozen. "Avery, now!" Ryan did not wait for her to obey. He grabbed her by the wrist and clamped his palm down hard. The sparks sent slicing currents up into her arm, and immediately the two were safely behind the attic wall.

"Ryan! The box! They are going to find the crystal!"

Ryan pulled on Avery's hand, indicating for her to look down at her feet. Between them, lay the box. Avery let out a sigh of relief. She looked up at Ryan and gave his hand a gentle squeeze.

They heard them enter. Their presence sucked every molecule that was left in the tiny stuffy room, and Avery felt herself gasping silently for air. Avery closed her eyes tightly. Through the wall, she could see them. They had the same androgynous look as Anastasia; cropped silver hair, translucent skin, and silver streaks flashing in their eyes. Goosebumps dotted her flesh when she saw the oozing sores that mirrored the same as Anastasia's. They too, she now understood, were also just pawns in Darius' master plan. But she also knew they were dangerous.

"This is going to take all day," one of them grumbled. "All Anastasia could see with her powers was that the crystal would be in a box."

"Yeah, but which one? There must be at least fifty up here. Our master will not be pleased if we do not return soon. He has sent me a signal that we must attend to our master's brother."

The two moaned. It was a grotesque sound, and Avery felt Ryan stiffen. Avery brought her hand up to his cheek and stroked him gently. She knew that even though Ryan claimed to hate his father, Alec was still a part of him. What she could not yet figure out was how Alec had wound up at Darius', and what sick and devious plan was being conceived. She had no way of knowing if the two brothers were in it together or if it was Darius on his own. But from the way the two goons responded, she guessed the latter.

From behind the wall, they could hear boxes being ripped open, their contents thrown onto the floor. With each setback, their frustration mounted. Dishes were smashed, and blankets were ripped into shreds.

Avery could feel herself begin to tingle with fear that they might soon be discovered. It was taking too long, and their powers could not keep them hidden indefinitely. Ryan could sense her mounting terror, and he returned the favor by now placing his hand on the small of her back and rubbing gently. She felt herself relax and mouthed, "thank you."

"It's not here. We have gone through every box. There is no crystal," one of the servants muttered.

"This could only mean one of two things," the other growled. "One, Anastasia lied to Darius, or two, someone else was here first! We must go now and face our punishment, for we have disgraced our master with our failure."

Avery closed her eyes again and could see the two servants touch their necks. She knew that they would be tortured, and the sorrow she felt for them was immeasurable. She could not begin to imagine what it would be like to live under Darius' control. At that moment, she vowed that she would destroy him. Ryan, reading her thought, squeezed her hand in agreement.

The weight of the air that surrounded Avery and Ryan lightened, and they knew that the servants were finally gone. Pressing their palms together, the two stepped out from behind the wall, taking the box with them. The room was in total chaos. Stuffed animals lay strewn across the wooden floor, their stuffing ripped out in clumps. Shards of glass were everywhere. The only box still intact sat quietly at their feet. Avery let out a sigh of relief. They had prevented a huge disaster from taking place.

"Let's clean this place up. I would hate for Ben and Peter to see all their belongings ruined," Avery said softly. She bent down to pick up a framed picture of Peter when he was a Boy Scout. The glass was cracked, and pieces were lying on the floor.

"Figures that *he* was a Boy Scout. He's always trying to come to your rescue and save you from me," Ryan muttered.

"Stop. Peter is a sweetheart. And I, of all people, do not need saving from anyone, especially from you. Just remem... Ouch!"

"What were you just saying?" Ryan knelt to Avery's level. She was holding her finger. Silvery liquid was dripping onto the floor. A piece of glass was jutting out from the gash. "Here, let me..."

"I can take care of myself!" Avery said stubbornly. She continued to stare at the glass protruding from the cut, internally deciding how exactly she was going to pull it out without fainting. She felt queasy, and it infuriated her that Ryan could tell.

"I said, let me help you." And before Avery could protest, Ryan swiftly pulled out that glass. He quickly placed his fingers around her injured one and held them there until the bleeding stopped.

Avery felt like her own heart had also stopped. The closeness was too much for her. The feelings that were building were so intense, and she was certain that Ryan felt the same way.

Ryan released his fingers and brought her finger up to his lips. He kissed the cut gently. Instantly the incision was sealed. And with that kiss, Avery knew that her love for Ryan was also sealed. He looked deeply into her eyes, teasing her at first, planting tiny kisses all over her face, like staccato notes being played on a piano. And then, bringing her in closer, he found her lips. They were smooth and moist, and he could detect a trace of a sweet fruity flavor on them.

Avery let herself give in. She was aware of Ryan's hands beginning to explore her body, stopping suddenly to look up at her, anxiously awaiting her approval. With each nod, Avery surrendered more and more to his touch; her body responding in a way that she had never experienced. His kisses were deeper, and Avery arched her back to meet his full and hot lips. Their tongues played tag, and Avery shivered when she felt a tiny nibble on her earlobe.

"I love you, Avery." Ryan's voice was husky and deep. "I have loved you from the moment I laid eyes on you." He felt her tense. "Avery, I know that by now you realize that despite what my father had planned for me, I could never have gone through with it. You are a part of me, and I will never let anything bad happen to you."

She nodded. "I do know that, and I will never let anything bad happen to you."

Ryan laughed. "You always have to get the last word, don't you?"

Avery took his hands. She placed them on her heart. "You will always have this." And then she slowly eased him down to the floor next to her, where she had cozied up on a heap of mismatched pillows and comforters. Her eyes told him what she wanted.

He sat up. Avery felt her face begin to redden. *How stupid she was to think that was what he also wanted!*

"Avery," Ryan said comfortingly. "If you think that for a second that I don't want the same thing right now, then you really don't know me." He jokingly poked her in the ribs. "But not like this. Not in Peter's attic." He could see her shoulders relaxing a bit and the redness disappearing. "When we are together, and I say *when*, it will be perfect. Believe me, it kills me right now to say 'no,'" Ryan said as he tousled her hair, "But it will be well worth the wait."

"Always the stud," Avery joked back, glad that the tension was quickly dissipating. And then quietly, placing her lips upon his, she murmured, "I will wait for you forever."

"Shouldn't they be back by now?" Steve asked, his tone hinting at more concern than he wanted to let on.

"Avery knew exactly where the box was. All they had to do was grab it and leave." Peter's voice had an edge to it. He knew he sounded like a sourly little boy, but he didn't care. It should have been him taking Avery back to the attic. It was *his* crystal.

"What if something has happened to them?" Talia's voice was strained, and immediately, Peter felt like an idiot for not even realizing that the two could be in real danger.

Korinna walked over to where Talia was standing. She had not left the window in over an hour. "They are fine. Between their powers and the power that Anastasia gave them, they are invincible."

"Let's hope so," Talia murmured.

At the sound of the front door banging shut, the group ran into the hallway. Avery was holding the box. "Where's Peter? I think it should be him to open the box and go through its contents." Peter was the only one that had lagged. He could not bear to see them together.

"He's in the family room, Avery," Korinna answered. "Why don't you go in first and talk to him. Find out whether he wants to do this alone or with all of us around him."

"Hey there," Avery said as she entered the room. Peter was staring out at the backyard. He didn't turn when he heard her voice. "So, I brought you your baby blanket," Avery continued, trying to sound upbeat.

Peter turned around. "Let's get this clear," he said gruffly. "We are not friends. We are not anything. If it takes my crystal to help, then fine. But that's it."

Avery could not blame him for what he was feeling. She was the one who should be blamed. Saving him from losing any more face, she simply handed him the box. "I am sorry, Peter." He watched her leave the room. He desperately wanted to hate her, but he knew that if push came to shove, he would use every ounce of strength in his body to protect her, and ultimately, die for her.

Chapter 32

Alec could hear the muffled cries of agony rising from where he sat in his locked room. After he had dressed, he tried to leave, only to find out that he was a prisoner.

"It was not there!" cried one of the servants. "We searched every box! Please, Master, please, we beg for your mercy." The wounds that had been scarred over and over were once again reopened, and Darius delighted in watching the silvery liquid drain out of them. "It is not my mercy you should be begging for. It is your life!" Darius growled at his servants. He hated to be outsmarted. He would now have to wait for Anastasia to come home. After he absorbed most of his servants' powers into his own body, he would be able to overtake his wife and make her tell him where the crystal was. He laughed bitterly to himself. She used to be so malleable; anything he wanted from her, he got. Now, she rebelled, lying to his face. *Well, that will all change*, he thought to himself. He watched his servants cower in the corner. Smiling smugly, he walked over to them. "Pick yourselves up and get our waiting houseguest. I am sure he is anxious to come downstairs."

"Our master is waiting for you," the servant said. Alec continued to stare out the barred window.

"He can wait as long as he wants because I am not going anywhere," Alec replied bitterly. "That man, if you can call him that; that despicable man is my brother, and this is how he treats me? You can go back downstairs and remind him that it was I who sought revenge for his death."

The other servant stepped in front of the window. Alec tried his best to avoid the fleshy opening that bulged in his neck. Drops of silvery liquid were still oozing from it, and the sound of them hitting the floor nauseated Alec. "Do you want this, Sir? Do you want to end up like us and Anastasia?" He roughly gripped Alec's face so that he could not look away.

"Why?" Alec said in a defeated tone. "Why did he do this sickening thing to all of you?"

The servants looked at each other. They knew that Darius' brother was also a devious and deceitful person. But they didn't realize that Alec was also a "servant" to Darius, and everything he had done was part of Darius' control over him. All they had heard from their master was how Alec had married Korinna just to create a child to carry on his plan to get back at Talia through her daughter Avery. But that, they both silently agreed, paled to all the atrocities that Darius was doing in order to achieve his goal. They nodded to each other and began to talk in hushed voices. The fear that Darius might find out that they were about to betray him would certainly result in a gruesome death for all of them.

The servants looked exactly alike except for one tiny difference. One wore a crystal pinky ring on the left ring finger, while the other wore one on the right. Alec knew instantly that they were from two very familiar clans.

"I am Orion. Like you and your brother, I am a Leirion." He gestured with his hand. "And this is Tereus. Like Anastasia and her sister Korinna, he is a Sethos. We were wanderers; two men without families. After the Leirion had left Oros Mountain, I was without any direction in life. For two years, I wandered aimlessly. I rented a shabby room above a butcher shop and worked there cutting the slaughtered animals into pieces of meat. It was a disgusting job. I would go upstairs at the end of a twelve-hour day and smell like dead animal flesh, my hands stained red from their blood. But I had no choice; there was nowhere else to go."

"What about your family?" Alec questioned.

"I had no siblings, and my parents had died five years prior to everyone leaving the mountain. They are still buried there."

The other servant now began to speak. "My story is very similar to Orion's. I, too, had no future. I lived day by day, performing odd jobs for people in the village."

"But you had your crystals? Why didn't you use them to create a better life for yourselves?"

They stared at Alec, their identical eyes sending shivers down his spine. "We are not like you and your brother," Orion said with dignity in his voice. "We honored our ancestors and the belief that we should not use our crystals for self-indulgent purposes."

Alec could feel the guilt surge through his body. His whole life seemed to revolve around self-indulgence. *And look where it got me*, he thought. He lost his wife and son and was the catalyst to the Leirion being forced to leave their beloved home. It was in that moment that he really understood the brevity of his actions and how he had ruined so many lives. Quiet sobs racked his body.

He felt a hand on his shoulder. It was Tereus. "You are cleansed now, my brother. Your sins are forgiven." Alec looked into Tereus's eyes. The relief he felt was immense.

"Thank you," was all he could utter. He felt a thousand years old.

"Come. Darius will suspect something if we are gone too long. We will talk later. Just remember. Darius does not know that we are against him. You must not, for the safety of everyone involved, including that beautiful girl downstairs, let on that you know our true feelings. We, too, have a plan. And that is to destroy him."

Alec bowed down in front of the servants. "I will give my last breath to help."

The three descended the stairs. Darius stood at the landing, tapping his foot against the last step.

"I hate to be left waiting," he sneered.

"We beg for your forgiveness, Master," the servants recited in unison. They were holding Alec up on either side by his armpits. The pain was excruciating, but Alec knew that it was necessary for his survival. It must look like the servants were against him. The servants then dropped their arms, and Alec fell to the floor.

Darius clapped his hands in delight. "Ahh, it makes me so happy to see my twin in a state of ultimate weakness." He walked over to where Alec was kneeling. "Stand up straight when I speak to you!" The tip of his shoe slammed into one of Alec's knees. Alec doubled over in pain. It felt as if his whole kneecap had been shattered. "I said get up!"

Alec struggled to his feet. He could not believe that this was his brother. He was a monster.

"Time for dinner. I am sure that you must be starving." Darius motioned to his brother to sit at the other end of the table. He snapped his fingers, and the two servants disappeared. "We can now talk privately." Alec limped over to the chair; his knee was throbbing, and sitting made it a bit more tolerable.

"What is your grand plan, my brother? Or should I say, *Master*?"

The force with which Darius slammed his fist down onto the table sent the china and crystal shattering to the floor. Immediately, the servants came rushing in to clean up the mess. "Out!" He roared. He turned to Alec. "You will never ever speak to me with sarcasm in your voice again! I will destroy you this instant if you do not obey my rules."

Alec nodded. He was powerless and detested that he felt so inferior to his twin.

"Good. Let's eat." He rang a bell, and the servants returned with new place settings and dishes of delectable food. Despite the delicious aromas wafting through the air, Alec wanted to gag. It took every ounce of strength in his body not to. The two ate in silence. Darius rang the bell, and the servants rushed in to clear the table. "We will go into the study to have an after-dinner drink. It is the perfect spot for us to chat."

Alec knew that his brother was enjoying this little game of his. It was always a game between them. But this time, the competition was fierce, and there would be only one winner left standing. Trying not to appear rattled, Alec followed his brother.

There were photographs of Leah and him in gilded frames on every marble tabletop. A huge portrait painted in oils was mounted above the fireplace. There was not one picture of Anastasia.

As if reading his mind, Darius let out a chuckle. "Anastasia merely serves as a mother figure to my beautiful daughter. Nothing more."

Before Alec could take back the words he blurted, "Your daughter? Doesn't it take two to create a child?" His other knee blew out from the electric current that hit it. Alec moaned in pain.

"I warned you," Darius said in a menacing voice. "I will not allow you to speak of my daughter and Anastasia in the same breath."

"I am sorry," whispered Alec. He felt faint, bile rising in his throat. "Please make this pain go away," he groaned.

Darius watched with satisfaction as his brother begged for mercy. Finally, he called his servants into the room. "Heal him," he ordered. They bent down, each placing a palm on one injured knee. Alec could immediately feel relief, and he mouthed the words, "thank you" to them.

Darius let out a manic laugh. "I would have done it myself, my dear brother. But when you left me to die, almost all my powers were destroyed. I must rely on Anastasia and my trusted servants to supply me with my power. And if that wife of mine will ever get home, I will surely be able to *recharge* myself.

"Now, where was I before you so rudely spoke? Ahh, I was just about to tell you about my beloved daughter, Leah." With the mention of her name, Darius' voice grew tender. "She is the light of my life and ultimately the one person in this universe who will benefit from my sole purpose in this world."

"And what is that?" Alec asked, knowing that he really did not want to hear the answer.

"It is simple. There will be no being on earth, human or otherwise, that will be more powerful than my Leah. Of course, she is not ready to be burdened with such power. It will take a couple of years for her to arrive at her full potential. Until then, my plan will continue its course. And when the day of Leah's eighteenth birthday arrives, she will be heralded as Queen of the Universe."

Alec stared at his brother in disbelief. He could not imagine that Leah would ever want such a life. She had a pureness about her, and the thought that her own father would want her to continue his lifelong dream of total control was inconceivable.

Darius' voice lowered. "Sadly, Leah was born a mortal, and it will take an enormous amount of crystal energy to create her powers."

At that moment, Alec wanted to vomit. He moaned softly to himself, wrapping his arms around him. "You can't do this."

Darius laughed. "But you see, I can. And I will. No one will be spared. Not your precious Korinna, not your son Ryan that you, Alec, held captive in your own devious plan. Not one person will remain. Although come to think of it, you should thank me. I am doing you a favor... even Talia and her daughter will be destroyed."

Chapter 33

"That's the baby blanket your dad and I would wrap you up in at night," Korinna said softly, as she knelt beside her son. "You always looked like a sleeping angel. Your dad and I would joke that we wanted to tie you to the crib in case your wings would take flight." Despite all the bottled-up anger, Peter felt himself smile.

"Can you get Dad? I want all three of us to be together when I go through the box." She knew what he really meant was when he got to the little silver box that held his fate.

Korinna smiled at her son. She had waited for words like those for such a long time. "I would love that."

The three of them formed a circle with the box in the middle at their feet. "From this moment on," Peter said to his parents, "We are a family again. I don't care what happened in the past. I need the two of you, and I know that you need each other." He anxiously waited for their reply. His eyes begged them to comply with his request. They nodded in agreement, and the three wrapped their arms around each other, hugging tightly.

"I have missed you so much, Korinna," Ben murmured into her ear. Korinna felt her tears flow.

"And I have missed you," she whispered back.

The two looked at Peter. He was so handsome. "We will never ever be apart," Ben said in a strong voice. He looked at Korinna. "I promise that I will never leave you again."

She clung to two of the three most important men in her life. At that moment, the relief that Korinna felt was like thousands of weights being lifted from her shoulders, but there was also grief that had pressed them back down again. "Ryan," she said softly.

The stinging sensation that Ryan felt throughout his body told him that something intense was going on in the family room. His jealousy was mounting, and Talia, sensing it, touched Ryan's arm. She knew exactly what he was feeling, and her heart ached for him. Despite his initial intentions of hurting her and her family, she knew that he would now do anything to protect them. She could see how her daughter looked at him; it was pure love. "I think you should go in now," she said softly. "They are your family." Ryan merely nodded and walked into the room.

The three turned towards him. Korinna's arms were outstretched, and Ryan ran into them. All his "coolness" was suddenly stripped away. He just wanted his mother. "Baby," Korinna murmured. "My precious little boy. I am so sorry for all that you've had to go through with your father." At the mention of his dad, Ryan stiffened. But Korinna drew him closer. "But you must understand that there is some goodness in your father, and I pray that wherever he is at this moment that he finds his way and makes it right."

Ben walked over to Korinna and Ryan. "I know that this is so strange for you." He glanced back to where Peter was still standing. "For you, too. But we must all try to put the past behind us now. From what Anastasia told us, we are all in danger, and I will not let anything happen to any of you." He put his hand on Ryan's shoulder. "Ryan, you are part of my family now. I hope you will let me in." Ryan found himself smiling. It had been so long since he felt any kind of parental love, and it surprised him how much he so desperately craved it. Ben motioned for Peter to join them. "You are brothers, and I pray that you can form some sort of bond. You don't have to be the best of friends but don't forget that there are people in your lives that you both would give anything to protect."

Ryan extended his hand to his brother. "I don't expect you to like me, but I am asking you to forgive Avery. You mean so much to her, and it is killing her that you might hate her."

"I could never hate her," Peter said in a low voice. "And she knows that." He shook his brother's hand. The crystal in Ryan's palm brushed against Peter's scar. He looked up at his mother. "It is time."

"Are you sure this is what you want?" Korinna asked her son.

Peter nodded. "This is my fate."

"You must use your powers wisely," Korinna replied. "Too much evil has come from those who have not abided by the law."

Peter shook his head. "I promise. I will take my powers seriously. I will not disappoint you." He shot a look in Ryan's direction.

Korinna opened the box and delicately scooped up the tiny silver tooth-fairy box. She paused, uncertain if this was what she should allow her son to do. But she knew that it was now beyond her control.

"I am ready, Mom. I want you to be the one to give me my powers."

"I wish it were that easy, Peter. The power in my crystal ring is no match for the power that lies in the crystals embedded in Ryan and Avery's palms. And since Avery is the most powerful, she must be the one to give you back your powers."

"That's crazy, Mom," Ryan protested. "My power is just as strong as Avery's. I will gladly help out Peter."

But Korinna shook her head. "I am afraid it is not, and Avery is the only one."

Peter could not wipe the smug smile off his face. It gave him huge satisfaction knowing that this was ticking his brother off immensely.

"What if Avery does not want to do it?" Ryan countered, knowing all too well that she would graciously abide by Korinna's wishes. But most importantly, he was certain that she would do anything to help Peter. Just because she said she loved him did not mean she had lost all feeling for Peter. Avery wanted so badly to win Peter's friendship back. It was killing her, knowing that he held any animosity toward her. And Ryan knew that he was now grasping at straws that seemed to slip magically through his hands.

"Why don't you get her now and ask her yourself, Ryan?" Peter challenged.

"Ask me what?" Avery had walked into the room. She sensed that she was being talked about; the tiny hairs on her neck were standing straight up.

Korinna walked towards Avery and took her hand. She then looked at Ryan and Steve. "We must leave them alone now." Avery felt her heart quicken. Still holding her hand, Korinna looked deeply into Avery's eyes. "I thank you in advance for giving this precious gift back to Peter." She then gently let go and motioned for the two men to follow her out of the room.

Ryan was furious. Sparks were shooting off his body. Korinna grabbed his arm and pulled it hard. "Out now!" she commanded. Ryan had never seen his sweet mother so forceful. He knew she meant business. Like a chastised dog with his tail between his legs, he followed her.

The two of them stood there, each afraid to be the first one to speak. Avery could already feel the sparks intensifying. She stared at the tiny silver tooth fairy box. It seemed like forever ago when they were in the attic. She felt so guilty. Her feelings for Peter were strong, but what she felt for Ryan was beyond strong. It was like someone had attached her heart to a kite string and let it soar. And the harder she tried to ignore it, the more intense it became.

Peter finally broke the silence. "I really appreciate you doing this for me." His cheeks felt hot, and he willed himself to keep his emotions in check.

"Peter, you know I would do anything for you." She walked closer, her eyes trying to fixate on the box rather on his sad eyes. "I know you will only use your powers when absolutely necessary. I am just so sorry that you had to wait so long for them."

Peter shrugged his shoulders. "I don't know. I kind of liked being a normal kid."

At the word normal, Avery seemed to freeze. She realized just how not normal she really was, and now the same would apply to Peter. "Are you sure you want to go through with this? Your life will be forever changed. It will be more difficult, and from what we are witnessing, very dangerous. You can tell your mom that you've changed your mind and do not want the powers. I know that she will understand."

"This is what I want," Peter said. "It is crucial for me to receive my powers. If what Anastasia is saying is really that horrible, then one more of us could not hurt. Besides, maybe now I can use my powers to win you back." Peter laughed, but Avery knew that it hurt like hell for him to see her with Ryan.

"I guess you have made up your mind." Avery walked to the entrance of the family room. She raised her palm and waved it towards the opening. Instantly, the room was sealed from the outside, allowing them total privacy.

"This looks pretty serious," Peter chuckled, trying to cover up his extreme nervousness.

Avery shook her head solemnly. "It is Peter. Contrary to popular belief, I never had to do anything like this before." She laughed softly. "I just thought that I was the only non-mortal kid living in suburbia. Boy, *was* I wrong." Avery took a deep breath and then let it out slowly. "In truth, I am terrified. No, let me restate that, I am more than terrified; I am utterly petrified." She took his hand in her own, and one by one, began to unclench his fingers that held the tiny tooth fairy box safely in place. She let her pointer finger outline the fairy that sat on top, protecting the crystal. "What if something happens to you? I could never forgive myself," Avery murmured. "Maybe you should just let things remain the same. Ryan and I can handle everyth..."

Peter roughly pulled away from her. "That is not the way it is going to be. I deserve to have my powers. I was born into this family as a warlock, and I demand I be given my rights." Avery knew that she had said the wrong thing to him. *I am forever saying the wrong thing*, she thought.

"I am sorry," she said softly. "You are right. She gently removed the box from his hand and opened the lid. "Are you ready?"

"Ready as I'll ever be," Peter said grimly. Avery traced the tiny, faded scar on Peter's palm with her finger. "Wait. If I was born a warlock, then why do I bleed red?"

Avery paused. She did not have an answer to that question. But as soon as her mouth opened to tell him that she didn't know why, other words spilled out. "Your mom used her powers to change the silvery liquid into mortal blood. She didn't ever want to risk that your real identity would be revealed." Avery knew that Korinna could hear her son, even though she had sealed them off from the others. And she could read Korinna's mind as well! Their connection was becoming stronger.

"I guess that makes sense," Peter agreed, although deep down inside, he felt the resentment that something had been stolen from him for so many years.

"Don't think that way. Your mom only did it for your safety." *Now I'm reading Peter's mind!* "I will need to reopen this," she said in a barely audible voice. "It is going to hurt a lot." The thought made Avery pause. "Peter, I just can't. How can I hurt you when I consider you my best friend?"

"I will be fine, Avery. I promise you," Peter assured her. Having his hand sliced open could not compare to the hurt that he felt from hearing the word "friend" from Avery's mouth. "Just do it quickly, kind of like ripping off a Band-Aid." He smiled. Staying mad at Avery was just not an option for him.

Avery returned the smile and took a deep breath. "Here goes everything." She placed the crystal that was embedded in her own palm over the scar and squeezed tightly. The instant heat that Peter felt was overwhelming. He sucked in his breath, and he could feel his eyes rolling back in his head. Avery saw the panic that crossed his face and paused.

Peter clamped his hand down harder. "Don't stop!" he managed to utter between gasps. They remained bonded for exactly sixty seconds, but for Peter, it seemed endless. Finally, Avery drew her hand back. Gazing down, Peter could see a gaping incision. Blood flowed freely. Red blood.

Avery used the bottom of her shirt to blot at it gently. "The first part is finished," she whispered. "Peter, you must know that what is about to follow will be a million times more difficult. Are you sure you are ready?"

Peter nodded. "Let's begin."

The crystal was tiny, but already it began to pulsate in Avery's hand. She trembled, not sure how to proceed. But the crystal seemed to have a mind of its own. As if by some magnetic force, it pulled Avery to Peter once more. She covered the crystal over the incision and pressed down tenderly. The crimson liquid that was oozing out the sides of the cut instantly became silver. Avery looked into Peter's eyes and smiled. It was working!

The sudden bond between them was indescribable. Her lips went to his, and electricity flowed between them. His lips were full, and they met hers eagerly. Their bodies were on fire. The room was illuminated with silver light as the two remained locked in each other's arms. Peter pulled back for a second only to murmur the words, "I love you." Avery, her eyes staring into his, responded with the same words. Peter's hands roamed freely, and the pleasure Avery was feeling intensified with each touch.

Suddenly, as quickly as they had come together, the two were violently forced apart. Avery was thrown against the wall. Peter cried out as his feet buckled under him, his broken leg looking like a discarded rag doll. Out of breath, Avery ran to him. "Peter!" she screamed. "Answer me, are you okay?" The wind had been knocked out of him, but a smile began to spread across his face. He held out his palm. There, looking as if it had always belonged, was the crystal, neatly and safely embedded in Peter's palm. "Congratulations," Avery said.

Peter picked at the dried silver liquid that had crusted up around the crystal. "So, does this mean I am now a full-fledged warlock?"

Avery nodded. "Full-fledged." She began to smile, but it quickly faded when she saw his leg. "Just this once," she whispered. She inched forward to place her palm on the twisted leg.

"No, let me." Peter began to move his palm closer to his leg, but the power from the crystal shot out like a rocket, and in a flash, Peter's leg was totally healed. The cast had split open, and his leg looked like new.

"Wow!" Avery exclaimed in amazement. "You didn't even have to touch the crystal to your leg." The realization of this was sobering. "Peter, you must be aware that your powers are the strongest of all of ours combined."

It was both exciting and a little bit unsettling for Peter to hear Avery say that. He sat there, staring at her beautiful face, aching to hold her again.

Reading his mind, Avery stood up. "Uh, I have to go and tell everyone that the process is complete," she said. "I am sure they are wondering what is going on in here," she laughed nervously.

"Avery!" Peter called after her. "Please don't go. Not yet. I think we need to talk about what happened to us in here."

Avery shook her head. "I can't talk about it, and please, if you really do care, please don't mention it to anyone."

"But it did happen, and what we felt was real."

"Peter," Avery said gently. "You know that I care for you deeply, but I just don't feel the same way that you feel for me. What happened was a result of the crystal's powers."

"But you said it back. I heard you," he insisted stubbornly.

Avery lowered her head. "Yes," she whispered softly. "Yes, I suppose I did.

Avery used her crystal to unseal the doorway. Six pairs of eyes were staring at the two as they faced the group. No words were spoken but Avery and Peter knew exactly what was on their minds. *Did it work?* Only Ryan was thinking of something else. He could feel the tension that was bouncing off their bodies and onto his. He knew something had gone on in there. Korinna was the first to rush up to the pair. She gently took Peter's hand and kissed the crystal. "Welcome to the Sethos clan."

Talia embraced her daughter and murmured, "Thank you for doing this." She, too, could sense that something was not right. Her daughter was subdued, and her body trembled as her mom hugged her tightly.

"Mom," Avery whispered. "His powers are the strongest I have ever seen. I am scared for him."

"Me too, Avery. Me too."

Ben slapped Peter on the back. "I am still going to kick your butt in basketball, crystal or no crystal," he joked.

Peter hugged his father. "Thank you for letting me receive my powers. I know this must have been really hard on you." Korinna and Ben exchanged looks. *If only he knew how difficult it was*, they thought simultaneously. They both knew that his life would never be the same. Danger lay ahead, and Peter, displaying the strongest powers, was going to be the primary target in Darius' plan.

"Congratulations, bro," Ryan mumbled. He shook Peter's hand and then, with the left, took Avery's. Avery could feel her face redden.

"I must go back now," Anastasia said, walking up to Peter. "I am certain that Darius is crazy with anger that I have not returned. There will be consequences for my delayed return."

The group was silent. By looking at Anastasia's gaping wounds, they knew only too well what those consequences would be.

"Don't go," Avery begged, running up to her and holding her tightly. "Stay with us. Now with Peter, our powers are unbeatable. Darius won't be able to hurt you anymore."

Anastasia shook her head. "If only it was that simple," she murmured. "But there is a beautiful girl that I must protect."

"A girl?" questioned Korinna.

A small smile crossed Anastasia's face. It felt like forever since she had last smiled. "Her name is Leah, and she is the only bright light in the darkness in which I exist."

"You do have a daughter!" said Avery excitedly. "How old is she? When do I get to meet her?"

"Avery! Slow down and give Anastasia a chance to talk," Talia once again scolded her daughter.

"She is a year younger than you, Avery. She just turned sixteen five days ago. We had a party for her."

"That must have been fun," Avery said.

Anastasia's smile faded. "Actually, I shouldn't even call it a party. There were no friends, just Darius, the servants, and me. But being the sweetest girl, Leah still had a great time. Darius has kept her like a prisoner. She has never been outside of the twenty feet high gated walls."

"But what about school?" Talia asked.

"Darius homeschools her. He uses the servants' and my powers to educate himself and then bestows his worldly knowledge on Leah." Anastasia laughed bitterly. "He makes himself out to be this amazing scholar. He has taught Leah five different languages, read to her Homer's Iliad and Odyssey, showed her how to solve the most rigorous calculus equations, and how to memorize the Periodic Table. She worships the ground that he walks on."

Anastasia placed her hand on her neck. "When I am around Leah, I must cover my wounds. The servants must do the same."

"Around Leah? What do you mean around? Aren't you her mother? Aren't you around her all the time?" Korinna questioned her sister.

"No, I am given limited time allotments. After the time is up, the servants bring me back to my room, where I must remain until summoned again."

"I do not understand this," said Korinna. "Why would Darius prevent a daughter from being with her mother?"

Anastasia closed her eyes and said with the softest voice, "Because I am not her mother."

Chapter 34

"Why would you want that for your daughter, Darius?" Alec questioned. "Can't you see how our powers have destroyed everything good in our lives?"

"The only thing that was ever good in my life was the birth of my daughter," Darius retorted. "And I will give her the power so that every second of her day will be amazing. She will lack for nothing, even if it means destroying everyone else."

Alec knew the gravity of the situation. Lives were at stake. If there was one thing that he could now do for redemption, it was to save the people in his life that mattered to him. He thought about Talia and Avery. Guilt began to seep into his pores until his inner core was racked with remorse. *What have I done?* He found himself thinking back to that dark night that determined the fate of all of them. He realized how deadly wrong his actions were. How could Talia not have retaliated? He and Darius were attacking her. In their warped game for total control, they were forcing themselves upon her. It made him sick to think about that horrific night. It was now his duty to save them as well. Darius' childhood game had not ended; it was only spinning more out of control.

"Don't look so shocked, Alec. On the day Anastasia went into labor, I was there holding her hand like any other dutiful husband. A midwife came to the house. Clearly, we could not go to a hospital. It was a long and excruciating ten hours for Anastasia, but all I could think about was seeing the face of my beautiful baby girl."

"But, you had to have known that there was a 50 percent chance the baby would be a boy." Alec stated.

"That was not an option," Darius jeered. There was such a venomous edge to the words he had just uttered that Alec could almost taste the poison that seemed to fill the air. "Finally, just as the clock struck three o'clock am, I heard the most wonderful sound. It was the sound of a newborn baby crying. I pushed the midwife aside, and there I was greeted with the most revolting sight. Gazing into my eyes was a baby boy!"

"But Darius, it was a beautiful baby that you and Anastasia created together. How could you have felt that way?"

Darius let out a loud laugh. "We all know that the only reason you had Ryan was to get revenge on Talia. To make matters worse, you manipulated Korinna to use her powers to have a boy. Don't you dare act all righteous with me!"

Alec closed his mouth. He knew that he was on the precipice of disaster. The pain that still racked his body was enough to tell him to be quiet.

"I prayed for him to greet the world in silence. But there he was, piercing the quiet with a hideous cry. The midwife offered for me to cut the cord, but I was repulsed by the sight. I turned my back and let her complete the task. My wife was sobbing quietly. She knew that she had betrayed me by having a boy. The midwife then proceeded to clean him off and wrapped him in the pink blanket that lay near the bed. She walked closer to the edge of the bed. Anastasia's arms reached out in longing to embrace her newborn son."

Alec remained quiet. He did not want to hear anymore. It was all too sickening. He knew that he was not innocent, but compared to his brother, he felt like an altar boy.

Darius' voice became higher, almost hysterical in nature. The words spilled out at an alarming rate. His face was glowing. "I snatched the baby from the midwife and ordered her to leave immediately. The terror on her face was priceless. Anastasia was screaming for her son. It was rather a quite unpleasant noise if I do say so myself."

Alec watched as his brother began to pace. The veins on his neck bulged, and it looked as though he was going to explode. It was terrifying, but he needed to know what Darius did next. The only way was to placate his brother and agree with everything he had done. Calmly, Alec took a deep breath. "I do not blame you at all, Darius, for what you did." At those words, Darius stopped dead in his tracks. The veins stilled, and he suddenly seemed subdued.

Pretending to be on Darius' side was the only thing that Alec knew would allow him to extract the deadly information from his brother's warped mind. "I do not blame you one bit at all for what you have done," he repeated in a reassuring voice. "You had no choice, my dear brother." He could feel the servants' eyes boring into him as he spoke his lies, and he prayed that his brother would not be able to use his powers to read his mind.

Darius seemed to relax. His features almost became boy-like as he motioned Alec to come closer. He put his arms around his brother and sobbed. "I knew that you would understand, Alec. I had no choice. The baby had to go."

The bile again began to rise in Alec's mouth, but when he cast his eyes towards the servants, he could almost hear them saying, "just go along with it, for everyone's sake." He let himself be embraced by his brother until the sobs subsided. Darius then released himself and took his brother's hand. "Come. Sit, so I may continue my story." With an abrupt flick of the wrist, he dismissed the servants. Alec could feel his heart begin to pound. He feared being alone with his brother. He turned his face towards the servants, his eyes pleading for help. But they averted his gaze and obediently left the room. Darius was an intelligent man, and they did not want to rouse suspicion.

"Now, where did I leave off? Ahh, yes, having Anastasia's darling little boy ripped from her arms." Darius shifted in his chair.

"These are quite comfortable. Only the finest for me and, of course, my dear Leah."

The wait was excruciating, but Alec knew better than to interrupt his brother when he was speaking. "Of course, only the best for you, Darius. You certainly deserve it."

Darius tilted his head to the side, not sure if Alec was mocking him. But then vanity took hold of him again and he continued. "The boy. He was the most disgusting little creature I had ever laid eyes on. Wailing on and on. It was ungodly the way he carried on. And then there was Anastasia. Her sobbing, I would have to say, was even more despicable." Darius paused and then let out a high-pitched laugh. "Especially when she realized she was never going to see her son again." Alec used every ounce of energy to remain silent. He could not fathom that this monster was his brother! As if reading his mind, Darius moved his chair closer to Alec's. "Oh, Alec, you actually didn't think that I would not let Anastasia get one last look at her son, did you? Come now, I am not that much of a meanie that you make me out to be."

He was being baited. Alec knew that Darius would just love to exert his powers over him again, so he continued to remain calm, taking shallow breaths to ease his racing mind.

"I held the boy out for Anastasia to take a final look. It was so much fun to watch her as she lay in bed trying to reach out for him, begging me to let her hold her newborn son. I moved him in closer until her fingertips barely grazed his shriveled skin and then took the utmost delight in jerking him back again. Even though I found him to be quite repulsive, I must admit he was quite the handsome young fella. A shock of wavy hair fell across his forehead, and when he wasn't squeezing his eyes shut, he revealed two dark green marbles."

"Sounds like he looked just like us," Alec said softly.

Darius clapped his hands together. "Exactly! And that is why I instantly knew that he must be destroyed!"

Alec wanted to cover his ears at the word *destroyed*. He knew that his brother had great malice, but he could not fathom that he would destroy a newborn baby, let alone the baby that his wife had just birthed. "Surely, that was just a fleeting thought. I know deep down inside you are too much of a good person to perform such a horrendous act of evil."

Darius let out a laugh. His eyes narrowed into slits. "There is no goodness left in me. That died when you all abandoned me on that mountain."

"You have it all wrong, Darius. We did not abandon you. By law, we could not change your fate. It killed me to see you lying there. It devastated me so much that I swore I would avenge your death. My whole life was devoted to making things right again. And as a result, I have lost everything that mattered to me. You must believe me."

Darius sprang to his feet. "I do not care about what you have lost. Your losses are insignificant," he spat. "My plan is in motion, and not you or anyone else will alter it." He sat back down again. "Now let's get back to the night that my darling little boy was born. As you said, the boy looked exactly like us. However, looking into those green eyes, I felt only hatred. It was the sheer hatred of seeing us and what we had let a woman do. If it were not for Talia, none of this would have happened. She taunted and teased us. She played games with our emotions. She wanted us to chase her."

Alec shook his head. "That is not how it happened. We teased and taunted her. We chased her." Alec was quiet. He then murmured, "We are to blame for what had happened."

He was on the floor before he knew what had happened. Darius was gripping his neck, choking him. What was left from the powers he had sucked from his servants was clearly enough to strangle him. "She is to blame! We were merely pawns in her game. And that is why I could not have a son. What if my own son ended up like us, his whole life ruined because of a woman? I would not allow that."

Alec was losing consciousness. He saw his entire life flash before him, the ugliness overshadowing anything that was remotely good. He welcomed death, and he said a silent prayer for forgiveness. Just as his eyelids closed for the last time, Darius let go. Alec's gasped for air, his body heaving in spasms.

"I am not going to give you the satisfaction of dying," Darius hissed. "You are going to hear the whole story, and then you are going to continue to help me carry out my plan." Alec's own breaths were suffocating him. His coughs came out only as shallow moans and saliva rolled down his chin. "I ordered my servants to take the boy and carry him to the top of Oros Mountain. They were to dig a small grave and bury him next to my own."

Alec vomited. He did not want to hear anymore. Darius grabbed him by the hair and snapped his head back. "I know what you are thinking. How could I bury my own son alive?" Darius let out one of his hysterical laughs. "I am not that heartless. I first ordered my servants to smother the infant with his own baby blanket and then gently wrap him in it before laying him in the cold hard ground. The same cold hard ground in which I was laid."

Darius looked at his brother. "You do look like a mess. How about you go upstairs and clean up, and we will continue in about an hour." Darius called for his servants to take Alec upstairs. He was not going to take any chances of his brother escaping. He knew too much, and he was not going to let him get in the way.

The servants forced their hands under Alec's armpits and dragged him up the stairs. Their looks told him to go along. Once inside, Orion took out a small pad of paper and a pencil. He wrote: Do not answer us with words. Just nod to acknowledge what we are telling you. Remember, Darius is listening. Alec nodded. The servant ripped off the piece of paper and with the crystal in his pinky ring burned it into ashes. They began to speak in booming voices. Alec cast them a bewildered look. The servant had just told him that Darius was listening.

Reading his mind, Orion held his pinky ring to his mouth. The words that spilled out were harsh. So harsh, that Darius would be quite pleased with his dutiful servants. But, by the time Alec's eardrums received them, they sounded quite different. "The boy lives."

Alec opened his mouth, but again Orion brought his pinky ring up to his mouth. "We couldn't bring ourselves to carry out such a hideous act. We decided that whatever happened to us, should Darius find out what we had done, would be worth it in order to save the life of the innocent child. We climbed the mountain. I held the swaddled infant tightly in my arms. I could feel his tiny heart beating, and it felt like raindrops on my chest. We dug a small grave and placed his blanket in it. And then, gazing around the mountaintop, we found what we had been looking for. There in the corner, lay the skeleton of a small animal. We were almost certain that Darius would not come to *visit* his deceased son's body, but we had to make sure. We wrapped the blanket around the skeleton and then covered it with dirt."

Alec's mind was racing. There were so many questions, but he knew that asking them now would bring danger to all three of them.

The other servant named, Tereus continued. "I then removed my tunic and began to wrap the baby in it. And that's when I saw them."

The sharp rap on the door brought the servants and Alec to their feet. "Open this door immediately before I break it down!" hissed Darius. "What is going on in here? You are taking entirely too long to change, Alec."

"I had to take a shower. You didn't want me to come downstairs smelling like puke, did you?"

Darius looked around the room. "Where are my servants?"

"After they so rudely shoved me into the room and took a few free punches at me, they disappeared. They really do worship you." Alec hoped that his voice did not convey the lies that he was telling his brother. Before they left, just to make it look it look authentic, the servants each landed a blow to Alec's face. Alec knew that enduring the pain was the price he had to pay for what he had just learned.

Satisfied that everything seemed to be in place, Darius took him by the elbow and led him downstairs. The grip he had on him was forceful enough to let his brother know that he meant business. He led Alec into to the dining room where the table was set for twelve. "Are we having company?" Alec asked.

Darius laughed. "No. Usually it's just Leah and me, but tonight she will eat in her room. I always have the servants set the table fit for a king since I am so deserving of that title."

"What about Anastasia? Doesn't she eat with you and Leah?" A blow struck Alec's left shoulder.

"I told you that I forbid you to speak of Leah and Anastasia together in the same breath! Do I finally make myself clear?" Alec nodded, his shoulder throbbing. "Now, sit so that we may eat and continue our discussion." He rang the bell, and the two servants came out carrying large platters of food. They avoided Alec's eyes and quietly placed the delicious offerings of food on their plates.

"That will be all," Darius said as he dismissed the servants with a wave of his hand. The servants bowed and left the room. "Where were we? Finally, the part that I love to speak about. My darling Leah." Darius' face softened as he spoke his daughter's name. "After I ordered the servants to take away that insipid newborn, I too, left the house. I could still hear Anastasia's desperate pleas for me to change my mind about our son." At the word *son*, Darius' face turned into a twisted grimace. "There would be no son in my house! I traveled to the outskirts of town. I knew that there was an abundance of women who lived in poverty. Many of them were not married and pregnant. I must have been there for three hours or so, inspecting this disgusting lot, when I finally came across *her*. She was lying on a small patch of grass that had somehow been overlooked when the rest of the street was paved. Her hair was matted and dirty, but I could see that it had once been golden. Her clothes were ragged, her skin dull. She lay motionless with her back toward me as I walked over to her. And then I saw *it*. At first, I didn't know whether the baby was a boy or a girl. The infant was wrapped in a rag; it looked like the mother had just given birth. There was no sound coming from either of them. I wondered if they might both be dead." Darius laughed, "I actually said a little prayer that just the mother would be dead. How absurd is that? Me, praying! But my task would be that much easier to complete." Darius looked at his brother. It delighted him when he saw Alec's horrified expression.

"Was she?" Alec asked, knowing that his brother reveled in having a captivated audience, and by Alec asking questions, it only made him more ecstatic. He was like a child, wanting center attention and pouting and stamping his feet in a temper tantrum when he did not get his way.

Darius frowned. "No such luck. As I bent down to take a closer look at the infant, the mother sprang to her knees, like a tiger ready to pounce on its prey. I could see her face then. It was streaked with blood and dirt, and she looked exhausted. But I could see that she was once beautiful. She held the baby tighter to her chest, and I could see the faint rising and falling of the infant's body. I knew then that the mother had certainly just given birth."

Darius paused and looked at his brother. Alec knew that this was his turn to ask another question. This game was sickening to him, but there was no other way to get answers. "Was the baby a girl or boy?"

"As if reading my mind, the mother looked up at me and said, 'I've named her Leah.' I peeled back the rag and saw the most exquisite face. She was perfect. Her lips were tiny rose buds, and her cheeks smooth and round. As if on cue, she opened her eyes. They were like two robin's eggs, the kind of blue that you knew would never change color. Her eyes fluttered, and then she returned to her slumber. The mother smiled weakly at me. I could sense the exhaustion that childbirth had caused her. I grasped the mother's hand. It was cold to the touch. Her fingers were long and slender, and I felt her desperately trying to hold on for her baby's sake. Her breaths were now labored. It was then that I saw blood pooling around her legs. 'Take good care of her,' she said to me, and her lifeless hand slipped from mine."

"And she died, just like that?" Alec asked incredulously.

Immediately, he felt the blow. "Do you question my integrity, my dear brother? How could you think that I could ever take that sweet child away from her mother?" At his own words, Darius began to laugh uncontrollably. "Contrary to what you may think, the woman *did* die on her own. Of course, her untimely and sad demise just made it easier for me. I know you want to ask me whether I would have taken the child against the mother's will. I will leave you to form your own answer to that question." Darius stood up and walked over to the huge portrait of his daughter that hung over the fireplace. "And the rest is history," he said with a lilt in his voice. "I have raised Leah as my own, and of course, she doesn't know that Anastasia is not her real mother."

"But when will you tell her the truth? Don't you think she has a right to know?"

"She will never need to discover that ugly fact because, you see, Leah will not have a mother for long."

Alec felt the hairs stand up straight all over his body.

"And when that time comes, I will be the one to stand by and comfort my daughter, the future Queen of the Universe."

Chapter 35

A myriad of emotions swirled through the air as Anastasia unraveled her devastating tale. Repulsion shook her sister's body as she spoke about her newborn son being abruptly snatched away from her and sent to die. Tears flowed down Avery, Korinna, and Talia's cheeks when she told the group how she didn't even get to kiss her baby boy. Anger wracked the men's bodies as she spoke about Darius leaving her that day to find a "replacement" baby.

"I wanted to die. There was nothing left for me. I can remember lifting myself out of bed and walking over to my full-length mirror. What had he done to me? My hair was cut short and made silver, my eyes were turned into vacant holes, and the gaps that were oozing silver liquid were pulsating. I took whatever energy I had left in my pinky ring and shattered the mirror into a thousand pieces. I continued to stare at my reflection. The torture that I saw was multiplied by the sliced fragments still held in place by the gilded frame. I was transfixed, immobilized. Suddenly, I could hear him calling me, '*Mama, Mama! I am hungry!*' He was whimpering, and I knew that my baby needed me. I deftly removed one of the jagged pieces from the frame and brought it up to my neck. It would be over in a flash, and we would be together for eternity. No more pain, no more suffering, just my baby and me."

Anastasia stopped speaking. Her eyes were closed, and her fingers were clenched tightly. "That's when he came in."

"'What is this?' I remember shouting at him. He told me that she was our daughter and that my duty would be to love her and cherish her forever. I tried to hand her back to him, but he pushed her into my arms. I did not want to look into her beautiful blue eyes, I did not want to breathe in her powdery baby scent, and I certainly did not want to see her lips making tiny sucking noises. But I did, and my desire to end my life subsided just a tiny bit. Darius gently backed out of the room, telling me that I should get to know our daughter. I just stared at him in disbelief. Was this the same man that just hours ago ordered our son to be killed? I knew that he was insane, and I feared for my life. But most importantly, I feared for this little girl's life. I knew how desperately he wanted a daughter. I remember feeling chills cascading down my spine because I knew he had some warped plan for her future. I brought Leah to my breast and nursed her, quietly promising that I would never let any evil come to her."

"But I still don't see why you were prohibited from spending all the time you wanted with her?" Avery questioned.

"It was part of Darius' devious plan," replied Anastasia. "At first, he made sure that Leah and I were inseparable. Darius brought in the most magnificent rocking chair, and I nursed her in that chair every three hours. A nanny would come in to change her and then hand her back to me. I told Darius that I was capable of bathing and diapering my daughter, but he insisted that my job was to sit in that chair and bond with her." Anastasia reached into her pocket and pulled out a faded and tattered photo. It was of her and Leah sleeping peacefully in the rocking chair. "This is the only picture that I have of her. After that, I was forbidden to be in any more pictures with her."

Korinna shook her head. "I still don't understand."

"When Leah turned six months old, I noticed Darius beginning to separate the two of us. He insisted that I stop nursing, and he was the one to give her the bottle. I was only allowed to put her to sleep two nights a week. The other nights, Darius would sing to her and rock her to sleep. I questioned him only once, and once was more than enough." Anastasia rolled up her sleeve. A jagged scar made its way down from her shoulder to her wrist. "He managed to save a piece of the shattered mirror, just in case. And as I was bleeding, Darius told me that the only thing I was needed for was to give Leah the strength to survive her first few months. She was so weak when she first arrived. My milk gave her the vital nutrients she so desperately craved."

Korinna ran to her sister. "You don't have to tell us anymore. Stay here. We will protect you."

But Anastasia again shook her head. "No, I must go back. Even though I do not get to see much of her, I still love her. It is my duty to protect her. Leah has no idea that one day she will be persuaded by her dear father to use her powers for evil. For now, she is just a carefree sixteen-year-old who loves her father immensely." She smiled slightly. "And I know she also loves me."

Talia looked puzzled. "But you said that Leah was not born a witch. She does not possess powers."

Anastasia was silent. This was the part she dreaded the most. She fixed her gaze on the three young adults that stood in front of her. She was shaking and felt like she was going to faint. Her voice was a whisper. "I can't tell you."

"You must," Korinna said softly. "They need to know of the dangers that lie before them."

She leaned on her sister for support, and then with a voice that sounded as thin as tissue paper, she said, "He plans on destroying all of you who have powers so Leah can complete the first stage of becoming a witch. First, he intends to release all your crystals' energy into her body. And then, the crystal that I was sent to find, Peter's crystal, will ultimately be embedded into her palm." She looked at Peter. "Yours is clearly the most powerful."

No one moved. The realization that they were dealing with a madman had finally hit them all. Fear flashed across Steve's face. "I will never let anyone hurt my family. I will die before that happens." Ben nodded in agreement.

Finally, Talia spoke. "How could even that work? She was not born a witch. How could he just think that using the crystals' energy and embedding a crystal into her palm would make her one?" she asked.

Anastasia shook her head. "These are his intentions. He is a madman. I have heard him rant and rave enough times to know that he seriously believes that this will work. He does not realize that he could kill his own daughter. Our daughter."

There was complete silence. The room seemed to spin around them.

"We have to destroy him!" It was Ryan's booming voice that finally broke the silence. The group turned to see him clenching his hands into tight-fisted balls. "I am ashamed that Alec is my father, but I am even more ashamed that Darius is my uncle." He looked at Korinna, Steve, and Talia. "I will never hurt you again."

Anastasia continued to speak. "I must now go back and tell Darius that I could not find the crystal. She turned and embraced her sister. "Or you."

The group looked at her, knowing what she was thinking. Fear was painted on all their faces.

"And I pray to God, he believes me."

Chapter 36

"Had I come home a minute too late, my dear Anastasia would have been spewing silver liquid all over our beautiful bedroom carpet." Darius let out a giggle that reminded Alec of that of a schoolboy. But coming out of his brother's mouth, it was hideous and demented. "And a good thing, too. The crystal in her pinky ring was of the utmost importance to my entire plan. I could not bear to think of her powers going to waste. And so, being the dutiful husband that I was, I placed my darling little daughter in her outstretched arms. At least that *wife* of mine was good for something; she was able to nurse Leah back to health."

"When is Mother coming home?" Leah asked her father as she joined Alec and him in the living room for a cup of tea.

"Soon, my darling." Darius cooed to his daughter. His voice had become normal again, and his mannerisms were those of a doting father. "Why don't you show Uncle Alec how you play the piano?"

Leah played beautifully, and Alec was in awe of his niece. How could Darius turn her into something evil?

The sun had set, and the moon rose high in the sky. Anastasia still had not returned. Darius had to stifle his disgust for his wife and continued to reassure his daughter that she would be home any moment. They heard the door open at the same time, and before Darius could hold his daughter back, she ran into her mother's arms.

"I have missed you so much!" Leah said, with her hands clasped around her mother's waist in a tight hug.

"And I have missed you," Anastasia murmured back softly. She was warned time and time again not to give Leah too much love. *It will only hurt her more in the long run,* Darius would tell her.

"We have a visitor, Mother!" Leah said excitedly. "Come in and see who it is!"

Anastasia let her daughter lead her into the living room. She had no idea who would be visiting them. No one ever came to the house to visit. It was a fortress, and they were Darius' prisoners. It only took one glimpse at the man standing next to Darius to know who he was. They looked almost identical. The dark green eyes met hers.

"You must be Anastasia." Alec tried with all his will to fight back the tears. He had done horrible things in his life, but there was no comparison to what Darius had done to his wife. She looked nothing like the pictures that Korinna had shown him of her sister.

"And you must be Alec," Anastasia answered. She could see why her sister had fallen madly in love with him. Although he and Darius were twins and looked very much alike, Alec stood a good three inches taller than his brother. His hair was thicker and blacker, and his eyes were the deepest green she had ever seen. He took her breath away. But then reality sunk in. She had heard the horrific stories her sister had told her about Alec's plot to seek revenge against Talia and her family. *Two brothers, two monsters.* Although she knew that it was all Darius' doing, it did not allay her disgust for him.

"Well, well, well, this is such a happy family reunion. All we need is Korinna, and our family circle will be complete. Anastasia, do you know when she will be arriving?"

Anastasia froze. When the servants had left her on the mountain, they had seen her pretend to torture her sister. Her "job" was to bring her sister and the crystal back to him. She was gone longer than she should have been, and she knew that Darius would be suspicious. *This is it,* she thought. *I am backed into a corner with no way out.* She opened her mouth to speak, but from the corner of her eye, she saw the servants point to her crystal in her pinky ring. She looked down at the crystal. Swirling above was one tiny word... *Lie.* Momentarily confused, Anastasia gathered up all the courage she could muster and said in her sweetest voice, "How would I know when Korinna would be arriving when I have not seen my sister in years?" When she looked back down at the ring, the word had vanished. From the corner of her eye, she could see the servants nodding in approval. *Could they be on my side?* She wondered.

Darius frowned, defeat visibly clear on his face. "Then it will just be the three of us catching up on old times."

"What about me, Father?" Leah asked. "I want to hear all the happy stories of your childhood."

"Not tonight, my darling. Uncle Alec, your mom, and I have much reminiscing. Perhaps tomorrow you can join in the conversation. Now come here and give your father a goodnight kiss." Leah kissed Darius on the cheek. But before leaving, she bent over and hugged and kissed Anastasia. Alec could sense the rage that was building up inside Darius as he witnessed this show of affection.

"I am so happy you are home." Anastasia accepted her daughter's kiss and hug but did not return the affection. Darius' words echoed in her ears… *It would only make things more difficult in the long run.*

"Now, stop stalling, my dear Leah. Up to bed you go." Leah quietly ascended the stairs.

In a flash, Darius' demeanor changed. His mouth curled into a snarl. "Where is Korinna? I sent the three of you to that mountain. She was there!" He screamed at his wife.

"Please, Darius," Anastasia whispered, backing herself into a corner. "I told you. I did not see her."

Clearly not satisfied with her answer, Darius used the remaining stored energy in his crystal to inflict pain. Anastasia moaned as her body shook in spasms. "And the crystal? Where is it? You were gone far too long! Where have you been?" He seethed.

"I tried to find the crystal, but there was something stronger blocking my way." She hoped that she sounded convincing; her life depended upon it. "I used my powers to envision where it or my sister might be, but all I saw in my crystal was a haze."

Darius paused for a moment. His anger seemed to have abated and Anastasia internally let out a sigh of relief. "Well, if that clearly is the case, my dear wife, then you are certainly not needed anymore." His voice was so calm that it created an eerie presence in the room. "You knew that this time would eventually arise. However, I didn't think it would be this soon." Darius let out a laugh. He rubbed his chin, as if deciding what to do next. "What will I tell Leah? She will be devastated. But she will survive. I will be there for her."

As Darius' words spilled out of his mouth, Alec could see the terror flashing in Anastasia's eyes. *Why didn't she use her crystal against Darius?* He thought. Suddenly it hit him... *She must have exhausted her powers for something; something so important that she would risk her own life.* He was now certain that this was the time for his redemption.

Darius grabbed Anastasia by the wrist and yanked the crystal pinky ring off her finger. Silver liquid oozed from her finger. "It is worthless. Just like you!" He spat. He threw the ring to the floor and, with his foot smashed the crystal into pieces. Tiny sparks flew into the air. "Servants, take her out back and do away with her! Bring back her heart so I can see for sure that she is truly dead."

Shocked, the servants exchanged glances. They knew that it was their job to obey their master. They also knew that if Darius found out that they were secretly betraying him, they would surely be tortured to death. And what about Leah? The two had grown to love her and vowed long ago that they would do anything to protect her from her father's plot. There was nothing they could do to help Anastasia. They walked towards the woman and grabbed her as Darius released his hold. They held her firm while they began to lead her out of the room, but Anastasia could hear them whisper in a barely audible voice, "We are so sorry."

Chapter 37

It was getting late, and the day's events had taken a toll on the group. Talia could see how tired everyone looked. "I think we need to call it a night," she said. "You all have to be up very early for school tomorrow."

"Mom!" Avery protested. "How can we just climb into our *safe* little beds when we know about Darius' plan? Anastasia is in danger. We all are."

Korinna stepped forward. "Your mother is right."

"But how can we just go to school and pretend none of this has happened?" asked Peter.

"Yeah, I agree with Peter on this," Ryan chimed in.

"Because I am your mother, and what I say, goes." Korinna went over and wrapped her arms around the boys.

"Korinna, you are welcome to stay with us," Steve said.

"For as long as you want," Talia added.

Ben walked over to the trio. He had been quiet for most of the day, but now he was shaking his head adamantly. "Thank you for the offer, but Korinna and Ryan are coming with Peter and me. They are coming home with us because that's where they belong."

Chapter 38

"My dear brother," Alec said. "Please let me help the servants carry out your wishes. I would love nothing more than to prove my complete and utter devotion to you." The words stuck in Alec's throat like daggers, but he knew that this was his only chance to try to right all his wrongs.

"I am so pleased that you finally see it my way. Of course. You may even partake in the killing if you so wish. Just make sure that you tidy up before you come back into the house. Feel free to shower in the pool house's bathroom. I am sure you will also find clothes that will suit you perfectly in the guest room's closet. I would hate to see my poor deceased wife's blood on your hands."

The four left the house, Alec leading the way. He took them past the pool and pool house, where a row of tall olive trees swayed gently in the warm breeze. The sky was clear, with millions of stars twinkling in the moonlight. Anastasia looked up and closed her eyes tightly. She had one wish... *Please let all those entangled in Darius' devious web be protected.*

The servants got down on their knees and bowed in front of Anastasia. "We are so deeply regretful for what we have to do to you," they said in unison. "We have no choice. We must obey our master, or more evil will ensue."

One of the servants pulled out a small vial. "Please, drink this. You will go to sleep forever and shall not feel any pain."

Anastasia smiled and nodded. With quivering hands, she took the vial from Orion's hand. "Thank you. I do understand that there is no other way. I am so sorry that you will be used even more for your powers. Please forgive me. Most importantly, take care of my beautiful Leah. Promise me that you will be her protectors, and shield her from her father's evil ways."

"We will," the two promised.

Anastasia brought the vial up to her lips. "Wait!" Alec shouted. "It is time that I make up for all the cruelty and heartbreak I have brought to your family. I have ruined your sister's life with my persistence for revenge. I twisted my own son's love for me by trying to coerce him into harming an innocent young girl as a ploy to get back at her mother for 'supposedly killing' my brother. I should be the one to die. I should be the one to have his heart ripped out of his body." He grabbed the vial from her hand and raised it up to his own lips.

"But I, *too,* have guilt. I am the one who *knew* everything," whispered Anastasia. "It was all arranged in advance."

Alec looked at her, puzzled. "What do you mean arranged?" A sick feeling was settling deep in his stomach.

"It was all part of the plan. Darius' warped plan. We led you to find Korinna, marry her, and produce a son." She was now gazing at the ground, summoning up the courage for the final blow. "Darius made you believe that it was your idea to seek revenge for his death. As much as you have done horrific things to your family, it wasn't totally your own doing. Darius constantly depended upon the servants' and my powers to replenish his own. All three of us were his pawns."

"What is this obsession that my brother has with making Leah Queen of the Universe?" He questioned the three.

They shook their heads. Tereus spoke first. "He is evil but very smart and convincing. He will ultimately persuade Leah to go along with his plan. He will play upon her sweetness and naivety, and she unwillingly will be twisted into submission."

"But she is mortal. Not even an embedded crystal or energy released into her body will allow her to become a witch and have powers," Alec challenged. "Darius should be well aware of that."

Anastasia stared at the ground. That was the same argument Talia had posed. "The crystal has been storing untapped energy for seventeen years. The powers that it holds are immense. Perhaps that will be the answer," she said.

"That will still not make her a witch," argued Alec. "The crystal is only the vehicle that enables the powers to surge and be released. But the blood of a witch must still flow through her."

The servants were as still as statues. Anastasia remained silent.

As if someone had flicked a switch, the realization hit Alec. "It is not just the crystals Darius wants. It's the blood! And he is going to get it from Peter, Ryan, and Avery, isn't he?"

The three shook their heads in affirmation.

"He must be stopped," said Alec. "But I am not the one." He placed his hand on Anastasia's shoulder. "You are." Then looking at the servants, he said, "It is time to tell her."

Before Anastasia could open her mouth to question Alec, he brought the vial to his lips. "Save them," he whispered.

The servants knelt beside Alec's still body. "He is gone," Tereus said. "Anastasia, you must run for your life. If Darius comes and sees that you are not dead, we will all be victims by his torturous hands."

"But I can't leave Leah. What will happen to her? And what was Alec speaking about? He said it was time to tell me something."

They all heard it at the same time. The footsteps were coming nearer. "Patience was never a virtue for him," muttered Anastasia.

"Go now," they hissed at her. "We will tell him that after Alec killed you, he felt it was his duty to return home and bring Talia and Avery back to him as the final brotherly offering."

Anastasia shook her head. "I can't let the two of you suffer the wrath for my freedom. I will stand up to him," she said defiantly.

Orion shook her hard. "No! You must go now! We will try our best to look after Leah. He will torture us, but he will not kill us. He depends upon our powers," he said wryly.

But still, she persisted. "There is something Alec said I needed to know."

He was coming closer. Anastasia had no choice but to run. The servants knelt. Tereus withdrew his knife from its sheath. It was over in seconds as the two worked feverishly. They had what they needed and tossed the body over the stone-wall that stood guard behind the olive trees. They returned to their master.

Chapter 39

"The time has finally come," she said to him softly. Her words were barely a whisper, but they felt like a locomotive barreling through his eardrums. He knew that the time would eventually arrive, but he always pushed that thought to the back of his mind. He didn't want to think about it. For sixteen years, he didn't have to.

"But I don't understand," said Cirio. "I can stay here with you. I am getting stronger by the day, and I know that you could use my muscles to help you fix up the convent. Just look at this place. It looks like it hasn't been remodeled for the past hundred years."

Sister Helena knew that he was trying to mask his true feelings by making a joke. She gently placed her hand on Cirio's shoulder and replied, "Cirio, from the day that I laid my eyes upon you, I knew that you belonged with us. You were a gift from God as I discovered your tiny body just lying there in front of the convent's steps. That is why I named you Cirio, which means Lordly in Greek. But you are now a man, and it is time that you say goodbye to us and begin your life."

Cirio gnawed at his bottom lip, trying to hold back the tears. He did not want to leave the convent. This was his home, and Sister Helena and all the other Sisters had become his family. They brought him up as their son, and he now felt as if he was being *discarded,* just like he had been on the day of his birth. "But where am I to go?"

"There is a university in America that has accepted you for this coming fall," said Sister Helena. "They were quite impressed with your application and agreed to let you start a year earlier than most incoming Freshmen."

Cirio's eyebrows furrowed. "What application? I do not remember filling out any university applications."

Sister Helena smiled. "Ah, but you did. Remember I had you write an essay two months ago? I told you it was to improve your English skills. Well, that essay, along with all the necessary information, was sent on its way to six universities in the United States. And as I predicted, you were accepted into all six."

Cirio's face reddened with anger. He could feel it starting. Sister Helena knew all too well what was going to happen. She placed both arms around him and tried to calm him down. "But why? Why would you want to send me away?" Cirio cried out. "Have I not been a good son? Tell me what I have done wrong, and I will do better." Hot tears flowed down his face. He didn't care that he was sixteen years old and was sobbing like a baby. The tiny sparks began to flow out of the crystals that were embedded in both of his hands. He didn't care that they shocked his body. He didn't care about anything.

Sister Helena could feel them but still held onto him. "Shh," she said soothingly. "It is not what you think. We love you too much to keep you here any longer. Cirio, we have taught you all that we could. Your intelligence and zest for learning is limitless, and now it is time to venture forth. We are not abandoning you. You will always have a home here." Sister Helena could feel the sparks subside. She knew that what she was saying to Cirio made sense to him, even though he did not want to admit it to himself.

"But, what about these?" Cirio was staring at the tiny crystals that were finally cool to the touch. "Who will settle me down when I get upset? Who will make sure that I don't do anything that I will regret because of these?" He continued to stare at the crystals. He did not know why he was born with them. He only knew that when he became upset, the powers that surged out of them sent tremendous currents through his body. There were times when the sparks would cause destruction; chairs would be sent flying, and windows shattered. Those were the times when he was especially terrified and sought Sister Helena's help. She was always there to calm him, to assure him that it would be okay.

"Your powers are a gift. You need to realize that. There will be a day when they will be truly needed. Until then, you must find a way to control them on your own." Sister Helena embraced her gift from God. "Now come with me, and I will tell you all about your new adventure."

Chapter 40

She heard the horn's beep. "Bye, Mom," Avery yelled.

"Avery, wait," Talia said as she came downstairs. "I want you to be able to enjoy your day. I want you to try not to think about what went on yesterday. This is your senior year, and you should make it a memorable one."

"You're kidding, right?" Avery looked at her mom in disbelief. "Nothing will ever be the same. Our lives are in danger. You want me to act like the other senior girls? All of them giddy about prom even though it's still eight months away, nervous about college acceptances, and totally *done* with school?" Before Talia could answer, Avery opened the front door, slammed it behind her, and ran down the driveway. She knew she was going to hear it when she got home, but right now, her anger bubbled inside. Her crystal sent out tiny sparks, and Avery had to take deep breaths to control them from escalating.

Ryan had reached over and opened the passenger door for her before she even got to the car. She climbed inside and slammed the door shut. "Hey, what's going on? I can see those sparks sizzling around your crystal. And from the looks of your scowling mouth, I know something is up."

Avery turned to face him. "You mean you don't know? After all, you can read my mind, can't you?" She questioned in a snarky tone.

"Whoa, calm down, Avery. I am with you, not against you. I will always be on your side."

"My mom thinks I should forget about everything that happened and act 'normal'."

"Yeah. Normal is *so* not us. My mom sat Peter and me down last night and explained to us that we need to put our differences aside and try to act like brothers. She also said that it was very important for us to enjoy our senior year. I guess she thinks that there will be enough rough times ahead once we find out what Darius has in store."

"But that's the point. We need to devise a plan now. We cannot let Darius continue without finding a way to stop his evil mission. We must destroy him. We don't know what Leah will do if she actually gets her powers. Will she become a tyrant like her dad? It is all so sickening. Don't you see? He is not going to stop until we are all dead! Ryan, we need to get Peter on board with us. We need his help. His powers are the strongest." Avery turned to Ryan to say something.

Reading her mind, Ryan said. "He took his own car. Mr. Saunders, um, I mean Ben, swung by my house last night so I could get mine."

"Was your dad there?"

Ryan shook his head. "Nope. I don't know what is going on with him and my uncle, but I am getting a sickening feeling in my gut. It can't be good."

Avery could tell that he was disappointed, so she changed the subject. "I guess he doesn't want to ride with us and feel like the third wheel." Now her disappointment found its way to her face.

"Give him time, Avery. He will come around. He loves you and will always want to be a part of your life, even if it means as a friend. And I agree. Peter needs to be involved. We have to make him realize that we can't just sit around and enjoy our senior year like everything is fine."

The two were silent for the rest of the ride, but Avery could swear that Ryan could hear her heart beating. Just being next to him made her excited.

Ryan parked and turned off the engine. He reached over and took her hand. He laced his fingers into hers. She stared at his side profile. *God, he is so cute*, she thought.

Ryan squeezed her hand and smiled. "So are you."

"Stop reading my mind!" Avery laughed, trying to cover up her embarrassment.

"Never," Ryan responded. "I just didn't know that I would be the center of it 24 hours a day." Avery rolled her eyes.

Ryan's face grew serious. He turned to face her. "I will never let anything happen to you or anyone that you love. You have my promise."

Avery leaned over and kissed him gently on the lips. "I believe you."

Chapter 41

She ran, not knowing where she was going. She only knew that she had to escape and somehow get back to her sister. Her crystal was gone, and she had nothing to help her. Her legs burned, and her lungs felt like they were going to explode. Anastasia finally stopped. Her arms and face were scratched from the tree branches and prickly bushes that blocked her way. But she didn't care. She had to get back to Korinna and explain to her the full extent of Darius' plan. Everyone was involved now. She also had to save Leah. Anastasia knew that Leah would do anything to please her father, even if it meant living a life of wickedness. She shuddered. She also knew that death was a grave possibility. The convent stood in front of her. Unlike Darius' pristine mansion, it looked ancient and in disrepair. The terracotta roof was crumbling, and the structure looked like it could collapse with one swift blow. But surrounding the convent was the most beautiful landscaping that Anastasia had ever seen. Cypress trees towered around the perimeter, and lilies of every color imaginable lined the walkway. It was clear that much love went into it. Although it was late, Anastasia could see that lights were still on. She had no other choice. She rang the bell.

Sister Helena wondered who could be calling on them at such a late hour, but she did not hesitate to answer the door.

"Please help me," Anastasia gasped as she collapsed at Sister Helena's feet.

Sister Helena called out for Cirio, and he came rushing to her aid. "Let's get her to the couch," she said with urgency in her voice. Cirio could not help but stare at the woman who lay almost lifeless in front of him. Her skin was so white, almost translucent, and her hair was so silver. But what really kept him transfixed were the oozing sores that seemed to have a life of their own. He watched with horror as the silver liquid trickled out of them. "Cirio, don't just stand there! Get a dampened washcloth."

When he returned, he placed the cool washcloth on Anastasia's face. Her breathing was shallow, and her eyes remained closed. "Who is she, Mother?"

"Only God knows the answer to that right now," she murmured.

Cirio stayed by the strange woman throughout the night. Something pulled him to her. As he watched her sleep, her body twitched in spasms, words tumbling out of her mouth that made no sense to him. The washcloth lay on her forehead, keeping the fever that spiked during the night, at bay.

Finally, as blackness gave way to a brilliant blue sky, Cirio heard a murmur. He could make out the name *Leah*. He knelt close in front of her, listening for any other words that might escape her lips. Anastasia's eyes began to flutter. Cirio leaned in closer, his face just inches from hers. It was then he saw her eyes open. They certainly did not look like the eyes of a human. He flinched and began to move away, but something held him.

Grasping Cirio's arm in a vice-like grip, Anastasia whispered, "It is you. You have come back to me."

THE END OF BOOK ONE

Made in the USA
Middletown, DE
29 April 2023

29709265R00186